COLDHEARTED BOSS

USA TODAY BESTSELLING AUTHOR

R.S. GREY

COLDHEARTED BOSS

Published: R.S. Grey 2019

authorrsgrey@gmail.com

Editing: Editing by C. Marie

Proofreading: JaVa Editing, Red Leaf Proofing

Cover Design: R.S. Grey

ISBN: 9781099457777

CHAPTER ONE

TAYLOR

I hang up my phone with an angry groan and let my forehead smack against the bar. The wood doesn't bite as much as I want it to. I was hoping I'd blackout for a couple minutes or—*even better*—experience a nice bout of amnesia. Nothing too crazy, just maybe I'd forget who I am and where I live and why my life is a bleak desolate nightmare.

Angrier than ever, I clutch my cheap prepaid phone in my lap and tighten my grip, wondering how close I am to pulverizing it. Surely it's not that hard. *Just...a little...tighter.* The phone stares back at me in one piece, gloating. I let out a defeated sigh just as a glass hits the bar near my head.

"These are on the house."

I crane my neck only high enough that I'm eye level with a shot glass full of maraschino cherries. They're nudged farther in my direction by the surly-looking bartender.

"Aren't those always on the house?" I remark with a healthy dose of snark. I'm taking my anger out on the wrong person.

"For *paying* customers," he mutters, reaching to take them back.

Shaken by the idea that he's going to revoke his offer and steal what will likely be my only dinner, I sit up quickly and swipe the shot glass away from him, aiming a grateful smile his way. It's been so long since I've felt gratitude that I don't think I achieve the desired effect. My teeth are clenched in more of a pseudo-snarl rather than an actual smile. He shoots me an odd look and then shakes his head, moving down to the other end of the bar to unpack some new bottles of liquor.

He's new here, a bear of a man as old as my father—or as old as my father would be if he were around. I reach for a cherry and pop it into my mouth. The sweet syrup coats my tongue and I wish the usual bartender were here. David gets it. He grew up in Oak Dale too. He would have heard my groan and seen my forehead resting on the bar and known, without having to ask, that another piece of my life had crumbled at my feet. He wouldn't have bothered with cherries, would have offered me a glass of the hard stuff, and tonight, I might have taken him up on it.

Then, he would have gone down the list.

"How's your mom?" he would have asked.

"Two years sober next month."

"Sister?"

"Still getting straight As and better now that she's on a new medication."

"Ah, so it's just life in general getting you down then?"

I'd have aimed a rueful smile his way. "Does a bear shit in the woods?"

He would have laughed at that and then gone on to serve another customer. There are never many in here. Most locals can't afford marked-up alcohol, which means the bar mostly caters to the travelers staying in the motel next door.

I glance over my shoulder at the group of suits that were here when I first walked in. There are four of them, as fancy as they come, definitely from out of town. These men are used to smelling rarified air, not trailer trash.

Comparing our lives would be comical.

I've bounced from odd job to odd job since high school. Currently, I make $7 an hour working as a maid at the motel.

That's below minimum wage, but our manager doesn't care. He says with tips, it should all break even. It doesn't. I can't complain, though, because there are already five of us splitting shifts, and if I don't like it, there's someone else ready to take my place.

These suits probably spend $7 on a cup of coffee every morning without a second thought. They toss the spare change into the tip jar, pick up their macchiato espresso chai teas, and glide through life like it's a fairytale.

A girl like me has no use for fairytales. They won't keep you warm or clothed or well fed.

The guy who's sitting in the chair facing the bar catches me watching them. When our eyes lock, my stomach clenches tight enough to give me instant abs.

He's the best-looking one among them, the one I noticed right away.

In their fairytale, he's the prince. There is no one on Earth more princely than him. His sharp cheekbones and square, clean-shaven jaw are set off by thick, dark brown hair. He's tan, as if he spends his days outdoors, but that can't be right because his suit fits his tall, muscular frame like a glove and his hair is too perfect. *Which is it? Are you stuck in a boardroom all day or splitting logs in the woods?*

He doesn't smile with interest like most guys would when he notices my unabashed perusal. Instead, he raises one dark brow as if to say, *Almost done?* and I realize I was wrong before. This one's not the prince in the fairytale.

He's the dragon.

I turn back around, too overwhelmed by my current predicament to feel any sort of embarrassment. So what if he's beautiful? When your car is falling to pieces and you're stuck in a dead-end job and the best you can hope for at the end of the day is a crappy couch shoved inside a too-small trailer, beauty of any kind loses its luster.

My phone rings on my lap and I answer it quickly.

"Mom?"

"Hey, why aren't you home yet?"

"I'm waiting for Jeremy to come pick me up."

"I thought you were getting the car back today?"

I'm careful with my sigh, not wanting her to hear it. "I was, until the mechanic called this morning and told me there's more to it than just the busted engine. It needs a ton of work. He spent the day getting a quote together."

"How much?"

I pinch my eyes closed. "Over $400 just for the parts."

Her heavy sigh breaks my heart, and I'm glad I didn't tell her the real number.

"I'm going to figure it out though," I insist, sounding sure of myself. "I've already started thinking of how we can get the money."

"Did you ask Mr. Harris for an advance?"

She and I discussed that possibility last night.

"Yes."

"And?"

My stomach twists as I recall my encounter with my boss at the motel this afternoon, his too-tight shirt stretched over his pot belly, his leftover tuna sandwich stinking up his dingy office. When I told him why I needed the small advance, explaining how much my family and I depend on our car—it's how McKenna gets to school, how I get to work, and how my mom gets to Livingston on the weekends to take classes so she can finally become a certified aesthetician—he leaned back in his chair, digging between his teeth with a toothpick. *Really* working at the tuna fish stuck between them.

"So it's a few extra bucks you want?" he asked, leering at my chest.

My uniform—a drab khaki dress—would have been formfitting if I hadn't sized up on my first day at the job. I did that to prevent this very thing: Mr. Harris looking at me like I'm an all-you-can-eat buffet.

"How badly do you need it?" he continued as his eyes dragged lower. His meaty hands clenched tight. He wanted to squash me like a butterfly.

Our conversation didn't continue after that.

"He can't give me one," I report to my mom, shivering at the remnants of that memory. "But there are other ways—"

"I'll pick up some shifts at Lonny's," she suggests, sounding like she hates the words even as they leave her mouth.

I sit up straighter and press the phone closer to my mouth. "No, Mom. *No*." I'm angry now, angry that we've been put in this position. "We'll figure out another option."

Lonny's always been my mom's worst vice. He's the one who got her into drinking so heavily in the first place, a guy who'd trade his soul for a bottle of tequila. The day she kicked him to the curb was one of the best days of my life. I won't let us slide backward, not when we're so close to getting our feet under us for good. My mom will graduate from her program this summer and then she can start her own salon and be able to support herself and McKenna without my help. I'll be free. Finally.

"All right. I just don't want you to feel like this is all on your shoulders."

I pick at a speck of dirt on my jeans, the pair I bring to work every day so I can rip that khaki dress off as soon as my shift ends. The day I quit, I'll burn it in a dumpster.

"It's fine. Really."

"When's your cousin supposed to pick you up anyway? It's already 8:30."

"He had a late shift."

"All right. Call me if he doesn't show up and I'll see if Nancy can come grab you."

The last half of her sentence fades as one of the suits comes up to the bar to order another round. I don't have to glance over to realize it's *him*. He's two stools down from me—far enough away that it isn't presumptuous, but close enough to send a message.

"Okay, I gotta go," I say, already pulling the phone away from my ear.

"Love you," she says, just before I hang up.

I drop my phone on the bar as the suit finally speaks.

"Can I get two Dos Equis with lime and two Bud Lights?"

His voice sends a warm shiver down my spine. It's smooth and refined, no hint of a twang.

The bartender grunts and starts reaching for beers so he can pop the tops.

I glance to my left just enough to see that the suit is checking out my shot glass full of cherries with narrowed eyes. It dawns on me that he probably thinks I'm underage.

"I'll take a Dos Equis too," I blurt out suddenly, without thought. Apparently, my pride is worth the five bucks the beer will cost me, though that's nearly an hour's wage. An hour of scrubbing toilets and making beds and trying to avoid weird stains left by weird people, all gone because of a childish impulse.

I don't want a beer, but now I have no choice because the bartender's already popping the top and reaching for limes.

Country music plays softly, filling the silence that stretches between me and the suit. If he's going to make a move, this is his time to do it.

I hold my breath, waiting for him to turn fully toward me and say something charming. I've heard a lot of opening lines from a lot of men in this town, nearly all of them unwelcome. It's got me curious to see what this guy has to offer. Surely he'd be better. Surely he knows how to make a woman forget about her troubles, even if just for the night.

I peer over at him from beneath my lashes. He's taken off his suit jacket, and his white collared shirt is rolled up to reveal his muscled forearms. His shiny silver watch winks at me under the hazy bar lights. Its dark brown leather strap is a good disguise, but I still recognize its value—likely more than the car I'm trying desperately to fix or even the trailer my mom inherited from her father that we've lived in my whole life.

That damn watch is a sucker punch to my gut after the day I've had, a visual representation of how different life is for some people.

Five beers clink on the bar top, and before the suit walks away with four of them, he tells the bartender to add my beer to his tab. Just that. Not a word in my direction. He just assumes I want him paying for my beer.

Arrogant bastard.

If I could afford to do it, I would refuse. Instead, I say nothing.

As he walks back to rejoin his friends, I dissect every possible motive he might have had for buying my drink. Maybe he was just being polite. Maybe he took one look at my thrift-store jeans and white t-shirt and felt a sense of pity. *Sure, there's a little hole in the armpit, but it's still a decent shirt!*

Whatever he was thinking, that beer tastes like piss as I down the first sip.

I want to leave it there on the bar, untouched, but I have nothing better to do than drink it as I sit and wait for Jeremy to come pick me up. He's late and not answering his phone. I try his number again and the call goes unanswered. I'm half convinced he won't show up at all.

I stifle a groan at the idea of having to find another way home. There's a ten-mile stretch of highway between our trailer and this bar, ten miles I'd have to walk in the dead of night. I've done it before, a few times, but I'd rather not do it today. I don't think I have it in me. I'd be better off heading to that booth in the corner and tucking myself in for the night.

When a round of laughter comes from the men behind me, I resist the urge to turn around. Another sip of beer warms my belly, and I realize it's starting to go to my head. I'm a lightweight. I don't drink often, and especially not on an empty stomach. The world gets fuzzy and my problems come into sharp focus.

I lied to my mom on the phone. When I told her we could figure out another option, I sounded hopeful, but what hope is there? What options are there in a town as small as Oak Dale? The truth is we're at rock bottom. We've been surviving down here so long, I'm not quite sure what life would feel like otherwise.

When I'm done with my beer, I push it away and polish off my cherries. I can practically hear my stomach groaning in protest: *Please, please put some kind of leafy green inside me before you die.*

Chairs screech across the floor as the suits stand to leave. One of them comes up to the bar to close out their tab, but it's not the one I'm interested in, so what do I care?

There's a sense of loss as I realize *he's* going with them, exiting the bar and leaving me behind.

As they walk out, I strain my ears, trying to listen for him, but they're all chatting at once and I can't distinguish one voice from another. The bar's door swings open and road noise from the highway rushes in, cars zooming past our small neck of the woods on their way to someplace better.

I pick at the label on my beer as the door swings shut again, leaving me alone with two regulars down at the end of the bar and the bartender who's still harboring ill will toward me about the cherries. I know because he keeps grumbling "ungrateful brat" under his breath. Altogether, we'd make a well-rounded cast for an antidepressant commercial, and I know I must be feeling down because even that thought doesn't make me smile.

"You need anything?" the bartender asks, speaking to the area of the room where the suits were sitting a few minutes ago, and my head whips over my shoulder so fast I nearly fall off my stool.

He's still there.

Alone.

Sitting at the table and telling the bartender he's all set. He doesn't want another drink…so then why is he still here? There's no game on the TV over the bar—it's been busted for years. There's no one around to offer up witty conversation unless you count the belching pair in the far corner. (I don't.)

Then his gaze finds mine and I get it.

He's here for me.

My heart lurches to a stop, misses a beat, and then starts to thump wildly.

He's not the answer to my problems. He'd be nothing more than a distraction, a short reprieve from the weight of life's boot on my neck.

I meet his eyes head on.

God, he's so good-looking with that rough edge to him. He's a man's man. Broad chest, veined forearms, tall frame. Even now, he's not smiling. His brows are furrowed and his supple mouth—arguably the only soft thing about him—is marked by a terse frown. It's like he's mad at me for putting us in this position, mad at me for making him want to stay.

I could aim the same resentment right back at him. I've never had a one-night stand before because I've never met a guy who made me *want* to do it. This man is seductive without even trying, sensual even as he sits half a bar away from me, partially reclined, assessing me coolly. In any setting, he'd turn heads. In this setting, he captures my full attention.

It occurs to me that I could walk out of the bar right now and keep my heart in one piece. Nothing good would come from this encounter.

Tomorrow, this stranger will be gone and my life will resume.

My life.

Four years since graduating from high school and I'm still here, unable to escape this nightmarish merry-go-round. We work and we save only to have some disaster strike—car breaks down, insurance doesn't cover McKenna's new asthma medication, A/C busts, roof needs fixing—and here we are again, right back at square one, just as broke as the day we started.

My hands shake and my throat aches from trying to keep these tears unshed.

I can't do it anymore.

This life is going to send me to an early grave. I need an emergency stop button, a safety valve that triggers a spring that will propel me from this barstool and send me to a deserted island where credit card bills and crappy bosses don't exist. Actually, let's scrap the island. I'm not picky. I'll take a quiet night in my mom's trailer, staring at a blank wall as long as no one reminds me of the doom that awaits me in the morning.

That emergency stop button doesn't exist, but this man does.

So, I will go down this path, just so I can step off the merry-go-round for one night.

I look pointedly toward the side hallway, the one that leads to the bathroom, making sure he gets the message. Then I slide off my barstool at the same time his chair scrapes across the wood floor.

There's no going back now.

CHAPTER TWO
TAYLOR

I'm in a daze as I walk to the bathroom, my body propelling itself forward one step at a time without me even realizing what I'm doing. I'm in shock. That's what this is, shock that I'm about to go through with this. My conscience tries to shout at me to stop, to turn and run while I still have the option, but then I'm in front of the door for the women's bathroom and a hand much bigger than mine is pushing it open for me.

I'd forgotten about the mirrors. I wish they weren't here, two of them sitting over old porcelain sinks. They're cracked and stained, but I still see my reflection well enough to be confronted by my actions.

My mother's brown eyes stare back at me, alluringly slanted up in the corners like I possess some untold mysteries.

My long brown hair hangs loose down to the middle of my spine in lazy waves.

My full lips are the stuff of dreams, or so I've been told. I suppose I have them to thank for bringing this dark stranger to me tonight.

I'm not unaware of the full package I present: the high cheekbones, cinched waist, and grown-up curves.

The way I look has never been something I've celebrated, though. In fact, it's caused me nothing but grief. My mother's boyfriends were always a little too interested in me. School teachers and parents assumed things about me based on the way I looked, like my sole purpose in life was to lure the men in this town off the path of righteousness. My bosses have never seen me as anyone with value beyond my appearance, my conversation with Mr. Harris earlier today a prime example. After all the unwanted advances and snide remarks—well, it's obvious why I don't wear much makeup or bother with tight clothes. There's no point in making the problem worse.

A hard chest hits my back, pushing me farther into the bathroom, and awareness trickles down my spine. He had a choice just like I did. He didn't have to follow me back here, but that door is already swinging shut and his presence is filling the quiet space.

His hand hits my bicep so he can direct me forward. In the mirror, I see how easily he towers over me. The distance between the top of my head and his chin could be measured in miles, not feet.

We make a striking pair: dark features perfectly matched, brown eyes of such varying shades they shouldn't even be classified as the same color. We're two beautiful people about to make some very bad decisions.

"How old are you?" he asks, meeting my eyes in the mirror. My body stills as I realize his tone is as sharp as his cheekbones.

"Twenty-two."

His brow arches in judgment. "Pretty young to be sitting in a bar by yourself."

I don't deign to justify my life to him. If he wants an explanation for why I'm here right now, he can ask nicely. Until then, I'll turn the spotlight back on him.

"Why didn't you leave with your friends?"

His free hand reaches for the hair hanging over my shoulder. I watch him in the mirror as he brushes it behind my back and an involuntary shiver racks through me.

"I didn't want to," he says quietly.

"Why?" I push.

His gaze flicks back to mine. "You looked sad sitting up at the bar all alone. I guess a part of me wanted to make sure you were okay."

That was the last thing I expected him to say. *Uh, 'cause you're hot* was about the response I thought I'd receive.

An avalanche of emotion collapses on me so suddenly, I'm trembling with the need to give up control of these tears, to let my shoulders slump and my spine crumble. I squeeze my eyes shut.

When's the last time someone wondered if I was okay?

I can't cry. I can't let him see me at my most vulnerable. He won't want to go through with this if I turn into a blubbering mess. *Oh, you thought we were coming in here to do naughty things? No, I'm actually looking to ugly sob for about thirty minutes while you rock me gently.*

He cares.

Why?

He's a stranger, someone I've only spoken a handful of words to, but I know instinctively he doesn't want to take advantage of me. Besides, he already could have.

We're alone in this bathroom right now. No one is going to come check on us. He could push me up against the wall and do as he pleases, and yet he holds perfectly still, waiting for me to respond.

My sadness quickly gives way to anger, just like it always does. Tears won't help me out of this mess. Self-pity won't solve my problems. I'm only standing here in this moment because of my strength and my sheer will to survive another day.

When I'm sure the tears are at bay, I blink my eyes open again and reach for his hand, the one that touched my hair so reverently it nearly burst my heart wide open.

"And what did the other part of you want to do? The part of you not worrying if I was okay..." I ask, my voice as sultry they come.

His gaze darkens in the mirror and I'm surprised to see he's not a man possessed by lust and desire. He looks troubled and confused, almost as if he's about to turn and walk right out the door.

I don't give him the chance.

I turn around, rise up onto my toes, and press my soft curves against him at the same time my lips touch his.

The gentle kiss shocks him.

His hand tightens painfully on my bicep, and then, just as quickly, he loosens it, brushing his hand up and down my bare skin, soothing the ache as if he's scared he hurt me.

He doesn't kiss me back right away, but I'm persistent, and when he finally does, our awkward, stilted movements turn into something sweeter: a kiss you share with your best guy friend the summer you turn fourteen, a kiss stolen when you know your parents aren't looking. It's tender and tentative, nothing but soft lips and unspoken possibilities.

We're not teenagers, though. This is a warm-blooded man I'm pushing my body against. No matter how much he might be concerned for my wellbeing, he can only hold out for so long as I continue to kiss him, seduce him, tempt him. My heavy breasts brush against his chest as I smooth my hand up over the cool fabric of his button-down. I make it past his collar and then my palm is against his neck, touching his skin for the very first time. He's so hot, I melt, and he must feel the heat too because he groans hungrily. The sound shakes me to my core, and suddenly I'm second-guessing myself, fearful about the situation I've put myself in.

This isn't a man you use for a night. This is a man you turn your life upside down to be with, one you crawl on hands and knees to please, one who touches you once and brands your soul forever.

I break our kiss on impulse, needing space, needing a moment to get a full breath. My chest is heaving. My hands are shaking.

This is crazy! I don't do things like this! I work and I scrimp and I save and I worry about the ways life is going to screw me over tomorrow. I don't let handsome strangers follow me into bathrooms!

There's no time for my conscience to grab hold of the situation because he's lifting me up like I'm filled with air and carrying me back toward the sink. My butt hits the porcelain lip and he pushes me up onto it then spreads my knees wide enough for him to step between. His suit pants brush against my denim-clad thighs and I let out a soft involuntary groan. Even with the added height, he still has to lean down to reach me, hands cradling my face and tilting my chin up so he can easily capture my lips. He turns his head to the side, slanting his mouth over mine and taking the reins oh so easily. I might have initiated our first kiss, but it's clear that every one that follows will be from him, by him, *for him*.

His tongue laps me up, sending pleasure through every inch of me.

I'm getting carried away.

I can feel reality nipping at my heels even as I try hard to bat it away.

I have to stop this.

This won't help me. This will only make me twice as sad come morning.

Unless...

A wild, stupid thought pops into my head: maybe I could get something out of this, more than just a pleasant evening...*money*. I could strike a bargain! Sell myself! Oh good, as if a one-night stand isn't bad enough, now I'm contemplating stepping into the oldest profession in the book. It's totally ridiculous, and besides, how does someone even initiate that bargain?

Oh, yes, hi, if you'd stop kissing me for a second, I'd like to discuss my terms of service for this transaction.

What do small-town prostitutes with hardly any experience go for these days? A hundred bucks and a coupon for a free milkshake?

The questions filling my head make it easier to separate myself from our kiss. His mouth is deliciously tempting, but it's no use against my impending panic attack. This impromptu bathroom make-out session was spontaneous and poorly thought-out. I'm only going to succeed in making a fool of myself.

If I wanted a one-night stand, I should have picked a lesser man, not this *suit* with his rock-hard body and come-hither kisses. He's going to tear through my sanity, show me pleasure like I've never experienced, and leave me lonely and bereft while he slides into a fancy sports car and kicks up dust as he peels out of town.

Even with my brain working a mile a minute, his sensual, teasing kisses are provoking every emotion I should be hiding. I know if he broke away and stepped back, he'd find my lips swollen and red, my eyes coated with a glossy love-me sheen, my chest heaving, my panties wet. If he brushed his hand down *there*, I'd come just from the sheer wrongness of this entire situation.

Even now, his hands brush up under the hem of my t-shirt, and when his warm palms glide over my skin, I momentarily lose track of my thoughts.

He squeezes my waist and I reach out for him too, scared I'm going to topple forward off the sink. My hands land squarely on his butt.

No, not just that…

His wallet.

Sitting snug in the back pocket of his suit pants.

My eyes spring open with the revelation as he bends to string kisses down my neck.

Take it, my survival instincts shout. *Take it now!*

NO.

My stomach twists with guilt and disgust that I'd even think of doing such a thing. I'm not a thief. Never.

This whole situation feels wrong and gritty and this bathroom smells and he's so tempting with his veined hands, warm and big, gripping my waist to bring us closer so that our hips rock together. I wish so badly we were kissing in his fairytale instead of a filthy bar bathroom. I wish so badly this was the grown-up version of that summertime teenage kiss, wish we were two lovers completely enraptured by each other instead of two strangers using each other in ways the other can't even begin to imagine.

And then a highlight reel of my future plays through my mind: overdue medical bills, broken-down cars, dead-end jobs. The money in this stranger's wallet wouldn't fix all my problems, but it would give us a much-needed boost, and it's with that thought that I realize my body has taken over the decision for me.

My fingers dig into his butt as a distraction and he doesn't protest. He must just assume I'm into butts, and I never really have been before this moment, but oh yes, I would be very into his. It's muscular and firm, not some kind of flat wussy cheeks that don't know how to fill out a pair of pants. His is ripe and *OH MY GOD FOCUS!*

Suddenly, I'm taking his wallet, working it out of his back pocket so slowly—millimeter by millimeter—that he doesn't notice and then I have no idea what to do with it. I have his wallet in my hand behind his back and my heart is pumping so hard, I'm going to be sick. It's convenient that we're making out so close to a toilet because I'm about to need one.

What have I done?!

At this point, I've stopped reacting to his kisses—I'm not that good at multitasking. He realizes something is wrong and pulls back to stare down at me, those warm brown eyes assessing me with worry. Then he sweeps his gaze around the bathroom, and he lets out a heavy sigh. Guilt replaces worry, but I can't let it fester. I can't let him turn into a nice guy, a gentleman who escorts me out of here and calls me a cab.

I'm still holding his wallet and there's no good explanation for that if he finds me with it. *Uhhh, I was looking for a condom? Pony up, big boy!*

No.

I do the first thing that comes to mind.

"Close your eyes."

His brows furrow and he doesn't follow my orders. Cocky men like him probably aren't used to being bossed around. The thought makes me smile, and the tension in his forehead lessons a little. I think he likes my smile, so I keep it there, pinned in place as I run a teasing finger down the front of his shirt.

"*Close your eyes.*"

He does it this time, though it's accompanied by a shake of his head and an annoyed groan. He tips his head back as if sending up a prayer.

I waste no time at all stuffing his wallet down the front of my shirt and into my bra.

"What's your room number?" I croon, sounding like a phone sex operator, my finger tracing down to the button of his pants. The bulge there is nearly obscene. I look away, scandalized.

One of his eyes winks open and I brace myself for him to notice his wallet stashed under my top. It's lumpy, but fortunately I'm packing enough cleavage that it nestles nicely in the middle, hidden.

"209."

"Go there and wait for me."

"What are you going to do?"

I panic as if I've been caught but then quickly recover with a coy smile.

"You didn't think I would make it this easy on you, did you? One beer and I'm yours for the taking?"

I keep expecting my seduction to work on him, assuming his hard veneer will crack. He still hasn't smiled at me. No flowery words or promises of pleasure. He's too smart for his own good, too skeptical of my bad acting. I can tell something about our encounter feels off to him. Still, I persist.

"I think you want a little chase, a little bit of time in that room, pacing back and forth, wondering if I'll come, and if I do—"

"*When* you do," he amends.

"Well, it will be worth the wait, and that reunion kiss will be all the sweeter. Don't you think?"

He tilts his head to the side, studying me.

I try to sit perfectly still, appearing cool and calm, when in reality I feel like a bug under a magnifying glass, about to go up in flames.

His mouth opens like he's going to say something, but in the end, he turns for the door and tugs it open, *hard*, without another word. His broad shoulders disappear out into the hall and the second the door swings closed behind him, I'm off that sink and hurrying for a toilet, just in time to throw up a winning combination of beer and chewed-up cherries.

It's disgusting and putrid and exactly what I deserve. Karma is on top of her shit these days. I haven't even finished completing my crime yet and I'm already being punished. My stomach rolls again and I squeeze my eyes shut, prepared for round two, but there's nothing left. I haven't eaten since breakfast.

I flush the toilet and move to the sink to rinse out my mouth and wash my hands. I don't have time to linger. I need to get out of here and fast. He's going to notice his wallet is missing as soon as he tries to get into his motel room and realizes he doesn't have his keycard, and the same parts of him that moments ago sent desire radiating through me will do the exact opposite when he storms in here boiling with rage at what I've just done to him.

With trembling hands, I open the wallet, ignore the hotel key and the thick black credit card, and move on to the cash. There's more in here than I expected, nearly $800 total. *Who keeps that much cash on them?!* I could skim $500 and he'd still be left with plenty. $500 is more than I make in a month. I move to take it, but my hand is shaking and I tell myself I should look at his driver's license first so I can memorize his address. One day, when I'm not surviving by the skin of my teeth, I'll send him back the money with interest and a thank you note. He'll get to feel good about himself. He'll get to say he helped the poor helpless country girl when she was down on her luck. He'll get to tell his buddies about it, and his wife, too. *No*—he wasn't wearing a ring. I can't add mistress to my growing list of sins.

According to his license, he'll turn thirty-one this year, but that's as much information as I can gather before I hear muffled voices out in the bar.

Is it him? Back already?

My heart leaps into overdrive.

It's now or never.

I have to get out of here.

I flip back to the cash and rub the bills between my fingers.

Take it. Take it and get out.

This money would solve your problems!

I want it. I want that money so badly my mouth nearly salivates, but instead of taking it out and slipping it into my back pocket, I sigh and slam the wallet closed.

In the end, I can't do it.

Instead of feeling proud that I'm doing the right thing, I chide myself as I walk out into the hallway. All that…for nothing. *Now what am I going to do? How's my mom going to get to her classes? How am I supposed to get to work?*

The voices I first heard in the bathroom grow louder and I relax, recognizing one of them as my cousin. I spot him leaning against the bar talking to the new bartender, asking where I am. When he sees me emerge from the hallway, he looks relieved—relieved and tired as hell. His beat-up baseball hat is tugged low on his head, nearly covering all of his ashy blond hair. His neon yellow t-shirt—his uniform at the lumber mill—is stained with sweat around the neck and arms. If this was a bad day for me, Jeremy's probably wasn't far behind.

"Hey, I've been calling you," he says, pushing away from the bar and straightening to stand.

I blanche. "Sorry. I wasn't feeling well."

He frowns and assesses me quickly from head to toe. Jeremy's always been a worrier. When our lives were at the most chaotic in my high school years, he was truly the only person I had in my corner. I was there for him too, someone he could trust, someone he could talk to. We formed a tight bond.

"Ready to go?" he asks, angling his head toward the door.

I nod then turn to the bartender, holding up the sleek leather wallet. "That suit must have dropped this. I'm sure he'll be back for it any second."

After I hand it off, I follow Jeremy out to his beat-up truck, decline the half-finished cheeseburger he tries to force on me, and don't look back in the rearview mirror even once as we pull out onto the old country highway.

CHAPTER THREE
ETHAN

Truth be told, when I make it back to my motel room and find my back pocket empty, my first reaction isn't even anger; it's shocked admiration. *How the hell did she steal my wallet without me even noticing?* That feeling doesn't last long, though. My anger settles rightly into place by the time I make it back to the elevator. The facts are impossible to ignore: I know I had my wallet when I got up to follow her into the bathroom because I remember reaching for it before Steven insisted on closing the tab. Sure, it could have fallen out at some point between then and now (something that has never *once* happened before), but the other piece of evidence glaring me in the face is the fact that the brunette bombshell isn't here right now, meeting me back at my room like she promised, ready to finish what we started in that bathroom.

No. Of course she's not. She never planned on meeting me here.

She took my wallet and ran like the little thief she is.

Rage curls my hands into fists. I can't believe I got played like that. I can't believe she pressed her supple body against mine and kissed me back, moaning like she was as shocked by the chemistry as I was and all the while, she was planning to rob me blind.

I want to find her and teach her a lesson for taking advantage of me.

I ignore the part of my conscience that tries to lay the blame at my feet. I knew something was off when I first laid eyes on her in the bar. My instincts shouted at me to leave after I'd spent half the night watching her. I'd written off the feeling, though, mistaking it as some kind of gentlemanly urge. I felt like I was taking advantage of her. She looked so fragile and helpless up there at the bar all alone, her shoulders slumped with defeat, head tilted down.

Now, I realize it was all an act, no doubt one she's performed a million times before considering how successfully she pulled it off. I could have sworn she was near tears at one point in the bathroom, right after I confessed that I wanted to make sure she was okay.

Jesus Christ. I'm an idiot. I can't believe I fell for that!

I yank my hands through my hair. My god, she seemed so into me, into the way I was touching her, *kissing her*.

This never should have happened. My partners and I are only in town for the weekend and we have a million things on our agenda. I had no business noticing the brunette when she first walked into the bar, but now I see the trap plain as day. The whole setup was arranged to tug at my heartstrings. It's so easy to pick it apart now that I have some distance. Casting aside her femme fatale beauty, I recall her faded jeans and thin t-shirt—clothes that looked like they'd been worn and washed a hundred times before.

She ignored all of us as she walked straight to the bar, threw herself up on a barstool, and heaved a heavy sigh. The bartender asked if she wanted anything to drink. She asked for some water but didn't order anything after that.

Instead, she sat, twirling her phone in her hands with her shoulders slumped over and her head bowed forward. She looked like she needed a savior, and some caveman instinct kicked on inside me, making me yearn to be that for her, even if just for one night.

My partners had all noticed her walk in too. In fact, one of them, Grant, tried to get me to change seats with him so he'd have a better vantage point from which to watch her at the bar. I didn't budge.

Then, later—still not quite ready to give up—he volunteered to go up to the bar to order our next round. Not happening. I clapped my hand on his shoulder and forced him to stay in his seat, much to the amusement of our two other partners. It's not often I make a fool of myself for a woman, if ever, but not a single one of them was surprised when they stood to leave and I opted to stay behind. They all wished me luck except for Grant, who shot me the finger and told me to go to hell.

At the time, it made sense. No man in his right mind would want to walk out of that bar and leave that angel behind.

No, I remind myself swiftly. She's a lot of things—con artist, thief, liar—but she's no angel.

I'm seeing red as I pull open the door to the bar and stalk toward the bartender, who's cleaning glasses.

"Is she still here?" I ask, my voice cutting through the air with the subtlety of a sledgehammer.

"The brunette you trailed into the bathroom?" he asks with a barely interested tone. "Nah. She left right after you did."

My ego takes another sucker punch at having my speculation confirmed. She never did plan on meeting me in my room.

"Great. Well, did you happen to see my wallet clutched in her hand as she ran out of here?"

Without a reply, he heads over to the cash register, grabs something, and then holds it up like a magician completing a trick.

I freeze, completely baffled.

So she didn't steal it? It really just slipped out of my back pocket—

No.

Fuck.

I haven't even finished the thought before I tear it out of his hand, look inside, and find every bit of my cash gone. I just pulled it out of the bank this morning, and I know I had over $800 because I didn't want to have to get cash out here in the middle of nowhere.

I curse under my breath and the bartender shrugs, totally unperturbed by my anger.

"Who is she?" I ask, biting out each word while my fingers curl into fists. Surely every man within a fifty-mile radius knows her name.

"Listen, I just started here. I've never met her before tonight and she didn't tell me her name. All I know is she walked out of the bathroom a few minutes after you and told me you'd dropped your wallet in the hallway."

"Yeah, well, she's a fucking liar. She *stole* it."

He shrugs as if to say, *Well, what can ya do?*

Then he resumes his duties.

"All I can say is, I hope she was worth it."

I shouldn't have told my partners what happened, Grant most of all. He won't drop it at breakfast the next morning.

We're all sitting around a table in an old diner named Lonny's. It's the only restaurant we could find that was open early. The food is only one minuscule step up from the crap I could have gotten in the vending machine back at the motel, but their coffee is strong and, after the night I've had, I need it. I ask the waitress for a refill just as Grant launches back into it.

He couldn't look more pleased with himself if he tried. I think he's soiled his pants.

"You thought she was into you and then she—" He breaks off into a fit of laughter so hearty and all-consuming that his next words are complete and utter gibberish. I don't pick up any sounds that resemble the English language until, "And then in the bathroom—" More laughter. He's wiping his eyes now. "Took your wallet!"

Grant is our youngest partner and the one I'm most likely to punch on a daily basis. It's that damn baby face. If it weren't for the fact that he keeps his blond hair buzzed short and stands close to my same height, I'd mistake him for a teenager. Our other two partners, Steven and Brad, sit quietly, sipping their coffee and keeping their attention down on the blueprints we're supposed to be discussing. I credit their resolve to their age. Both of them are well into their 40s and married, each with a couple of kids under their belt. Then I notice the smile Brad is trying desperately to hide and that idea flies out the window. They're all assholes. Every one of them.

Steven nudges my shoulder. "So you got scammed—who cares? Jesus, with that face, any one of us would have fallen for it."

Brad agrees, and even Grant stops laughing long enough to nod along.

He reaches across the table as if wanting to shake my hand, cocky smile in place. "Hey man, I actually owe you one. It could have been me in that bar getting duped—"

Steven motions across his neck for him to cut it out. "He's been sufficiently shamed," he says, nodding back down to the blueprints. "Let's move on and focus so we can get the hell out of here."

"How far is the site from where we are now?" I ask, itching to leave.

Steven narrows one eye, thinking it over. "As the crow flies, not too far. Unfortunately, it's all backcountry roads. It'll take us over an hour."

"We'll need to leave soon. The reps are meeting us there at 9 AM and I don't want to be late," Brad adds. "That should give us plenty of time to walk the property and go over final details before we head back to Austin."

"And if they approve?" I ask, knowing they will. Permits have been stamped. Steven personally oversaw the design, and in our final proposal—the one we presented two months ago—the hotel chain's entire wish list was fulfilled and then some. "When do we break ground?"

"A month from now if all goes as planned."

"Still up for the challenge?" Steven asks, eyeing me with skepticism.

I don't really have a choice. Lockwood Construction is a well-oiled machine because we each play our part: Steven is the principal architect and creative director; Brad heads up acquisitions, sales, and financial modeling; Grant oversees the engineering department; and I'm the one on the ground acting as principal contractor and senior-most project manager on our large-scale commercial builds. It's an unusual setup. We've taken the industry standard and turned it on its head. Usually a client has to outsource every piece of a project from architectural plans to soil reports to construction. We wanted everything done in house by a staff capable of streamlining projects and cutting down on lead time.

In Austin and the surrounding areas, we usually have two or three projects going at once: shopping malls, university expansions, hospital complexes. We're an emerging force in the world of design-build firms, and as of this month, our office in downtown Austin employs over a hundred people.

That's part of the reason why this project excites me.

We've been working our asses off the last few years. I've been forced into the office, stuffed inside boardrooms, and crowded around conference tables entirely too much for my liking. When our client on this new project strongly requested that one of the four partners not only manage but be present through the fruition of the build out here in East Texas, I didn't hesitate before jumping on board.

So what if that means I have to live out here in the middle of nowhere? So what if there aren't *real* accommodations on site? I like roughing it.

So what if that brunette vixen is still on my goddamn mind even after I swore I'd forget about her?

In a month, by the time we're breaking ground, she'll be long forgotten.

CHAPTER FOUR
TAYLOR

I had no plans to stay in this town after I graduated from high school. I wanted to go to college, but that path wasn't in the cards for me. For one, my mom was still dating Lonny my senior year of high school, and I couldn't leave McKenna on her own with them. The other reason—the one so many of us battle around here—is that I just didn't have the grades to get into any schools, let alone qualify for scholarships or financial aid.

I can remember going to talk with our school's counselor my senior year. At the time, I was still carrying around a bud of hope for what my future could entail. Maybe I could still get into college, and maybe I could take McKenna with me. I could find us a small apartment and get a part-time job. I was sure I'd be able to juggle it all if only I could get us out of Oak Dale. My naivety at the time still makes me laugh.

Our high school's counselor was a heavyset woman with an affinity for floral patterns. Her gray hair was always swept up into a severe bun and her thin lips rarely curved into a smile, at least around me. It's why the whimsical dresses always threw me off.

"Put the idea of college out of your mind," she said almost as soon as I walked in that day. *Well, hello to you too, lady.* "Your grades aren't where they need to be. You have far too many absences and no extracurricular activities of any kind."

"I was on the soccer team for a few weeks my freshman year," I said with a self-deprecating smile. Truly, I just wanted her to throw me a bone. Unfortunately, this lady had none of those to spare.

She straightened her glasses on the bridge of her nose and flipped through my file. "I talked to some of your teachers. You do well on exams, but you don't seem to care about the other part of your grades: homework assignments, projects, papers. Anything you do manage to turn in is only halfway done at best. You should be glad you're even graduating."

It wasn't that I didn't care. I wasn't a slacker. My senior year, my mom was drinking heavily and more in love with Lonny than ever. I spent most of my time outside of school trying to avoid our trailer and making sure McKenna stayed away from it as well. Sometimes we stayed with Jeremy. Sometimes we slept out in our car. If we did stay at home, I had to be watchful and alert, scared something bad would happen if I ever let my guard down.

That year, McKenna was getting sick a lot too. She was wheezing and coughing in her sleep, and we thought she had a lingering cold. My mom didn't have the money to take her to the doctor. She hoped McKenna would get over it on her own, but she didn't, and I had to skip school a few times to help out on the hard days.

Things only started to turn around when we were able to get McKenna in to see a doctor. Her diagnosis of asthma came with an expensive price tag, but at least it was treatable.

The next major breakthrough came when my mom finally ended things with Lonny.

Unfortunately, it was too little too late for me.

McKenna has it different, though. She's just now a freshman in high school, and I'm working hard to make sure she doesn't have to bear the same weight on her shoulders that I did. With the approval of her doctor, she even tried out for the freshman soccer team, and she has a small group of friends, girls who care more about grades than boys. She brought home straight As on her report card last week, and my mom put it up on the fridge.

She's doing better than ever—thriving, really—and I'm going to ensure it stays that way. It's why I'm back at Oak Dale High School today, back in the familiar hallway that leads to the counselor's office. I have a meeting scheduled with the same oh-so-lovely woman from four years ago. I find that she's just the same as I remember after I knock on the door and enter her office: red-cheeked and tired. How many students has she watched pass through this school? How many dreams has she dashed? I used to resent her, but now I actually kind of pity her. She has a hard job.

"Ms. Larson," she says, eyeing me over the rims of her glasses. "I'm surprised to see you here."

I smile and pass her the tin of cookies McKenna and I made especially for her last night. There aren't many and they're just shortbread—the cheapest cookie you can bake—but they still serve the purpose. They're a bribe of sorts.

"I'm here to talk about McKenna's future."

Her brow quirks with intrigue as she opens the tin and inhales. Ah yes, that buttery smell would bring anyone to their knees. When she pushes them aside and turns her attention back to me, I swear her gaze is slightly less severe.

"Your sister is only a freshman, if I recall. It's a little early to be talking about—"

I lean forward and ensure my words are enunciated. I want her to understand me and take my words to heart. "It's not too early. I want to ensure that McKenna stays on track all four years. I want to ensure that she's in the right extracurriculars and keeping her grades up. I want to make sure she's taking as many advanced courses as she wants to take. When it's time for her to take the SAT, I want you to look into free classes or guides she can use to boost her score. I'll do my part too, but—"

She waves her hand to cut me off. "I understand what you're saying, and while I will happily help your sister in any way I can, I don't think you have to worry. Just last week, she was in my office, pestering me about taking dual credit courses in her sophomore year so she can earn college credit early. Your sister seems to be far more focused on her schoolwork than you were at her age."

I try not to let her words dig at me. Even still, they hurt.

"And what about you? What are you doing now?" she says, peering down at the sweatshirt I'm using to hide my maid's uniform. I have to go straight to work from here, and unless Jeremy can extend his lunch break at the lumber mill, it looks like I'll be walking there. "You've been out of high school for a while now."

I'm too embarrassed to answer, so I don't.

She still gets the message loud and clear. "There are still options for you." She turns and grabs a pamphlet for a community college she keeps on a small stand behind her desk. The campus is a few hours away. I know because I've looked into it before, years ago.

She unfolds the flaps and I'm confronted by the smiling faces of co-eds throwing frisbees and performing experiments in lab coats. It looks like a Gap ad and I'm not sure where the girl from the trailer park fits in. *Oh, there I am—the custodian in the background taking out the trash.*

"They have online classes," she says, sounding hopeful.

I don't have a computer.

"And flexible course schedules in case the weekends work better for you."

It doesn't really matter what days I'd have class because I still don't have a car.

Even so, I don't want to be rude by rebuffing her kind suggestions, so I accept the pamphlet and stand, thanking her for her time and insisting she notify me if McKenna's grades start to slip or she seems to be losing track of her studies.

Then I walk out into the hall with that pamphlet burning a hole in my palm.

What business do I have thinking about college? I don't even know what I would want to be, if I *could* be something other than what I am in this moment.

Just the idea of hope hurts.

No. I put away that dream a long time ago.

College isn't in the cards for me. All I can do is focus on McKenna and make sure, out of the two of us, she's the one to make it out of this town for good.

A week later, I'm sitting at the kitchen table in our trailer, counting my tips from my shift at the motel. I lucked out earlier. One of the women I work with clocked out at the same time I did and offered to give me a ride home. I had to pay her for the gas, but it was worth it considering I've had to walk home a few times now and my tennis shoes aren't holding up all that well.

"How'd you do today?" McKenna asks, dropping a small plate of spaghetti beside my pile of tips, and by tips, I mean garbage—literally. I think most people just reach into their pockets and leave behind anything they happen to grab.

Surely the maid who's had her face level with the shitter all week wants my lint-covered candy wrapper!

Other than that, there's a few dollars, some change, and one very pleasant note scrawled on the back of a receipt:

Hey, saw you cleaning. Your hot. Call me if you want to grab a beer.
- Mike from #113

Mike from room 113 doesn't know the proper usage of you're, but I'd be okay with that if he hadn't also left his room a complete wreck. Leftover pepperoni pizza *under* the pillows, Mike? Why? *How?*

"Do we have enough to get the car out of the shop now?" McKenna asks, sounding hopeful. I can't bear to look up at her. She's all the things I didn't get the chance to be: innocent, doe-eyed, sweet. I want to hold her against my bosom and keep her there forever. I want to squeeze her soft cheeks and tell her the world is a beautiful and happy place. I do not want to tell her that with the $14.50 in tips I got today, we're not even remotely close to getting our car back. In fact, this money won't even be going into the car fund. We need it for groceries.

I force a smile and nod. "We're getting there. Have you finished your homework?"

She rolls her eyes halfheartedly and sits back down at the table across from me. Her biology textbook is open and she continues her reading assignment while she eats her dinner. Seeing her there, looking so much like I did at her age, makes it hard to get a full breath. It's like seeing what could have been in another life.

A pounding on the trailer's door jolts me out of my thoughts and I turn, frowning, wondering who could be coming by here at this time of night. My mom's still working her shift at the grocery store and not due back for another hour at least. My brain immediately thinks of Lonny, but then I quickly cast that thought aside. He's moved on. He has no reason to come snooping around here.

Still, I tell McKenna to stay put and then I peer tentatively through the faded curtains over our couch. I heave a sigh of relief when I spot Jeremy's truck parked in the grass beyond our front door.

"You could have called first," I joke as I tug the door open.

He holds up his phone, an annoyed expression across his face. In his other hand, he holds a plastic grocery bag knotted at the top. "I have—three times."

I blush. Cell reception isn't the best out here. "Sorry. What's up?"

His eyes immediately home in on my plate of spaghetti on the table as he pushes through the door, dropping his bag and kicking off his dirty work boots. "I'm starving. You have any more?"

McKenna holds up her bowl. "You can have mine."

Jeremy and I both say "No" at the same time then I head over to our small kitchenette to grab a spare bowl so I can split my portion with him. This is unusual. He doesn't show up at our trailer out of the blue much these days, especially now that he's dating Khloe. If he's not at work, he's usually with her. A year into their relationship, they still have stars in their eyes. I'm happy for him, but I refuse to say so because then he'll start rambling on about her for an hour and I'm tired and I need a shower and I don't have all night to hear about how he's saving up money to buy an engagement ring.

I let him eat a few bites of spaghetti before I question him again. "So…to what do we owe this pleasure?"

He finishes chewing, wipes his mouth, and then levels me with a toothy grin. I haven't seen him this happy in a long time.

"I have a solution for our money problems, cuz."

Uh huh. Not likely.

"Jeremy, please tell me Nick didn't convince you to start dealing." I immediately point a finger toward McKenna. "Pretend you didn't hear that."

She makes a motion like she's zipping her lips then pretends to go back to reading.

"Not even close," Jeremy says before he proceeds to eat three more bites of spaghetti, leaving me sitting there, impatiently waiting for him to continue.

Eventually, I yank the bowl out from in front of him and hold it far enough away that he's forced to look up at me.

"Tell me."

He chews slowly, swallows slowly, sits back slowly. I'm going to kill him.

"You remember when some big-time developer snatched up the old summer camp out that way, heading toward Louisiana?"

I nod. "Yeah. We all thought they were going to do something with it, but nothing's happened."

He leans forward, his green eyes aglow. "Well they *are* doing something with it. Apparently, they're going to turn it into some fancy resort. Massive hotel, golf course, pools—the works."

My heart drops. This isn't the first time this town has gotten its hopes up like this. A few years back, Walmart was planning on building a distribution center out here. It never happened. Then a few oil companies wanted to set up some speculative drill sites. They promised Oak Dale and its residents would have so much money pouring in, we wouldn't know what to do with it. That was right before the boom happened over in West Texas. I've learned my lesson.

"And when is this '*fancy*' resort supposed to get built? Next year? Year after?"

He shakes his head, his toothy grin staying in place. "Tomorrow, Lockwood Construction is having a recruitment day over in the grocery store parking lot. Line's supposed to be long so I'll be getting there around 8 AM."

I'm struck silent.

He leans forward, yanking his bowl of spaghetti out of my hand. "They're paying $25 an hour, more if you can prove you've been around a construction site before."

$25 an hour?! I can't even imagine. To me, that's movie star money. That's tossing dollars in the air at a nightclub money.

"Why are they hiring people out here?"

He gives me an isn't-it-obvious glare. "Think about it: it's cheaper than carting in a boatload of guys from across the state. The subs will be their guys, of course, but they still need a crew—unskilled labor for the grunt work."

I'm so jealous I can hardly breathe. Jeremy will be hired in an instant. He's young and in shape from his work at the mill. He's worked construction in the past and has a clean record. Getting paid $25 an hour, he'll have Khloe's ring in no time.

"I'm happy for you," I say, impressed that I'm able to sound remotely sincere. Inside, I'm a bitter Betty. I rise from the table and take my untouched plate of spaghetti over to the counter to store it for later. I've lost my appetite.

"I want you to come with me and apply," Jeremy says suddenly.

I laugh and glance at him over my shoulder. "You think they need maids on the construction site? Cleaning out porta-potties—now there's every girl's dream job."

"I talked to my buddy and he said they're desperate. They'll take any and all help they can get. If you're an able-bodied guy, you'll get hired."

I smirk. "I know you prefer not to notice seeing as we're family and all, but I'm afraid I don't fit that 'guy' requirement. I've had boobs since middle school."

He screws his face up like it grosses him out to acknowledge my female body then he rises to his feet so he can retrieve the grocery bag he left by the door.

"Don't you think I've thought of that?"

He unties the knot and dumps out the contents onto the floor. There's a faded blue baseball hat, two old flannel work shirts, a pair of jeans, and tan work boots that have seen better days. In fact, I'm not sure they've got any days left in them.

"The shirts are mine. The boots and jeans I bought off a friend at work. He's a lot smaller than me, so they should fit you okay."

He can't be serious.

I hold up one of the boots and tug at the rubber heel, which is no longer fully connected to the rest of the shoe. "I hope you didn't pay much."

He grunts in annoyance and yanks it out of my hand.

"Jeremy, it's not the shoes or the clothes. It's the idea. You think if I dress up like a guy they'll be willing to hire me? Just like that?"

He glances at me, narrows one eye, and tilts his head as if imagining the possibility. "Well, you'll have to tuck your hair up under the hat, and maybe add a fake mustache."

McKenna cracks up at that. I shoot her a glare over my shoulder and she whips her attention right back to her textbook. She's not supposed to be listening to any of this absurd plan.

"It won't work," I say definitively.

His shoulders sag in defeat. "So you don't even want to try?"

"Pfft." I reach down for the jeans and hold them up against my waist. I'll have to tighten them with a rope or something, but they should stay up. "I didn't say that—of course I'll try. Just don't be shocked when they send me packing."

CHAPTER FIVE

TAYLOR

The decision to dress like a guy was impulsive and half-baked. I passed on the fake mustache and any other over-the-top disguise, but I still look completely ridiculous, like I've stolen my big brother's clothes for a Halloween costume. My jeans are rolled up twice at the ankles and cinched at the waist with a thin piece of rope. On top, I layered one of Jeremy's flannel shirts over a plain white t-shirt. Even with the sleeves pushed up to my elbows, it shrouds my body like a blanket. There was no other option, though; with it tucked in, it revealed too much of my figure. Even though it looks rather absurd, it has to stay untucked and baggy.

McKenna helped me spin my hair into a bun and pin it down underneath the baseball hat. Last night, as we discussed the plan, Jeremy grabbed a pair of scissors from our junk drawer and suggested I just chop it off. McKenna and I both screamed at him to put the scissors down. Needless to say, my long hair is staying put underneath the hat.

Fortunately, the only-slightly-too-big work boots have held up as we've stood in line, shuffling forward slowly over the last hour. Jeremy was right to get here early, but other guys still beat us to the punch. There has to be a hundred of them, all ready to sign their life away for the hope of earning triple what most jobs around here pay an hour.

A lot of the men are from surrounding towns and counties, guys who were willing to drive quite a distance to be here today. I'm glad for their presence, though, because they don't know me, which means they're less likely to see past my disguise. Unfortunately, there are still quite a few guys I do know, some I went to high school with. One, I used to date.

I really don't stand a chance with Max. He works with Jeremy at the lumber mill so when he sees us waiting in line, he comes over to say hi right away. I try to keep my head down, seemingly very interested in the parking lot—*Huh, is that concrete? Cool stuff*—but that doesn't help.

"Taylor?" Max asks, leaning down to peer under the brim of my hat.

I act deeply shocked to see him there. "Max?! No way. What are you doing here?"

His brows furrow in confusion.

Max was the "it" guy at my high school. Universally attractive with his boy band haircut and winning smile, no girl was immune to his charms. He also happened to be slightly more well-off than the rest of us thanks to his mom's job as the middle school's principal. He was the one with the cool new shoes at the start of every school year while all the rest of us were rocking hand-me-downs that had someone else's feet imprinted on the soles. He and I only dated for a few months our sophomore year, but I've always had the impression that Max would change that if I gave him the chance.

His confusion gives way to intrigue. His dimples pop.

"I'm applying for a job. What are *you* doing here?"

Jeremy grunts loudly. Max looks toward him, and I barely notice my cousin shake his head in warning. The guys around us in line are starting to take notice. I don't blame them. It's been pretty boring so far, and I'd be curious about the man-child drowning in adult clothing too.

"Taylor and I are both applying," Jeremy says simply as we all shuffle up one place in line.

A few of the guys behind us observe Max and the fact that he's lingering. "Hey bud," one of them says gruffly, "we've all been waiting here for an hour. If you want to get in line, get in the back."

Max holds up his hands in surrender. "All right, all right, I'm going." Then he aims one last smirk my way and adds a wink. "I'll catch you *guys* in a little bit."

Jeremy and I exchange a glance but otherwise keep silent. It's obvious we're both having second thoughts about going through with this. It's going to be so embarrassing when we get to the front of the line and the recruitment team calls me out in front of everyone.

She's a woman! Get her!

I've spent my time carefully assessing the situation so I can limit my chances of failure. Ahead of us, there's a large white portable construction trailer, which Lockwood Construction staff has been filtering in and out of all day. In front of the trailer, there are three tables, each manned by a recruiter. When an applicant reaches the front of the line, he (or in my case, *she*) steps up to an available table, hands over his completed paperwork with his ID, answers a few questions, and if all goes well, he's then given a small sterile cup for a urine sample. Ah yes, drug testing. I'm actually glad they're doing it because a handful of guys awkwardly shuffled away and headed home once they realized that was the case, which shortened our wait time by a little bit.

To the left of the tables, there's one of those fancy porta-potties—the kind with a mirror and sink inside. A man in scrubs stands at the door, allowing one person in at a time and subsequently collecting their urine samples after they're finished.

That's all I've got to get through. There's nothing that should call undue attention to me. They're not forcing us to perform daring feats of strength or prove our skill with a hammer. *You there! Flip over that human-sized tire with one hand!*

Nothing will call attention to my gender unless a great gust of wind whips my hat off and my hair goes tumbling down my back.

Just the thought makes me pull the brim down so it sits a little more snuggly on my head. Any lower and I'll be blind.

The line moves forward and dread fills my stomach. It feels like I'm doing something wrong, but nowhere on the application does it specify that women aren't allowed to apply for jobs today. It's just heavily implied. When's the last time you pulled up to a construction site and saw a bunch of ladies rockin' hard hats? Oh right, *never*.

To be clear, I'm not pretending to be a man. I'm just trying to blend in like a chameleon. Yup, don't mind me, just your average red-blooded American construction worker with a heart-shaped face, button nose, and pouty mouth.

"Next!" one of the recruiters shouts.

The line moves and we're only a few people away from the front now.

My hands start to tremble, and Jeremy notices.

"You okay?" he asks, keeping his voice low.

I nod, but I'm not…really. A strange sensation grips hold of my spine and I swear I'm being watched. *No shit, Sherlock. You look like a doof.* I glance over my shoulder, but there's nothing out of the ordinary, just a bunch of guys shuffling around in line, bored. Some of them are chatting amongst themselves. Some are on their phones. One guy is ferociously tearing into a cinnamon roll, and I think I like him the best of all. If I get hired, I hope we work together.

Jeremy nudges me forward as the line moves and when I turn back around, my attention catches on the trailer behind the tables where Lockwood Construction staff is presumably watching the events of the morning take place.

That's why I feel like I'm being watched—we probably *all* are.

Before I know it, I'm at the front of the line, heading toward a recruiter who looks like he's ready to call it a day. I don't blame him. He's dealt with dozens of guys already and he doesn't even look up right away, just asks for my ID and application while he continues typing on his laptop.

"Name?"

"Taylor Larson."

He confirms that's the name on my ID and application then continues typing, filling in things like my date of birth and address, asking me to clarify the name of my current employer since my handwriting is so bad. Then he turns back to my ID for some other piece of information and stalls, hands hovering above his keyboard, no doubt finally noticing my photo. Was it really so important that I wear my hair down to the DMV that day? No one on Earth would confuse me for a dude in that photo.

His eyes cut up to me and then narrow, studying my face. I sit perfectly still, waiting. Hoping. Prepared to call his bluff. I *know* he's about to say something like, *Uh, lady? Scram and stop wasting our time*, but then someone walks up behind him. He's a short, squat guy with a thick beard, wearing a Lockwood Construction shirt. He leans down and whispers something into the recruiter's ear. The man behind the table nods quickly and reaches for my application without hesitation. Then the bearded guy turns on his heel and climbs the stairs to the trailer so he can disappear inside once again.

"What was that about?" I ask, more paranoid than ever. There've been no whispers in ears about any of the other applicants, at least none that I've seen.

"Nothing for you to worry about," he says with a clipped tone.

I laugh. "Oh, well…that sounds slightly ominous."

He doesn't find me funny.

"You know you'll be the only female on the crew," he says, stamping one of my forms with a green check and then shoving the papers back in my direction along with a sterile cup. "The only female staying in the bunkhouses too. You must really need the job."

I frown, having a hard time keeping up. "What do you mean 'bunkhouses'?"

He holds up his hand, looks over my shoulder at the line of people behind me, and shouts, "Next!" so loudly that I get the gist. If I have questions, I should direct them elsewhere.

CHAPTER SIX
ETHAN

"There's a ton of guys out there," Hudson says, standing at the window and peering out at the parking lot. He's tapping the windowpane with his finger like he's actually performing a head count. It's annoying as shit. "Yup, over a hundred, though I think I missed a few."

Good God, if he tries to start over with his count, I'm going to break his finger off.

Ignorant of the daggers I'm aiming his way, Hudson goes right on rambling about the turnout, and I go right on ignoring him. I've been doing a pretty good job of it so far this morning. I'm sitting at a desk in the trailer, working, and Hudson should be doing the same seeing as he's my assistant project manager for this build. Off the top of my head, I can think of five things he should be doing right now, none of which include standing idle at the window.

"Have you called to confirm the builder's risk insurance is active?"

"I did that yesterday," he replies, easy breezy.

"What about dumpsters? We'll be starting demo first thing on Tuesday."

"They're being delivered Monday. I'll be there to make sure they're in the right spots."

"Excavators?"

"Already on site."

I narrow my eyes.

He turns and smiles.

Hudson's only a few years out of college and nearly as annoying as he is helpful. We didn't even have a job listing posted when he walked into the Lockwood Construction office and asked to speak with one of the partners. Of course, that didn't happen—we're busy guys—so he came back the next day…and the next. In the end, I had no choice but to give him an internship, which he quickly finagled into a full-time position.

"Wait, wait, wait." He starts laughing, leaning forward and narrowing his eyes to get a better look at whatever's caught his attention.

I pound away loudly on my laptop, hoping to get the message through his thick brain: *Stop bothering me.*

"Holy shit. Either that's the hottest dude I've ever seen or it's not a dude at all."

I frown, stuck between a rock and a hard place. If I stand up and go over to look at the person he's referring to, he'll have been successful in distracting me. If I don't look, my curiosity will eat away at me.

With a reluctant sigh, I push up to stand and make my way over to the window.

"There. You see him?"

I see a sea of recruits, none all that noteworthy.

"There, in the blue baseball hat." Hudson points. "Hold on, wait until he turns."

I spot the guy, but he's facing the opposite direction, glancing back down the line behind him. Even still, I can tell he's a pipsqueak, basically half the size of his peers. It doesn't help that his clothes are four sizes too big.

I wouldn't be surprised to find out it's a kid trying to pass himself off as legal. We've had that happen a few times in the past, but at the least those guys *looked* eighteen. This kid hasn't even gone through puberty yet from the looks of it.

The guy finally turns when the line shifts forward and his buddy nudges him. He lifts his head, the brim of his hat no longer hiding his face, and right then, a fist collides with my stomach.

I know those eyes.

I know those lips.

I know that face.

I. Know. That. Face.

The shock leaves me completely immobile. Then, just as quickly, adrenaline seizes hold of me. My blood pressure skyrockets. My heart starts racing. I can barely believe it. I never thought I'd see the girl again and now here she is, in line to get a job working for my company…pretending to be a guy. Oh, it's too good.

"See what I mean?" Hudson asks. "There's no way *that's* a dude."

My brain is working overtime, trying to figure out what I want to do with this gift. Yes, *gift*. In the month since I first encountered her, I've been unable to push her out of my mind. My inability to forget about her has only made the wound she inflicted on my ego fester. I don't know why she's proven unforgettable. Sure, there's the possibility that our searing kiss in the bathroom left its mark on my memory, but more likely, my pride wants some kind of resolution.

"Look at those lips." Hudson is still talking. "No, I refuse to believe that's a guy, because if it is…" He scratches his neck. "Well, I guess I might be into dudes. Who knew?"

Without a reply, I forcefully push him toward the door of the trailer.

"I want you to make sure that guy gets hired."

He trips over his feet trying to match my pace.

"Why?" He turns back to look at me. "What aren't you telling me?"

I open the door and move to shove him out, but he leaps down the first few stairs just in time to avoid my "gentle" nudge, which is for the best. I'm not trying to hurt him. Much.

"Go."

He holds up his hands in defeat. "Okay! *Okay*!"

And then he's out the door and I'm back at the window watching the girl in the blue baseball hat sitting at a table with a recruiter. Hudson rushes over to whisper something in his ear and just like that, she's hired.

I know I'm not handling the situation the right way. I should drag her down to the police station and report her crime, let the authorities take care of her—I'm sure she's wanted for a multitude of other offenses—but something about that course of action doesn't feel right. Maybe I want to handle my own problems. Maybe I like the idea of toying with her a little, teaching her a lesson. Maybe my pride has finally found a way to seek resolution in the form of retribution.

I feel like the big bad wolf setting a trap.

I almost feel bad for her.

Almost.

CHAPTER SEVEN

TAYLOR

"You didn't say anything about bunkhouses when you told me about this job!"

Jeremy deflects the punch I aim at his shoulder and manages to continue driving just fine. "That's because I didn't know about them, but I actually think it sounds fun."

"Fun?!"

Another punch dodged.

Now he's holding me at arm's length to keep me away. My puny arms can't reach him. Stupid wing span.

"Yeah. I mean, it makes sense. The jobsite is an hour and a half away from Oak Dale, even more since your trailer is on the other side of town. Driving back and forth every day would waste too much gas and too much time. Besides, they're giving people the option. You can either stay in the bunkhouses or commute every day."

"Well, you're my ride and you're staying there."

He smiles wide. "So then problem solved. What's there to worry about?"

Oh, I don't know…*everything?!*

This is how Jeremy explained it to me: Lockwood Construction is building a luxury resort on the old grounds of Pine Wood Camp. They have the resort laid out so that the new hotel complex will be built over the existing stables, obstacle course, and meeting hall because those areas all have lakefront views. The bunkhouses we're supposed to be staying in will eventually be turned into luxury cabins, but that phase of construction won't happen until much later.

Thus, until then, they've given the crew the option to live in them while we work.

"You of all people shouldn't want to do it. When will you see Khloe?"

I think I have a very convincing argument until he shrugs nonchalantly.

"On the weekends. As it is, I'm too busy working the late shift at the mill to see her much during the week anyway. Nothing will change except for my paycheck—or have you forgotten that part?"

I cross my arms and glare out the window. Of course I haven't. I might not think it's a good idea to go camp in the middle of the woods with dozens of gruff construction workers, but the money is too good to walk away from, not to mention I'll have Jeremy there as a buffer between me and the guys.

"Well I don't know if I can leave McKenna during the week like that. Who's going to make sure she gets her homework done?"

"She's a good kid. You worry about her more than you need to."

"Who will cook dinner?"

"I think she'll manage to make her own peanut butter and jelly sandwiches just fine."

Wow. Okay. Harsh, but true.

"Still…I don't think it's a good idea. For other reasons…"

He shrugs. "Then don't do it."

Wait—he was supposed to convince me otherwise. I thought that was what we were doing here, a little routine where he goads me into this so I can blame him when it all goes up in flames.

I turn to face him, brows furrowed. "You don't think I should?"

He shakes his head. "Eh, I've thought about it. The work will be hard, and it'll be hot out there in a few weeks when summer hits. Better just keep working at the hotel. At least that's air-conditioned."

I know exactly what he's trying to pull and yet my pride still rears its ugly head.

"So you don't think I can do the work? That's what you're saying?"

He gives me a teasing smirk. "Wouldn't want to get splinters in those dainty hands of yours."

Of all the insufferable, misogynistic...

Right. Well, it should come as no surprise that when Jeremy drops me off a few minutes later, before I close the door and stomp into the trailer, I lean back into the truck and tell him very matter-of-factly to pick me up on his way to the jobsite on Sunday evening.

I guess I'm going camping.

My mom and sister cried a lot as I packed a duffle bag full of necessities. There I was in our tiny bathroom, trying to decide how many rolls of toilet paper I wanted to bring with me (just in case) when McKenna came up behind me, wrapped her skinny arms around my middle, and squeezed me so tight my dinner threatened a second showing.

"I'm going to miss you so much."

I patted her hand, trying hard not to chuckle. "You know I'm not really moving away, right?"

Her little sniffles did the answering for her.

Meanwhile, my mom leaned against the doorframe doing a poor job of wiping at her cheeks to hide her tears. Between the two of them, I wouldn't have been surprised to find a puddle at my feet.

"Jeremy will be coming back on the weekends to visit Khloe, so I'll get a ride with him," I assured them. "With school and work, weekdays go by so fast anyway. You won't even notice I'm gone."

McKenna shook her head back and forth against my shoulder blade. "Not true. I'll notice."

I try to push the memory of her sad voice out of my mind as Jeremy puts his truck in park. It's Sunday evening and those of us who'll be staying in the bunkhouses are arriving to get the lay of the land so we can hit the ground running tomorrow morning.

I've grown up in East Texas—a part of the state known for its logging industry—my whole life and still, pockets of deep forest like this amaze me. Outside the truck's windshield, pine trees grow as far as the eye can see, soaring so tall and mighty they look like they've been here since the dawn of time. Underneath their branches, the forest floor is covered in dense green foliage. Any paths that might have wended their way through the trees while the camp was up and running are gone now, stolen back by nature.

Jeremy opens his door to jump out and I follow suit, grabbing my bag and making sure my hat is in place. We talked about it on the drive and both agreed it's a good idea for me to continue wearing the hat and clothes he lent me for as long as possible. If everything goes as planned, I'll find a position that doesn't require too much brawn, keep my head down, and work. Sure, there's a good chance the guys will start to notice I'm not one of them, but hopefully by then, I'll have been a part of the crew long enough that it shouldn't matter.

We walk past the long row of cars toward a clearing in the woods. Up ahead, an old wooden sign marks the entrance of Pine Wood Camp, but flowering vines have wound their way up the posts, concealing half the painted letters. The rest are dull and faded. Our boots crunching fallen leaves seems like the only sound for miles.

"Kind of creepy," Jeremy says, throwing me a smile over his shoulder.

I think it's cool. We've only been outside walking a short while and already, I know this place could get into my soul if I let it. The air is crisp and cool. The smell of the trees is nearly overwhelming. *Okay, forest, now you're just showing off.* There's a reason so many cleaning products come with a "pine fresh" scent, but they don't come close to replicating this. You can't. There are too many undercurrents: damp earth and wild jasmine and blooming honeysuckle.

Maybe this won't be so bad, I think just before we come upon the first signs of the old camp and my fleeting optimism flies right out the window. There's already a ton of guys here, more than I thought would be staying during the week. Apparently, a lot of them agreed driving back and forth was a waste of gas, but that means there's no way Jeremy and I will have our own bunkhouse. I know it was kind of delusional of me to think that was an option, but it's the only way I could convince myself to get into his truck back in Oak Dale.

I don't want to sleep in a room with a dozen guys I've never met!

Where will I change?

Where will I shower?!

Jeremy must notice my hesitation based on the fact that I've stopped walking forward and am now actively retreating back toward his truck.

He rushes back to wrap an arm around my shoulder and nudges me forward. "C'mon, before you throw in the towel, let's go check out the room situation and we'll figure out what to do from there. I swear it won't be so bad."

It is so bad.

Since stupid Jeremy *had* to have dinner with Khloe before we left Oak Dale, we don't exactly get the cream of the crop when it comes to sleeping quarters. Fortunately, there's still a bunkhouse with two beds available. Unfortunately, the beds are on opposite sides of the room from one another. When I drop my duffle onto my bed and turn back to look for Jeremy, I can't even see him there are so many bunk beds in the way.

My only hope is that a very clean, very quiet man will be sleeping above me, but based on the gentleman sitting on the bunk to my right, I'm not sure that will be the case.

He's currently putting every ounce of energy he has into hocking up a loogie before he spits it into an empty cup he drops on the floor near my feet. I nearly gag. When he's done, he returns to his activity of choice: sharpening a rather large hunting knife. When he sees me staring, he offers up a sneer that includes what I can only describe as a breathtaking row of teeth. Truly, they are breathtaking in that the stench wafting from his mouth is making it very difficult for me to draw a breath.

"Name's Carl," he volunteers in a heavy Southern drawl.

I nod and turn back, pretending to look for something in my duffle bag. Oh right, it's called hope and I find none among the oversized clothes and toilet paper rolls. "I'm Taylor."

"You don't look like you've done much construction work before." I can feel his eyes drag over my body, assessing me.

"I haven't," I reply honestly.

He nods. "Well I'm around if you need anythin'. I've been workin' construction since I was old enough to hold a hammer."

"Thanks, I appreciate that," I say, surprised by his kindness, just before someone casts a heavy shadow over me.

"Can I see your card?"

I glance up, and up some more, until I reach the face of a young bald guy frowning at me.

"My card?"

He holds up a card with a name—*his* name, I presume—and a number written on it.

"Yeah, does your card say bunkhouse 2? Because I already asked around and—"

"I don't have a card," I say, suddenly panicked. "I assumed the bunks were first come, first served."

Carl and the new guy groan.

Apparently, even though we aren't twelve-year-olds on a middle school field trip, Lockwood Construction deemed it necessary to post bunkhouse assignments for the crew. That way they'll know where everyone is located in the event of an emergency. I know this because I asked the employee passing out the cards for the room assignments.

"Insurance wanted it that way too," he says as he finds the one with my name on it. I recognize him from the hiring event, the stout guy with a beard so thick it makes him look like an extra for *Game of Thrones*.

"What'd you get?" Jeremy asks, leaning toward me to read my card. "Rose Cabin? No shit? I guess you lucked out. I'm in bunkhouse 3."

"Why'd I luck out?" I ask, confused.

"The cabins have been reserved for the higher-ups, but there were a few vacancies," the employee answers for him. "You'll be filling one."

I nod, not quite sure what to make of this turn of events. On one hand, I'm glad I won't have to share a bunkhouse with twenty Carls. On the other hand, there is a sort of security in numbers. I don't want to be stuck in a tiny cabin with someone I hate. At least before, I knew Jeremy was in the same building. Now, he could be half a camp away.

Jeremy senses my hesitation and holds out his card. "Want to switch?"

The employee clears his throat loudly. "Unfortunately, that's not allowed."

This guy. I turn and smirk. "What did you say your name was?"

He sits up, squares his shoulders, and holds out his hand. "Hudson Rivers, assistant project manager."

So, he's Dwight. I want to ask if he's the assistant *to* the project manager.

I shake his hand instead. "Where exactly is Rose Cabin, Hudson?"

After I'm armed with directions for how to get to my cabin, Jeremy and I split off since he still needs to go claim his bunk.

"You good?" he asks, walking backward in the direction we just came from.

"Yup." I wave my card in the air. "Have fun in the bunkhouse. I'll be thinking of you as I'm living it up in *Rose Cabin*, enjoying my life with the 'higher-ups'. I bet they serve breakfast in bed!" I say, voice rising with mock hope. "I bet we have a butler!"

He shakes his head as if he isn't sure what to do with me and then turns to head off.

For the first time since we arrived, I'm alone in the forest.

Well, kind of.

Where I stand, the forest surrounds me on all sides, but at a distance. A large swath of land was cleared for the original campgrounds, and it looks like Lockwood Construction spent some time clearing out any regrowth in the weeks leading up to our arrival.

The old camp is set up based on the four cardinal directions. The old parking lot where Jeremy left his truck is on the northmost side, which gives way to a main walking path. Due south of the faded sign we passed under, there's the center of camp composed of an old infirmary, a large mess hall, and a main office, all of which look like they've been cleaned up recently to accommodate our crew. It's where I currently stand. South of these buildings, deeper in the forest, there's apparently a large lake and the site where the future hotel will be built. I squint and try to spot the body of water, but it must be pretty far away. East of the central camp buildings is where the row of bunkhouses are located, where Jeremy is headed now, and to the west is where I'm supposed to go to find my cabin. It sounds easy enough, but the camp is sprawling and encompasses untold acres of forest. The farther away from the central buildings I walk, the more dense the forest becomes and the less people I encounter.

I'm also aware that early evening has given way to dusk, and the sun is starting to fade behind the tall trees, casting the path in front of me into shallow darkness. I'm kicking myself for not forcing Jeremy to leave Oak Dale earlier. I sure hope he enjoyed that dinner with Khloe because I'm going to get lost in the woods as a result of it. I just know it. In fact, I take a mental note of what's in my duffle just in case I need to survive on the contents alone. I have the clothes Jeremy lent me, toiletries, and the granola bar McKenna stuffed in my bag on my way out the door.

"In case you get hungry on the drive!" she said.

I'm more grateful than ever that I forgot about that granola bar until just now. It will likely be my only sustenance for the next week as I play out a real-life version of *Naked and Afraid*—except I'll be fully clothed, so I guess just *Afraid*.

An owl hoots in a tree nearby and *oh my god is that my shadow or a mountain lion?* I remind myself I'm not in the mountains and then proceed forward, having successfully talked myself down from panicking. Then I remember that just because I'm not in the mountains doesn't mean there aren't other forest creatures roaming near me, licking their chops. I pick up the pace and am nearly hysterical with joy when I spot a log cabin up ahead. *Finally!*

I run toward it like it's my salvation and don't realize until I'm right upon it that it has a wooden sign dangling from the porch roof that says Daisy. Or rather, D-A-I…half-falling-off-S-Y. Not only that, it's in quite a state of disrepair. One windowpane is shattered. The other is completely gone. It's missing a nice chunk of its metal roof, and the front door is only attached by one hinge, leaving it to sway ominously in the wind, creaking at just the right interval to send a tingle of terror down my spine.

HELLO, LOCATION OF MY NIGHTMARES.

My heart is a speeding bullet as I run back to the path and force myself to continue in the direction Hudson's scrawled map is leading me. I walk/run/skip (anything to get me away from Nightmare Cabin) down the path for what feels like 45,000 yards and still have not come across another structure, and then I reach a curve in the path and decide if I don't see a cabin once I turn the corner, I'm bolting. I'll find Jeremy, steal his keys, and sleep in his truck. That actually sounds lovely, right up until I make it around the bend and there she is: Rose Cabin.

CHAPTER EIGHT

TAYLOR

My expectations after seeing the first cabin are at an all-time low, but this one is the exact opposite of its predecessor. It's actually...*adorable.*

Small and square with a metal roof and two symmetrical windows framing the front door, the log cabin sits surrounded by wildflowers on all sides. Sure, some might call the unruly things weeds, but I'm not cultured enough to tell the difference. To me, they're lovely, and I think that's the first time I've used that word in my adult life without a single note of sarcasm.

The setting sun leaves just enough light to illuminate my path to the front porch. I know this is the right cabin because of the sign that proclaims it to be and also because the door is painted a dusky pink hue. *Rose*. Sure, there's dust caked around the doorframe now, but I can tell that at one point, this cabin was well-loved. It's the stuff of fairytales. In fact, I half expect Snow White to poke her head out one of the windows and invite me in for tea. *"Yoo-hoo, scruffy young lad! Do come inside!"*

I hold on to the wooden railing as I walk up the stairs that lead to the porch, just in case one of the steps decides it's had enough and wants to disintegrate beneath my feet. The wooden boards do groan under my weight as if they're waking from a long slumber, but they hold steady.

I'm about to reach out to open the front door when I stop short and decide to knock first. I won't be living here alone. I'll have at least one or two roommates, and I'd rather not barge in on one of them in a compromising position. I don't know. I've never lived with a guy, but I feel like 9 times out of 10 when left alone, they're up to no good.

"Knock knock," I say, *while* knocking. I roll my eyes at myself and am actually grateful when no one answers. Maybe my roommate hasn't arrived yet—or better yet, maybe he doesn't exist.

I push the door open and step inside tentatively, and once again, I'm impressed by what I find.

The place is larger than it looked from the outside. On the right, just past the door, there's a bunk bed. Beyond that sits an outdated wooden dresser that looks to be heavier than I am. Across from the bed, there's a small wooden desk and chair. Then in the corner, near the desk, there's an empty aluminum trough large enough for someone to sit back and recline in. My eyes widen. Oh god, is that where I'll have to bathe? *Out in the open?*

Then my eyes belatedly fall on a half-open door and I realize there's a bathroom directly across from where I stand. Inside, I spot a small wall-mounted sink, a toilet, and a shower. There's no curtain rod for the shower, but the floor is graded toward a drain in the corner so water won't get everywhere

I give the place an approving nod. This is shaping up to be quite a luxurious little abode. As far as I know, the guys in the bunkhouse have to share communal bathrooms. I get one all to myself. Well…kind of.

I do have a roommate, and he's already been here. I know this because there are personal effects neatly stowed around the cabin. On the sink, there's a toothbrush and some toothpaste sitting in a cup. A towel hangs on a hook by the shower. Behind me, on the bottom bunk, I spy an open paperback halfway tucked beneath a pillow. On the dresser, there's a worn baseball hat. When I gently tug open the top drawer, I'm greeted by a stack of black boxer briefs. My cheeks burn and I immediately shove it closed again, embarrassed. I am apparently a ten-year-old. *They're just underwear!* I chide myself. Then the child in me shouts back, *Yes, but a stranger's underwear!*

I have no idea how long he's been here, but it seems like he didn't just arrive today if he's already been showering and reading.

Maybe he's the one who cleaned the place up. Compared to the bunkhouses, this cabin is practically sterile, in a good way. The dark wood floors are shiny as if they've been mopped recently. The beds have linens on them that seem relatively new. There's no mold or ambiguous green sludge collecting in the bathroom.

Overall, I decide this cabin will do just fine as I start to empty my duffle bag into the empty bottom drawer of the dresser. It takes me all of two seconds and then I sit back on my heels wondering what I'm supposed to do now. It's nearly 8:30 PM. There's no point in wandering back out into the woods. The guys are probably all settling into their bunks, and Jeremy's probably on the phone with Khloe swearing he misses her already. My roommate will probably be here soon and then we can meet and I'll have to look him in the eye knowing what color underwear he's wearing.

My neck grows warm.

I'm being ridiculous.

Still, maybe an early-morning introduction is best, rather than a late-night one. I decide to get ready for bed, but it's proving kind of difficult now that the sun has fully set. My eyes have adjusted slowly, but it's too dark now and I fumble around quite a bit until I manage to turn on the electric lantern I spotted on the desk earlier. It produces the same amount of light a small lamp would and makes it easy to navigate around the cabin as I quickly brush my teeth and change into my sweatpants and t-shirt.

I wouldn't mind a quick shower, but I don't want to chance it. What if my roommate arrives while I'm bathing? What if he assumes I'm a dude and waltzes right into the bathroom to go pee without even knocking first? No. Nope. I'll have to wait until the morning.

As it is, without A/C, the cabin is a little stuffy. I pry open the windows to let in some air, but Texas is Texas, even in spring, and there isn't a breeze cool enough to bring this cabin down to a temperature conducive to heavy sweatpants. Unfortunately, they were the only thing I could find to sleep in that would cover my legs. I couldn't exactly pack a pair of tiny sleeping shorts. My main objective is to fly under my roommate's radar, not flash him my butt cheeks.

After I wash my face with cool water, I turn the lantern off, drop my baseball hat on the dresser beside my roommate's, shake out my hair (*Ah! Freedom!*), and climb the ladder up to the top bunk. There's a wave of relief as I lie down on top of the cool sheet and stare up at the ceiling.

I did it.

I survived the first day.

Kind of.

Tomorrow is the real first day.

This was nothing, really.

Still, I'm here, and it's an accomplishment for a girl who's never spent a night outside of Oak Dale in her entire life. I'm embarrassed to admit there's a tight ball of tension in my stomach I've been trying to ignore: homesickness. Ridiculous, I know. I'm too old to feel homesick. Besides, there's nothing I can do about it. I can't call home—there's no cell reception out here. I've been trying to pick up a signal since I first arrived, and now, as I try to call my mom's phone yet again, it won't go through.

I wish I could distract myself, but I didn't bring a book and the light is off anyway. I try to close my eyes and tell myself to go to sleep, but I'm too hot and I'm not tired and I'm still on pins and needles waiting for my roommate to arrive. Surely he won't stay out much later.

That's when I hear the cabin door creak and my heart leaps into my throat.

He's here!

Or a bear is sneaking in.

Either way, I play dead, eyes closed and everything.

In an ideal world, he'd dive straight into his bunk and start to snore.

No such luck.

Light suddenly filters past my closed eyelids and I realize he's turned the lantern back on, though it must be on a different setting than I used because it's a softer glow, barely enough to let him see what he's doing.

I hear him over by the dresser and I peel one eye open just enough to see the top two inches of his dark brown hair as he reaches into the drawer for something. BRIEFS. *BLACK BRIEFS.*

The drawer closes and he steps back and I jerk toward the wall, using some of my pillow to conceal my face and hair. I know he notices because I hear a faint chuckle before the bathroom door closes, taking the lantern light with it. Water cuts on and the sound drowns out the loud hum of the cicadas outside.

He's showering and I have to listen, which feels oddly intimate: the sound of the stream as it hits different parts of his body. He could be a monster with two heads and five hands for all I know, but that's not the way I imagine him in there. Mr. Black Briefs.

The water cuts off a few minutes later and I'm under the sheet now with it tugged right up to my nose so I can peer over the top without my whole face showing. It's absolutely absurd, this game I'm playing, but it seems too late to turn back now. Besides, I've already decided I'll introduce myself in the morning. Right now, I just want to get a quick peek at him and put a face to the man who will be sleeping directly underneath me for the foreseeable future.

And I do get a peek at him. *All of him*.

Well, save for the low-slung shorts he apparently sleeps in. The rest of him, though? *Bare*. His broad, tanned chest. The smooth, rigid muscles composing his shoulders and arms. The impossibly sexy rows of abs and the sprinkle of hair leading down. Dark hair, enough to confirm he's a man but not so much that I'm worried he's part werewolf. He's tall and trim and I'm so hung up on that body—the sharp difference between my curves and his seemingly endless *firmness*—that it takes me a moment to drag my gaze up to his face.

When I do, the earth falls out from underneath me.

He can't be here.

In this cabin.

My eyes are playing a trick on me.

There's no other explanation.

Because it looks like *him*.

The man from the bar, the man I took into the bathroom and seduced…

The man I stole from.

No.

Technically, I did take his wallet, but then I gave it back. No harm, no foul.

Except, that can't be right. There must have been a foul because I'm here now and there's no way it's a coincidence. My body whirs to life as if preparing for fight or flight. I have a panicked urge to kick off my sheet, jump down from the top bunk, and bolt right out the cabin door. I spiral through a list of possibilities so quickly: *he found me, and he brought me out here on purpose, and now he's going to—*

What?

Kill me?

For some reason, finishing the thought actually forces me to stifle a laugh. It's totally crazy.

The fact is, coincidences *do* happen. Actually, now that I think about it, it's not really all that much of a coincidence at all. He was probably at the motel in Oak Dale a month ago because it was the only place to stay within two hours of this jobsite. He and the other suits must all work for Lockwood Construction and they were in town that weekend working on some aspect of this project. There, that feels better. Talking myself out of paranoid hysteria is the right thing to do.

The alternative just doesn't make sense.

It's not feasible that he set this whole thing up to exact some kind of revenge.

It's just not.

The light from the lantern cuts out and the cabin falls back into complete darkness, made even blacker by the fact that my eyes haven't adjusted. I lie perfectly still and listen to him as he pads across the floor and folds himself into the bunk beneath mine. He settles in place and the cicadas hum loudly, acting as a white noise that drowns out the sound of my heart thumping hard in my ears.

I don't know how long I stay awake, thinking, contemplating, breaking down possibilities and next steps.

The only thing I know for sure is that I *cannot* be here in this cabin when he wakes up.

CHAPTER NINE
ETHAN

The little thief is gone in the morning. I'm a pretty light sleeper, which means she was as quiet as a mouse on her way out, trying her hardest not to wake me. I'm not surprised she was successful. If she was stealthy enough to steal my wallet without me noticing, I'm sure it wasn't all that hard to sneak out without rousing me.

I know she saw me last night. I *wanted* her to see me when I walked out of the shower. I wanted her to have to lie there all night wondering how the hell we came to be bunkmates in this tiny cabin in the middle of nowhere. I wanted all the possibilities to fester in her mind, the more sinister the better.

I sit up and let my bare feet hit the wood floor, digging the heels of my palms into my tired eyes. I could use a few more hours of shuteye. Last night, I tossed and turned longer than I usually do, unable to put her out of my mind. That wasn't part of my plan. I was supposed to be sleeping like a baby while she stayed up worrying.

Even now, she's gone, but her scent still lingers. It's sweet and feminine, like a ripe juicy peach.

I smelled it all night.

I need to get out of here.

I brush my teeth and stare angrily at my reflection. This isn't like me. I'm not a vindictive asshole in my normal life. I mean, sure, I'm not the most easygoing guy. In fact, even suggesting that would make my sister, Isla, die from laughter. She says I'm more of a "strong silent type," whatever that means. I talk…when I feel like there's something worth saying. I guess I've always been a little reserved and more serious than my friends. I don't know. My parents tell me I was a shy kid. Maybe I never really grew out of it.

The point is, just because I'm not Mr. Happy-Go-Lucky doesn't mean I walk around conjuring up revenge plots. I would have let it go with Taylor. Yes, *Taylor*—I know her name because I read her application. I know for her last job she worked as a maid at the motel where I stayed last month. No doubt it was a convenient location for her, right next to the bar and all. I wonder how many guys came before me, how much money she's stolen.

A part of me feels pity for her, but then I remember she's here, working for my company and lying about her identity.

Surely conning guys at the bar is a much quicker way to make a buck than an honest day's work, but then again, I haven't been assured that's the reason she's here. It's why I have her rooming with me. I want to keep an eye on her.

Unfortunately, my work gets in the way of that a little. I don't exactly have all day to follow her around like I'm a secret agent on a stealth mission. I'm up at the jobsite all morning ensuring things are good to go for the crew to start demolition tomorrow. Right now, they're all trapped inside the mess hall watching OSHA training videos. I head there at lunch because I'm starving, but also because I know she'll be there.

I walk in the back and scan the rows of bodies facing a large projection screen. More than half the guys are wearing baseball hats, so she blends in surprisingly well. I'm about to give up when movement near the back catches my attention and I spot her profile as she leans in and whispers something to the guy beside her. He chuckles quietly and shakes his head.

She presses her hands together pleadingly, but he crosses his arms over his chest then nudges his head toward the video like he wants her to be paying attention.

Interesting.

I wonder if she's taken his wallet yet.

"This food isn't half bad," Hudson says, coming up to stand at my left with a full plate. We hired a catering company to provide meals for the crew during the duration of the project. It's not gourmet dining by any stretch of the imagination, but there shouldn't be any complaints. For lunch, they've prepared baked potatoes with chopped beef. Hudson has so much barbecue sauce poured over his it's about to spill over the sides.

"Bring mine out to the site, will you?" I ask, already turning for the door. "And go easy on the sauce."

Hudson's job doesn't usually involve preparing my lunch, but today it does.

I wanted to check up on Taylor and I have. I've confirmed she's where she's supposed to be, even if she's not doing what she's supposed to be doing: paying attention to the training videos. Out of everyone on the crew, she's easily the least experienced when it comes to construction. She should be up in the front row taking notes, acting like a star pupil. I guess it doesn't really matter though. She won't be anywhere near heavy machinery starting tomorrow.

That evening, I make it back to our cabin before Taylor, though I'm not surprised. In fact, if she comes back here at all, I'll be shocked.

I take a quick shower and change into a pair of lounge pants and a t-shirt. The sun hasn't set yet, and I owe my sister a call, so I take my phone out onto the front porch of the cabin and sit on the top stair before I dial.

"Well, well, well, look what the cat dragged in," she says, unable to pull off sounding truly menacing.

I smile. "Hey. Did you get that email I forwarded yesterday?"

"Yes. It was hilarious. I sent you back an interesting article I stumbled across during our morning meeting. It's about pandas. Seems random, but just read it. Trust me."

I shake my head as she launches into a full summary of the article, therefore making it unnecessary for me to read it myself.

Isla is my twin sister and we're close, mostly due to her persistence and relentless pursuit of a relationship with me. Growing up, I wanted my distance from her. I wanted my friends to be my friends and my life to be my life. Our parents didn't think that was necessary. Whatever afterschool activity I did, Isla did too. Track, swimming, basketball—even though she doesn't have an athletic bone in her body, not to mention she's only 5'3". The team photo of the JV basketball team includes a dozen girls close to six feet, and then there's Isla standing off to the side like someone's kid sister. I have it framed in my office back home.

By our senior year of high school, I finally realized she's actually pretty funny and I like being around her. If she weren't my twin sister, I'd still want to be her friend. We ended up at the same college, and even now, we hang out in the same circle of friends. Her apartment is ten minutes from my house in downtown Austin, which means she routinely shows up unannounced, but I never really mind because she usually brings beer or some kind of dessert. She bakes a lot, which is by far my favorite hobby of hers.

"This sucks that you're in the middle of freaking nowhere," she says, shifting gears now that she's exhausted the panda topic. "Jace and Alice want to go get drinks tomorrow, but I don't feel like going because you know how they get."

"I bet they hold hands the whole time."

She groans. "Handholding is one thing! At dinner the other night, she did this thing where she rubbed his earlobe between her fingers for like for five minutes. It was the weirdest shit I've ever seen. They need to get over each other already. Enough with the eternal love crap."

I smile. Isla functions in extremes when it comes to love and relationships. If she's in one, true love exists and we'll all find it. If she's just broken up with someone, love is a sham and anyone who says otherwise is a brainwashed idiot who needs to turn off the Hallmark channel.

"So Randall didn't work out?"

"*Randall.*" She puffs out a breath of air. "Don't even say his name."

"How many dates did you guys get to? I forget."

"Four, and then he told me he's not really looking to put labels on anything and love isn't binary and 'Would it be cool if we kept this unlabeled relationship open to others?'"

I groan. "I knew he sucked. When are you going to give in and just date Tanner?"

She laughs. "I have no idea what you're talking about. Anyway, enough about me. What about you? Does Tinder still work way out there? Maybe you'll meet a nice country mouse."

"The closest town is an hour and a half away. I don't think I'll be doing much dating."

"You say that like you do a lot of dating when you're in Austin."

"I do," I say, sounding defensive even to my own ears.

"That's hilarious."

"Kayley," I say as proof, reminding her of the friend she set me up with back in the fall.

"Yes, Kayley, who you took out on two horrible dates. She said during dinner you barely looked up from your phone. Then, you called her Candace when you dropped her off, before giving her a *side* hug."

I frown. "That was back in October. I was probably preoccupied with the Zilker project."

"When are you *not* preoccupied with a project? Whatever. I'm not setting you up with any more of my friends. Kayley swore she wasn't bothered that you didn't seem that into her, but whenever I see her in the office, she bolts in the other direction. Last week, I think she hid from me in the maintenance closet."

I rub the back of my neck.

"So what I'm saying is," she continues, "you better sign up for Tinder and get to swipin' cause I'm not helping you out anymore."

It's sad to say I haven't felt all that inspired to date in the last few years. I've put myself out there—mostly due to the insistence of friends—but the routine has become a little stale. Slow, awkward first dates. Good-but-not-great sex. Nonexistent banter. It's my fault. I'm the asshole on my phone during dinner. I'm the jerk who doesn't call back. I'm the guy who apparently forgets his date's name. Yikes, that's…not good. I just don't know how to stop myself from focusing all of my attention on work. It doesn't help that I've built up this illusion in my mind, this idea that I'm just biding my time, waiting for someone to shake me out of this stupor.

Even worse, I did find that woman.

Taylor.

Our encounter last month was like a slap to the face. *WAKE UP, YOU IDIOT. Look at her! Look at her sitting at the bar and realize that if you don't crawl over broken glass to get to this woman, you will regret it for the rest of your life.* So, I followed her into that bathroom, and I kissed her with an all-consuming need. Her smooth curves pressed against mine, her full lips tempting me toward insanity.

She was different, wild, beautiful. She was…stealing my wallet while I was thinking only of how I could convince her to spend the night with me.

The reminder twists my gut.

Ah yes, she was different because she was a seductive actress.

Not real.

I push to stand.

The sun is hanging low in the sky now, behind the canopy of trees. Soon, I'll need the lantern to find my way around, but Isla drones on. Isla is always droning on. Fiery meteors could be raining down from the sky and she would want to chat about it, preferably for two hours.

"Isla," I say, interrupting a story about her boss. "I gotta go."

"Oh! Okay. I'll let you know how drinks go tomorrow. Chances are I'll be texting you vomit emojis."

After we hang up, I head inside the cabin, turn on the lantern, and lie down on my bunk to read. It's kind of nice being out here. My computer is back in the trailer near the jobsite where there's power and a boosted internet connection. In the cabin, the wireless internet on my phone is slow and not worth bothering with, which means no work. I have to read, and when reading proves a poor distraction from thoughts of Taylor, I change into workout clothes and go for a run, setting a punishing pace. I like the trails around the camp, though it was stupid to run this late. By the time I make it back, it's pitch-black outside and I've nearly tripped over my feet ten times.

I'm dripping with sweat when I push the door open, and my eyes immediately rove to Taylor's bunk.

Empty.

I stomp toward the bathroom and jerk the shower knob until icy water rains down on my head. It's my second shower of the evening, my towel still wet from the last one. I scrub my hair and arms and legs and avoid the urge to touch myself anywhere that's not perfectly necessary. I've closed my eyes and stroked myself, dreaming of her, all month. I don't want to give her the satisfaction tonight, even if she'd never know about it.

When I step back out in my lounge pants and no shirt, Taylor still isn't back.

I worry about her walking around out here in the middle of the night, but then I remind myself that she's not mine to worry about.

I turn off the lantern and get in bed. I'm lying on my bunk with my eyes closed, willing sleep to take me, when the cabin door creaks open. She tiptoes in on light feet like she's trying not to wake me. I listen as she carefully takes off her boots, a soft hiss escaping her lips. I'm not surprised—they're too big on her, and I'm sure she has blisters by now.

I open my eyes as she starts to tiptoe past the bunk, grabs something from the dresser, and then disappears into the bathroom. She doesn't turn a light on, but she runs the sink on a gentle stream. At first, I think she's brushing her teeth, but then I realize she must be trying to wash off without having to turn the shower on.

It's ridiculous, these lengths she's willing to go to.

A few minutes later, the bathroom door opens silently and she tiptoes toward the ladder. I thought she was going to get her things and leave, but it turns out she's staying. Interesting.

"What's your name, man?" I ask suddenly.

She jumps out of her skin and knocks something off the dresser—my hat, probably. She replaces it then quickly scrambles up the ladder to her bunk.

"Oh…uh, Taylor."

She speaks so softly I can barely hear her, and I wonder if she's worried I'll recognize her voice. As it is, I'm surprised she gave me an honest answer, though it's probably because the name Taylor is pretty androgynous.

"Like Taylor Swift?" I ask, wanting to tease out a little more conversation.

"Or like Taylor Lautner," she clarifies.

"Who?"

"The werewolf from *Twilight*," she mumbles, followed by a low groan.

I'm smiling now, despite myself.

"You done much construction work in the past?"

There's a long pause here, as if she's working through a million thoughts in her head. Then finally, she replies softly. "No."

"What made you start now?" I ask, no longer playing a game.

I want to know why she's here. I want to know what possessed her to dress up like a guy and interview for a job in which she'll be hauling lumber and slogging through mud in the sweltering heat and dealing with a hundred ill-mannered men.

"It seemed like a good opportunity."

The way she says it is final, cut and dry. Then her sheets rustle and a few moments later, her breathing evens out and I know she's fallen asleep.

Or, she's pretending.

CHAPTER TEN
TAYLOR

First thing yesterday morning—after finding out the suit was my roommate—I realized I had two options. One, I could quit and leave immediately, run as far away from this jobsite as possible and never look back. Two, I could find Jeremy and try to convince him that instead of sleeping here during the week, we should commute back and forth every day. That way, I'd still get to keep the job, but I wouldn't have to room with *him* every night.

"It just makes sense," I said while we walked toward the mess hall for breakfast. "You probably already miss Khloe, and I really need to check on McKenna. You know I don't even get cell reception out in my cabin? Isn't that crazy? Anyway, if we leave at 4:45 every morning, we should be able to get here before…"

My words trailed off as I realized he'd stopped listening. In fact, I don't think he paid attention to any of my argument.

I tried another tactic.

"I really don't like my roommate. That's why I don't want to stay here."

I thought my honesty would appeal to him.

"Why? Does he know you're a woman? Is that it? Because he's going to find out and it shouldn't be that big of a deal—"

"It's not that."

I know the men here will slowly start to realize who—or rather *what* I am. I'm not going to great lengths to hide it. These boobs and hips don't lie, people.

He shrugged and held the door for me. "Then why don't you just ignore him and sleep? I'm not driving home every day. Just suck it up. You only have to be with him at night. What's the big deal?"

The big deal is that night is the worst time to be with the man! I'm supposed to get shut-eye with *him* lying directly underneath me? It's impossible. I barely slept. I was an overly caffeinated psycho by the time lunch rolled around, so I doubled down on trying to convince Jeremy to go along with my plan while we were watching the never-ending training videos.

"C'mon, 4:45 AM isn't *that* early!"

My words fell on deaf ears.

I realized then that I wouldn't be getting my way with him. We weren't going to commute every day, so I needed to find a new place to sleep.

I found Max at dinner, or rather he found me. I was sitting outside the mess hall with Jeremy, eating a turkey sandwich when he joined us.

He flicked the brim of my hat and smiled.

"You really aren't fooling anyone with this—you know that, right? I've already heard a couple guys asking about you."

I frowned, and he must have sensed my unease because he continued, "Nothing bad though. They were just curious about why a girl would sign on for something like this. I told them to mind their own business."

I aimed a grateful smile his way. "I appreciate it." Then the idea sparked. "Wait, where are you rooming?"

He nodded his head in the direction of the bunkhouses. "The last one there at the end."

"Is there a spare bed?"

He smirked. "No, and the guy next to me snores so loudly I had to throw a pillow at his head last night. Besides, Jeremy told me you're over in one of the cabins. That's probably the best place for you, away from all this."

I frowned, disheartened.

I'd managed one night in that cabin; there was no way I'd survive another unscathed. I'd be better off just quitting and going home, and I was tempted to, *really* tempted, up until that night when my phone finally picked up a signal in the center of camp and I called my mom. The place was cleared out. Most of the guys were showering or back in the bunks, getting ready for bed. I'd been delaying my return to the cabin, trying to think my way out of this mess I'd found myself in when the call connected.

It felt so good to hear her voice, tears burned the edges of my eyes.

"I've been thinking about you so much since you left," my mom said, a smile clear as day in her voice. "How are things going? Have they put you to work yet?"

My throat squeezed tight and words were hard to come by. I dragged my toe along the dirt, drawing a line. "Not yet. Tomorrow."

"HI SIS!" McKenna shouted in the background.

My mom laughed. "Your sister says hi."

I chuckled and wiped my eyes. "Yeah, I heard. Tell her I said hi."

"You sound off. Are things all right?"

I heaved a big, clearing breath. "Just a little homesick, that's all. How are things with you guys?"

I was planning to introduce the idea of quitting and coming back, of returning to my job at the motel, but I didn't get the chance. The grocery store had apparently cut my mom's hours. "Just not enough work to go around, and I'm the last one added to the schedule since they have to work around my classes on the weekends," she explained.

My heart sank as I squeezed my eyes closed, knowing I was truly stuck here. There was no way for me to quit. How would we make ends meet without this job?

"That's okay, Mom. I should be getting my first paycheck soon. Some say it might even come at the end of this week."

McKenna grabbed the phone then, jumping into any and all updates about her life, little things, nothing bits. Her friend has a new crush. Her English teacher read her essay aloud because she thought it was so good. Soccer practice was hard and her asthma flared up a little, but she didn't have to sit out for long.

I could have listened to her talking forever—it was the first time my stomach had unclenched all day—but right in the middle of her stories, the call dropped. Whatever fleeting signal I'd nabbed, I couldn't recapture, so I stuffed my phone in my back pocket, mentally repeated Jeremy's advice to suck it up when the tears threatened more than ever, and headed out for the cabin. I took my time, appreciating the quiet, dark forest. It would have spooked me the night before, but not anymore. I was grateful for the distance between the main camp and our cabin; it meant the sun was all the way down and night had fallen by the time I opened the door. I was grateful he was probably asleep by the time I walked inside, grateful I only caught a fleeting glimpse of my roommate's naked torso as I flew past him into the bathroom.

I thought I was in the clear until he spoke.

I can't believe he was awake.

I can't believe I didn't correct him when he said, "What's your name, *man*?"

Does he truly not know it's me?
Could I get so lucky?

Tuesday, bright and early, we're all due at the jobsite near the lake. It's our first official day getting our hands dirty, using tools—y'know, whacking nails and…*stuff*. Honestly, my mission is simple: stay out of everyone's way and try to seem as if I belong.

I survived the second night in the cabin and snuck out again at the crack of dawn, so I'm the very first person at breakfast. Good news: I get my pick of the scrambled eggs and bacon from the caterers because no one else is awake. Bad news: to fill the hours before work, I drink a lot of coffee. I've had so much caffeine by the time we're heading to the jobsite, I'm a jittery mess. Also, I'm due to pee my pants any second now, but I feel slightly better about my situation. The blisters on my feet have become so painful that my brain is numb to them. I've survived two nights sleeping in the same cabin as him. HIM—I really need to learn his name, but to do that I'd have to talk to him. So, Him is never getting a name. Sorry Him.

Anyway, the point is I've survived, and even though I'm operating on very little sleep, thanks to excessive amounts of caffeine, there's hope on my horizon that this might all work out.

Well, right up until we get to the jobsite and I'm greeted by the sight of heavy machinery. There are half a dozen diggers and excavators and Transformers.

"Oh god, what if they put me up in one of those?" I ask Jeremy.

He follows my finger to see that I'm pointing at a bulldozer. He finds the idea highly comical. "You need a license to operate those. I don't even have one."

Thank God. Could you imagine the damage I would cause?

Honestly, they should just put me on refreshments like the water boy for a football team. I'd get this crew so hydrated they'd be peeing their pants right along with me.

The crew gathers around Hudson and another tall man with a white mustache and a booming voice who introduces himself as Robert, the foreman. While he explains that we'll be split up into teams to tackle the demolition for each building, I surreptitiously search the crowd for my cabinmate. No such luck.

Hard hats and neon green safety vests are dispersed through the crowd. The guy handing them out pauses when he gets to me and he narrows his eyes curiously. I'm still wearing my hair hidden up under my baseball hat, but my flannel shirt is tucked in today because the billowing fabric seemed like it'd be hazardous on the jobsite. I don't need it getting caught on a bulldozer or something. No thank you. That's not the way I've leaving this earth.

"You're the girl, aren't you?" he asks. "The one everyone's talking about?"

"Yes," I reply tentatively.

And then he nods, hands me my gear, and moves on.

Jeremy and I exchange a relieved glance.

That's when I hear my name being shouted. It's the foreman, telling me I'm needed in the office. A hush falls over the crowd as heads turn in my direction. It seems, even if I don't know the names of 99% of the crew here, they all know mine. It's not shocking. I'm the only one with boobs.

I arch my brows at Jeremy and the crowd parts to give me a clear path to the white trailer nestled in a cluster of pine trees back in the direction of camp. It's command headquarters for Lockwood Construction, an ominous place I'd hoped to avoid at all costs. In fact, as I start heading in that direction, it feels almost as if I'm back in high school being summoned by the principal.

I brace myself as I knock on the door. A deep voice bids me to enter, but I linger there on the precipice for a moment longer, trying to gather courage. If they're going to fire me just because I'm a woman, I'll fight it. Somehow. Maybe I can find a lawyer who accepts Monopoly money.

With that thought, I push the door open and am arrested by the sight that greets me: Him, the suit, my cabinmate standing behind a desk with regal posture and a formidable presence.

Somehow, it's shocking, though it shouldn't be.

Of course he's not a common construction worker. He wasn't with the rest of the crew back at the jobsite. He's not staying in the bunkhouses with the other men. He was wearing a suit all those weeks ago, and that thought propels me toward another: right now, he doesn't look all that different than he did that night in the bar. It's more like looking at two sides of a coin. One version seemed perfectly composed, gentlemanly even. This other version might be wearing jeans, boots, and a blue Lockwood Construction shirt rolled to his elbows, but his hair is the same shade of dark brown. His jaw is still carved from marble. His eyes are just as piercing as he looks up and pins me to my spot by the door.

"You asked to see me?" I ask, my voice wobbly.

His eyes scan me quickly, halt at the hard hat and safety vest I'm clutching in my arms, and then he nods toward the chair at my right. "You can drop that gear. You won't be needing it."

So this is it.

He's finally connected the dots and is going to send me on my way—or worse. Maybe there's a police squadron hovering in the bushes outside waiting to leap out and haul me to jail. *Ten-four, we've got the wallet thief.* How many years in the clink do you get for taking someone's wallet but not actually stealing anything out of it?

I set my gear down then stand back up and catch my elbow behind my back to conceal the fact that my hands are shaking.

His attention has already fallen back to his work. To me, his desk looks like a chaotic mess. Blueprints curling at the edges. A laptop obscuring the paperwork underneath it. A cell phone precariously positioned at one corner, millimeters away from toppling to the ground. I want to step forward and nudge it to safety, but I stay right where I am.

It comes to my attention then that we've both been quiet longer than is socially acceptable. It almost feels like he's forgotten I exist. Isn't he going to come right out with it? Tell me he recognizes me as the woman from the bar? Fire me? Imprison me?

"You won't be working on the jobsite," he finally says as he continues to write something on a construction drawing.

"Are you…are you firing me?" I blurt out, sounding almost panicked. I immediately think of my phone call with my mom last night, how desperate I am to keep this job.

"No," he says with a tight shake of his head. "But you'll have a different position than the rest of the crew. You'll be working here. With me."

When he says "me", his brown eyes flick up and lock with mine. My stomach dips and *wait, wait, wait, this makes no sense.* Does he really not recognize me? My disguise has proven to be terrible. I'm like Hilary Duff wearing that tiny mask in *A Cinderella Story*, acting like no one could possibly recognize her. *Spoiler: we know it's you, Hilary. Your mask is one inch wide.*

"I need a personal lackey," he continues with a wave of his hand. "An errand boy."

I swear he emphasizes the word *boy*.

"You know…right?"

His eyes narrow and there's the flip of that coin. This is the shrewd businessman again, the man who should be poured into a black suit and sipping a fine scotch. The jeans give me a false sense of ease. "*Know*? What should I know?"

Yes, what should he know?! If he doesn't recognize me then I'd be an absolute fool to bring it to his attention. If the lion has decided not to eat the gazelle, the gazelle doesn't need to lie down on a bed of lettuce and put an apple in its mouth, just to make sure. *Take the gift for what it is, you silly gazelle!*

"That I'm a woman," I say, rushing the words out quickly. "So I can't be your errand 'boy', but I'm happy to fill the role of your personal lackey."

I'm even attempting to smile now, really putting in an effort with my new boss.

So what if he doesn't recognize me? That's a good thing! I shouldn't be offended that our steamy encounter meant so little to him that he can't even seem to recall it. For all I know maybe he has bathroom trysts all the time. Maybe he gets his wallet stolen biweekly.

This is the first time his face has been anything but an impenetrable mask of indifference. I swear, *swear* he's very nearly smirking as he glances back down at his desk. Then he nods once.

"Yes, I know you're a woman."

Those words seem to be dripping with so much meaning that I have to fight the urge to squirm with pleasure.

In this moment, I want him to remember me. I want him to be so consumed with remembering me that those blueprints tumble to the ground and that phone goes with it. It's just begging to fall, and I've had enough. I step forward and push it farther onto the desk then glance up and find his icy gaze frozen on my hand. I jerk it away and laugh self-deprecatingly. "Sorry. It was bothering me." I step back to give us both a healthy distance from one another. With that scowl in place, it looks like he'd appreciate it. "Anyway, what exactly would my duties be if I were to be working for you, Mr…ah…"

I leave the sentence dangling so he can pick it up.

"Ethan."

"Mr. Ethan?"

Odd, but okay.

His brows soften and I think there's a shadow of a smile hidden on his rugged face. I lean forward on my toes just a smidge, waiting…wanting to see it. But then his mask is back and he shakes his head sharply.

"Ethan Stone."

So there it is, the name I can hang over this face in my naughty dreams—and there will be dreams now that I know the nightmares can recede. Everything is going to be okay. He doesn't remember me from last month. He knows I'm a woman. We can move forward now. I can prove to be the best employee he's ever had and maybe by the end of the week, I'll be walking away with a nice little raise.

"So what exactly will I be doing for you, Mr. Stone?"

CHAPTER ELEVEN
ETHAN

"Just call me Ethan," I say, picking up my phone and putting it in my pocket, annoyed she touched it in the first place. Had I not been watching her, would she have taken it? A sharp bite from my conscience tells me I'm wrong to think so little of her, but I can't seem to help it.

She had the opportunity to tell me the truth just now, to fess up to her deeds, but she didn't. Of the two lies she's carrying around—her theft and her gender—she only admitted to one, and declaring she's a woman isn't exactly all that earth-shattering. Anyone with a pair of eyes already knew. To go on pretending would have only made her look stupid.

She really committed to the role, though. Those jeans are hanging off her frame, and that shirt looks like it's my size. She's still suffering in those work boots—they're so ridiculous, they nearly look like clown shoes on her.

Still, her beauty is so obvious that hat does nothing to diminish it. Her tempting curves are still visible beneath the baggy clothes, her pouty lips just as alluring as they were a month ago.

She tips back on her heels. "Right. Well, Ethan, what exactly would you like me to do?"

In truth, I don't actually need an assistant. I've never used one in the past. I can answer my phone and reply to my emails myself. I'm pretty good at pouring coffee into a mug and picking up my lunch from the mess hall. I don't really want someone in my space, but I don't know what else to do with her. I should fire her and be done with it, but I won't. I saw her moment of despair earlier when she thought I was letting her go. It almost looked like she was about to cry, which makes sense. If she's forced to leave, all her plans go up in smoke—plans I'm still curious about.

Still, if I'm going to keep her around, I can't have her out at the jobsite. It's a safety issue. Everyone else we hired has had some experience in construction, but not her.

So, she'll work directly for me.

Just…elsewhere.

"I'd like you to take this note to Robert. When you're done, see if he has anything he needs you to do."

She frowns, confused. I've just told her she'll be working for me and now I'm sending her away.

Even still, she accepts the note without another word and is quick with her task. Unfortunately, Robert doesn't need her assistance at the moment, so in less than ten minutes, she's back in the trailer, staring up at me with those big brown eyes.

"What would you like me to do next?" she asks with an eager-to-please tone.

I'd like her to leave me alone, but I guess that's not an option.

"Have you ever been an assistant before?"

"No." She shakes her head before offering up a small smile. "But to be fair…I was hired to be a construction worker." When it's clear I won't be joining in her teasing banter, she changes her tone. "Mr. Stone, I'm a quick learner and I'd like to be useful, so maybe if you took some time to train me or gave me a list of tasks you'd like me to complete…"

Tasks? I have plenty of them. I want her to stop calling me Mr. Stone. I want her to stop wearing those ridiculous clothes. I want her to tell me why she's here.

Beyond that, I have nothing for her to do, and I see no reason to train her to be useful because she won't be around long enough to make it worth it.

So, I keep her busy with menial tasks, things that keep her away from me. I snap at her to refill my coffee, run notes to the site, clean a pair of my boots that got muddy yesterday, check on lunch, take out my trash.

Each time I tell her to do something slightly more degrading, I expect her to respond to my command with a look of disdain or at least a subtle complaint, but instead, she's quick and eager, always looking for more work when she's finished.

Annoyed, I finally tell her to take the rest of the afternoon off, and that night, I stay away from the cabin until dark, working in the trailer, keeping myself busy, beating back thoughts of her. When I finally walk into the cabin, well past dark, her floral scent slams into me. I pause on the threshold, wondering if it's a good idea to go inside. Then I see she's asleep in her bunk, her feminine features so sweet and docile in her slumber, her dark lashes fanned across her cheeks.

An owl hoots, jarring me out of my careful study of her, and I'm angrier than ever as I storm into the bathroom to take a shower.

In the morning, she's gone before I wake. It appears neither one of us is eager for a close-quarters cabin encounter. I'm glad.

Wednesday and Thursday follow the same pattern. I send her out to do things that will put as much distance between us as possible, but my inspiration is dwindling quickly. I don't own that many pairs of boots, don't generate that much trash, not to mention I have actual work to do. I don't have all day to come up with arbitrary tasks for her. On Thursday afternoon, I have a conference call with my partners, and I tell her to sit outside until I'm done. So, she does. She sits right up on the top stair with her chin in her hands, observing the progress of the demolition taking place in front of her.

It's unnerving.

It wrecks my entire vindictive plan. The small part of me that wanted to enact revenge is quickly losing steam. The fire that burned when I saw her standing in line, hoping to be hired as part of my crew is quickly turning to ash. Apparently, I'm not half the asshole I thought I was.

It annoys me.

She might be playing the kitten now, but a month ago, she wasn't quite so innocent. In that bar, she had a plan. She seduced me on purpose. She took my wallet and stole my cash. That wasn't an accident.

It'd be so much easier if she just showed her true nature so we could be done with this. I want something in my office to go missing. I want one of the guys to report a stolen item from the bunkhouses. She's had plenty of unsupervised time throughout the last few days, ample opportunity to play the thief if she wanted to.

And yet by lunchtime on Friday, she's still the docile kitten, so I have no choice. I won't continue this charade into next week. I won't keep tiptoeing around the cabin and sending her off on fool's errands just so I can bait her into committing a crime.

Paychecks go out at the end of today.

After I sign hers, I include a small note: *Now we're even.*

I'm not surprised to hear footsteps banging up the steps of the trailer that afternoon. A moment later, the door slams open. Ah yes, the kitten is gone. She's seething now, an angry little spitfire as she throws the note in my direction. It flutters to the ground pitifully slowly, like a feather, which only angers her more. With a growl, she reaches for it, storms over to my desk, and slaps it down on top of a new rendering Steven just completed. The paper wrinkles under her hand.

"You knew who I was this whole time?!" she asks, smoke billowing off her.

I lean back in my chair, surprisingly calm now that she's not. This is the fight I've been waiting for, the truth-telling I've been eager to hear.

"You mean, do I remember you seducing me in that bar and stealing from me?" I ask, tone deceptively bored. "Yes."

Her eyes widen and she rears back. It takes me a moment to realize she looks shocked.

Shocked?!

Why the hell should she look shocked now? Maybe before, yes, when she first opened her paycheck and found it was $800 less than it should have been. I'm sure she was surprised to find she's only taking home a paltry $45.32, but she should be glad I left her with that much. I was tempted to send her home with nothing, just like she did me.

"What do you mean 'stole from you'?" she asks carefully.

Oh good grief. I thought we were done with this game. We've been playing it all week and its long lost its appeal. "Do you have amnesia? Or are you just playing dumb?"

She practically snarls, those high cheekbones bright red with anger now. She looks ready to strangle me. I wonder how she managed to pull off the innocent act all week.

"Fine. Since you've apparently pulled the same stunt so many times you can't even pick them apart anymore, I'll recount that evening for the both of us. Last month, I stayed in Oak Dale for one night with my partners. We decided to get a drink at the bar beside our motel. You happened to be there too."

She blinks and her anger gives way to another, indiscernible emotion while she listens to me speak.

"When my partners left, I stayed, curious about the sad girl alone at the bar. You turned back to glance at me over your shoulder and the invitation was clear. You wanted me to follow you into that bathroom." The red from her cheeks spreads all the way down her neck. "And of course, I did. You had me eating out of the palm of your hand, didn't you?"

The memories from that night are too hard to beat back—hot mouths, impatient hands, explosive chemistry. She must be remembering now too because she shakes her head and steps back.

"It's not a crime to kiss a man in a bathroom."

"But it *is* a crime to steal money from him."

Her jaw drops. "I didn't take any money!"

Her words are so clear and convincing, I almost believe her. "You've clearly had practice. That almost sounded believable."

"It should sound believable! It's the truth!" she cries, throwing her hands up in defeat. She's pacing now, walking back and forth in front of my desk, fisting her hands.

"When I went into the bathroom with you, I had my wallet," I point out dryly.

"Yes!" she says with a huff. "Okay, I *did* take your wallet, but—"

"After you seduced me."

"I did *not* seduce you!"

"What was it you were doing then?" I ask, standing and rounding my desk. I hate that she isn't looking at me right now. I can't stand her pacing. I want her to meet my eyes as she lies to me. I want to see her for what she truly is, once and for all. "That was an act, right? A way to distract me from your real goal?"

She's taking one step back for every one of my steps forward. Soon, she's back against the door, chin lifted, eyes blinking up at me. Black sultry lashes frame a pair of knock-you-on-your-ass brown eyes. I put up a wall against them.

"Yes," she says on a long exhalation. Then she catches herself. "*No!* That's not why we went in there. I didn't plan on stealing from you!"

Her words are so convincing something inside me nearly breaks. Then I realize what she let slip before she caught herself. Yes, it was an act. Yes, she was only kissing me that night because she wanted my money. Who cares that she's backtracking now? In fact, it almost makes it worse.

I keep a careful distance between us, enough space that I'm not in danger of touching her. I don't trust myself—not because I'm feeling the passion I felt in that bathroom, not because it's nearly eating me alive to keep my hands off her, but because I'm so enraged, I don't trust myself to act like a gentleman.

"And what about now? Why are you here, pretending to be a man on my crew? We both know you're not here to swing a hammer. So, what is it? Are you going to steal from the guys while they're out working on the jobsite? No one would expect it from an innocent thing like you, but I know better." My hand reaches out so I can curve my pointer finger under her chin and force her to meet my eyes.

She yanks her face away from my touch and shoots daggers up at me. "I'm not here pretending to be a guy. I never lied," she insists, teeth gritted. "I just decided it was best not to advertise that I'm a woman. There's a difference."

"Is that what you were doing in the bar that night? *Advertising*?"

Her hand shoots up, but I catch it before it makes contact with my cheek.

I toss it away just before she turns around, trying to yank the door open.

She reaches for the handle and there are tears on her cheeks now when she glances back at me. "You're wrong. I am here to work, even if you don't believe me."

"No." I shake my head, back to sounding as if this whole confrontation is beneath me. "I don't believe you." And just before the door slams shut behind her, I think, *Good. We're done.*

Except it doesn't feel that way.

Not even close.

CHAPTER TWELVE
TAYLOR

So this is what pure unadulterated rage feels like. There's so much built up inside of me, I could lift a car and throw it across a football field. I could rip a phonebook in two. I could get out of this truck right now and run the whole way home, and not a pretend-you're-running-because-your-P.E.-teacher-is-watching situation. I mean arms pumping at my sides, wind in my sails, all-out sprint. That's how I feel sitting in Jeremy's truck on the way home to Oak Dale on Friday night.

Meanwhile, he's happy as a clam. His paycheck is in the cup holder between us. It's made out for over a thousand dollars with Ethan's signature in the bottom right corner. Jeremy asked me about mine, and I told him it was roughly the same.

"Really?" he seems surprised. "They gave me a little extra because I have construction experience."

"Oh, well they pay me extra because working for the boss is such a hard job," I snap back.

My anger flies over his head. "Huh. I saw him a few times around the jobsite, and he didn't seem so bad. I mean, I can see why people are intimidated by him—he's got that look about him—but he wasn't barking orders or shouting at people or anything."

"Can we talk about something else?"

Literally anything.

I will listen to a long multifaceted discussion about the current state of politics in America between people talking at half-speed if it means I don't have to continue discussing Ethan Stone.

Just his name causes a visceral reaction. I wouldn't be surprised to find I've broken out in angry red hives.

The things he accused me of!

The way he spoke to me!

The disdain dripping off his words!

I wish I'd tried to slap him a second time. He probably wouldn't have seen that one coming, and *oh*, it would have felt *so* nice. Of course, it probably would have hurt me more than it hurt him. I'd have broken every finger thanks to his sharply honed features. Still, it would have been worth it.

After I left the trailer, I stormed back to our cabin, gathered my things, stuffed them back into my duffle, and told Jeremy I'd be waiting for him at the truck. I couldn't wait to leave. I never want to go back to Pine Wood Camp ever again.

I can't believe Ethan knew who I was the whole week and didn't say anything. I slept on the bunk over his for five nights while he pretended I was a complete stranger. He called me "man" the night he asked for my name! The memory has me fuming all over again. I bet he was so pleased to find me trapped like that, to get to poke fun at me right to my face.

Even worse than the fact that he played me this entire week, there's another massive problem: I can't believe he really thinks I stole from him! I know I'm splitting hairs here, but there is a difference between *almost* stealing from someone and *actually* going through with it. Is he so rich he doesn't realize all his cash was still in his wallet when he came back to retrieve it? Does he think I skimmed some off the top?

I freaking wish! At this point I wish I'd taken every cent from that man just to flush it right down the toilet.

There's the possibility that the wallet never made it back to him in the first place, which might be why he thinks I stole from him, but I know he has it. I asked the bartender about it a few days later while waiting for Jeremy to pick me up after a shift at the motel. He said Ethan came back to grab his wallet that same night. Everything should have been smoothed over. The only thing Ethan should have been upset about is that I never showed up at his motel room like I promised I would.

God, I'm more glad than ever that I had a change of heart. I can't imagine what would have happened if I had joined him in his room that night. A man like that? With a temper like that? And a frame that size? Hands that big? Eyes that dark? I'm getting carried away. The point is, everything worked out for the best.

I won't be seeing Ethan Stone again.

No, wait, I *will* see him once more—in seventy years, when I find his grave and do a little jig on top of it.

When I get home, McKenna bursts through the front door of the trailer, nearly tripping down the rickety wooden stairs on her way to get to me.

"You're home! You're home!"

Her arms wrap around my middle and she lugs me up off the ground. I laugh and tell her to put me down before she hurts herself.

"Here, let me get your bag," she says, very gallantly, grabbing my duffle from the front seat of the truck before waving goodbye to Jeremy. He's heading to meet Khloe and I know he's excited because he talked about it for most of the way home. I heard it all. He misses Khloe. Khloe misses him. They hardly talked. Cell reception was bad near the bunkhouses too. He had to borrow Max's new iPhone to get a good signal, but apparently absence made the heart grow fonder because one-fifth of his first check is going into his engagement ring fund. By comparison, one-fifth of my check will cover the cost of a Taco Bell dinner.

I am really looking forward to that grave-top jig.

"Tell me everything!" McKenna says, tugging me toward the couch. "Was it weird being away? I tried to call you a few times and it said the call couldn't be completed as dialed. Are you really that far from civilization? In the middle of the woods? Did you see a bear?!"

It's no surprise my sister doesn't stop asking me questions until well past dinner. I'm exhausted since I haven't slept well all week and I could probably stay asleep all the way through Sunday if given the opportunity, but I am not given that opportunity. She talks to me while I kick off my boots, wince in pain, and head for the shower. She talks to me while I wash my hair, close my eyes, and let the water rinse away the last vestiges of my fury. She talks to me while I rub antibiotic ointment on my blistered heels and then cover them in Band-Aids. And she's still talking as I lie down on the couch and close my eyes, telling myself I'm only going to rest for a little while. I conk out.

Saturday morning, my mom wakes us up at 5:30 AM with pancakes. I want to hate her for it, but I can't. She has to leave extra early because she's catching a ride with a friend to get to Livingston for her classes and she has to get on the road by six. This way, we get to have breakfast together before she leaves. She doles out pancakes on my plate and kisses my hair, and it's still dark out and we don't even have syrup, but I don't mind one bit. My heart is full.

As soon as she's gone, McKenna and I run for the couch and huddle under blankets. We spend the whole morning watching whatever random shows our antenna manages to pick up, trying hard to become fused with the couch fibers. We do a pretty good job of it until I have to begrudgingly get up to make us lunch.

McKenna proves to be a perfect distraction from the worries of life, one I didn't even realize I needed until she announces that she's going out with some friends for milkshakes. Nothing crazy—they're just going to hang out at Whataburger. Ah, the life of a teenager in rural Texas.

"No drugs," I emphasize as she heads out the door. "And no drinking."

"Taylor, I'm going with *Lillian* and *Brittany*. Lilian's mom will be with us the whole time."

I know McKenna's friends. Lilian's in band and the president of the freshman honor society, and Brittany is on the robotics team and captain of the freshman soccer team. Sure, that could all just be a front for the fact that they're really all drug-addicted partiers, but I think they're too smart for that. They've made a pact. They all want to go to the same college, and I know they can make it happen if they stick together.

I give her a few dollars—money we don't really have to spare at the moment—before waving her off. Then I head back inside the quiet trailer. My mom was supposed to be home by now but a coworker called in sick at the grocery store so she picked up an extra shift after her class. I feel guilty that she's having to do it. I know she's probably exhausted. I wish I'd come home for the weekend with my full paycheck instead of the measly few bucks Ethan threw my way. It would have gone a long way to getting us back on our feet, especially considering I'm not sure what I'll be doing for work now.

I've been avoiding the dilemma all day, but tomorrow is Sunday and I have to make a decision.

I can't just go back to the motel. I had to put in my notice there when I accepted the job with Lockwood Construction. Sure, I could go back and grovel at my manager's feet, but just the thought makes my dignity scream out in protest. I hated that job and I hated how little they paid me.

I could apply for work somewhere else, but I've been in this town long enough to know that's a dead-end road. There are a few decent jobs around Oak Dale, but not for someone who barely graduated from high school. The familiar twinge of resentment over my lack of education settles in the pit of my stomach.

If we could afford to get our car out of the shop, I could drive into Livingston or another nearby city to look for work, but even that would be a major waste of gas and time, and there'd be no telling how well the car would hold up if I was driving it around that much.

With a heartbreaking sigh, I realize I'm just as stuck now as I was four years ago. I've been working so hard trying to claw my way out of this hole life tossed me into only to slide right back down to the bottom time and time again.

My job with Lockwood Construction was the first sign of hope I'd had in a long time, and I hate Ethan Stone even more for taking the opportunity away from me.

But then I realize—maybe he didn't.

He didn't *technically* fire me, and I didn't *technically* quit.

So what if I hate him? A lot of people hate their bosses.

The fact is, right now, I don't really have another option, so Saturday night, I come up with my plan. The first step? Call Jeremy and demand we make a stop on our way out of town tomorrow afternoon. I'm spending every last cent of my paltry paycheck on a new pair of boots—ones that actually fit.

The second step in my plan is to find Hudson as soon as we make it back to camp the following evening. This proves more difficult than I thought it would because while searching for him, I also am trying hard to avoid Ethan. I'm forced to hover near buildings and trees in case I need to duck and cover. Work doesn't start until tomorrow morning, and I'd rather not cross paths with him until then. Of course, this method means I draw quite a few concerned glances from passersby, but I put on my best smile and wave like everything is all good. *"Don't mind me, just checking the hardy plank on this building." Knock knock. "Yup! Good as new!"*

I eventually find Hudson when he walks through the center of camp with a backpack. He's just returned and is probably heading to unload his stuff, but I can't afford to lose track of him. We have important things to discuss.

"Hudson! Hi," I say, leaping into his path.

His eyes widen as he takes me in.

Oh right, I'm not wearing the baseball hat, and the baggy flannel shirt is gone too. I'm wearing a light blue t-shirt and a pair of my own jeans. My hair hangs loose down my back. Apparently, it's really throwing him off.

"I'm Taylor," I offer, trying to alleviate the awkwardness. "Ethan's assistant."

I don't embarrass either of us by pointing out that I am, indeed, a woman. If people were duped by my hilariously poor disguise, that's on them.

He nods and quickly reins in his reaction. "Right. Of course. What do you need?"

I haven't had much interaction with Hudson, but he seems like a loyal servant to Lockwood Construction. I have to play my cards just right.

A gentle smile spreads across my face. "I know you're probably very busy and likely don't want to be dealing with this right now, but I was wondering if there was any way for me to transfer to a different position on the crew?"

He frowns. "What do you mean?"

"Just…I was wondering if there was anyone else looking for an assistant?" My eyes flick up to his face. "*You!* Maybe? Do you need an assistant?"

His cheeks redden and he tugs at the collar on his shirt. "I'm not authorized to shift personnel around like that." He's looking away, planning his escape.

My smile turns pleading. "Oh, I know I'm being a nuisance, and I would never want to get you into trouble. I'm just not sure this position with Ethan is the right fit for me. Maybe you and I would work better together?"

I need him on my side. I need him to want—no, *need*—me as his assistant. I wish I could prove my skills right here on the spot. *Wait! Listen to how well I take a message! Watch how good I am with the copier!*

As it is, he fidgets and shuffles his feet, angling to get around me. I've really put him on the spot. He can barely look me in the eye.

"It's Ethan you need to discuss this with," he says, sounding resolute.

"And if I can't speak with Ethan…for reasons I'd rather not say…does he have a boss? Or a supervisor of some sort?"

That question elicits a hearty laugh from Hudson. "No, Ethan does not have a boss. He has three partners, but they won't override a decision like this."

"And what about an HR department? Do you guys have one of those?"

I didn't see any HR-looking people around the camp last week.

"Not here on site. There are a few people back in Austin." He narrows his eyes now, skeptical of me. "We've never had a crewmember request to meet with them. Are you looking to make a formal complaint about Ethan?"

A formal complaint? That sounds official and permanent. No, I don't think I want to go down that path yet, not only because I'm not sure what chain of events that would set off, but because I don't exactly have my hands clean in this situation. If I called HR, what would Ethan do? Call the police? At this point, it's his word against mine.

With a tight smile, I step back and shake my head. "You know, maybe I'll try to handle this by myself first. Who knows, maybe we just have a few growing pains we need to work through."

He's smiling again, happy to see I'm going to be a team player. This guy is Ethan's loyal pet, through and through. Noted.

I scratch through that part of my plan and move on to the next important step: finding somewhere else to sleep. Obviously, I can't stay in the cabin with Ethan.

So, before night falls, I set up a pallet on the floor in Jeremy's bunkhouse. I even thought ahead and brought a spare blanket and pillow from back home. I have all sorts of fantasies about how well it will go, how soundly I'll sleep until morning. Unfortunately, Jeremy's spot is in the middle of the bunkhouse, therefore I have to set up my pallet in the middle of the bunkhouse. He caves and offers to let me have his bed, but I insist that's not fair. I'm all for equality. He doesn't have to sleep on the floor just because Ethan and I don't get along. A few other nice guys offer their beds too—some try to insist upon it—but I turn them all down and continue setting up my pallet.

"It's nice! Homey, even!" I say, pointing down to it.

It's a bald-faced lie. It's a thin blanket on top of dusty wooden floorboards. After I lie down, half of me is sticking out into the walkway. In the middle of the night, while I'm up listening to God-knows-what scuttling across the floor near my head, someone gets up to use the bathroom and steps on my foot. It feels as though they break all my bones and my barely muffled shriek wakes up half the bunkhouse.

"Sorry! *Sorry*," the guy whispers, feeling bad for accidentally stepping on me.

"It's my fault," I whisper back, and then for the remainder of the night, I lie awake with my legs tucked up against my chest in the fetal position and my hand outstretched over my head, ready to swat away any creepy-crawly bugs that want to come near me.

Admittedly, it's not the best night of sleep I've ever had, and I'm not my best self on Monday morning. Limping softly and yawning often, I'm wholly unprepared for round two with Ethan. But, I'm not quite ready to make nice either. So, I settle on being cordial as I step past the open door of the trailer.

He's inside meeting with Robert and Hudson. Robert's by far the oldest member of the crew with white-gray hair and tan, wrinkled skin. His face gives him the appearance of being open and honest, probably owing to his light blue eyes. Something about him makes me wish he could guide me through life. It's probably the smile he's aiming my way. The gentlemen flanking him have very different reactions.

Hudson stands there with wide eyes and mouth gaping, still not quite over the fact that I'm a full-fledged woman.

Ethan is doing some kind of unsmiling facial expression, I'm sure, but I'm too chicken to look his way.

"Oh sorry," I say with a tip of my head, looking right at Robert. "I didn't realize you guys were meeting in here." I step back toward the door. "I'll just wait outsi—"

"Take a seat," Ethan says, tone hard as stone. He really lives up to that surname of his.

The seat he's referring to is right beside the door, and I don't wait for him to offer it up to me a second time. I leap into that chair and stay perfectly silent while the three of them finish up their meeting. They're going over the schedule for the week, what equipment will be used on what day, which of the dumpsters are full and need to be replaced, what torture techniques Ethan will employ on me first. Okay, that last one is just in my head.

I listen to them carefully. Ethan is the highest ranked among them and yet he speaks the least. When he does, my body hums with energy like I'm hooked up to an electrical current.

"The site needs to be cleared by next Friday so we can start leveling," he tells Robert. "I have concrete trucks scheduled in three weeks."

"It'll be cleared, easily. The crew worked quickly last week. Most of the guys have more experience in construction than we were anticipating."

"Think we'll need to bring in more fill than expected to level the pad?"

Hudson chimes in then, and I finally work up the courage to peer at Ethan from beneath my lashes. Either he somehow grew over the weekend or my fear of him has blown him up to epic proportions. He stands a foot taller than the other two men, his broad shoulders and chest covered in a gray Henley shirt with a plaid flannel on top, rolled up to his elbows, of course. His jaw is clean-shaven, and I study its sharp contour all the way down to his chin. Then my gaze flicks up to his lips without my consent—lips I've felt before, lips I'd kill to feel again if they weren't attached to a man I despise.

"All right, that's all for now."

I jerk my gaze back down to my lap.

The men file out quickly and Hudson thankfully leaves the door open. That way everyone will hear our fight to the death.

"I can assume by your presence here that you'd like to continue working for Lockwood Construction despite our conversation on Friday?" Ethan asks, cutting right to the chase.

How was your weekend, Taylor?

Oh, great! I imagined ten different ways to murder you with my bare hands.

"Taylor?" he prods impatiently.

"Yes," I reply curtly, my gaze on the floor.

Papers rustle on his desk like he's in a rush. "I have no position to offer you besides my personal assistant."

So he's really going to force this issue then? He's really going to make me suffer? I square my shoulders. "That's fine. What would you like me to do first?"

"First?" he says, and the word hangs for so long that I finally look up at him. Our gazes meet with a blaze. "I'd like you to admit you stole from me."

You know what, Hudson? Maybe I would like to file that formal complaint with HR after all.

"I'm afraid that's not possible because I didn't steal from you. As I told you on Friday, I—"

He shakes his head then, cutting me off with a look of pure disdain. "Forget it. I don't really care to hear you lie your way through an explanation. The fact is, I don't have a spot for you on the crew—you'd be a hindrance more than an asset—and I don't need a personal assistant."

"Please."

There's no hint of tears in my voice, no sniffling or whining. It's a word spoken with a steel spine at a meeting of enemies, a word he surely knows I would never utter in his vicinity unless I was truly desperate.

"I'll spare you the details, but the fact is, I need this job. I need it badly enough to work for a man I can barely tolerate."

I probably would have done better to leave out that last part, but he's thrown out so many barbs this morning, he deserves to feel the sting of one as well.

His brown eyes are still on me, hot as flames. I wonder if it would have been wiser to keep my hat on. I don't like the way he's looking at me, like he can see things I haven't consented to showing him.

There's no easing of his scowl, no gentle smile unfolding across those lips. He really intends to dig in his heels, and I can't allow it. For my mom and for McKenna and for my own future, I need this job.

"I'm asking you nicely to please find something for me to do here."

CHAPTER THIRTEEN
ETHAN

I want her out of my hair and away from my construction site. In short, I have no idea what to do with her. I should tell her to march out into the forest and start counting trees. *Don't come back until you reach 10,000.*

I could send her on a pointless errand, but then I'd have to lend her my truck. I happen to like the way it looks without her digging a key into the side of it.

"I need you to wash my laundry."

Laundry? *Really?* Jesus, why don't you ask her to get in the kitchen and make you a sandwich while you're at it?

I know I sound like a sexist pig, but the fact is, I actually do need my laundry done. I didn't leave the camp over the weekend. I stayed and worked, appreciating the quiet.

Not to mention, laundry is just about the only thing I trust her with. I don't think she's going to try to steal my briefs.

"Laundry?" she confirms.

Her tone is disbelieving. She thinks this is a trick.

I raise one brow.

She shoots to her feet. "Right, laundry. Fine. Any specifications? Cold water only? Hand-wash delicates?"

I resist the urge to ask if I look like the type of man who owns delicates.

"There's an old washer and dryer in the back of the mess hall. If they don't work, use a sink."

Then she's gone, flying out the door of my trailer like her feet are on fire.

I watch her go. I watch the sway of her hips. I watch her high ponytail swishing back and forth. I watch her walk in those new boots that actually fit her. I'm glad for that. Wait—I'm *happy* she has new boots? Jesus. I jerk my attention back to work and don't look up again until lunch.

The mess hall is noisy when I walk in. I had Hudson stagger lunch breaks for the crew so there wouldn't be a line out the door, but even still, these guys like to eat. The catering team hustles to fill plates with burgers and fries. The smell has my mouth watering, but I bypass it all and keep moving through the kitchen back into the adjoining washroom. I figure the camp used to use the washing machine in here for towels and dish rags used by the kitchen staff. Whatever the reason, I'm glad it's here.

I hear voices before I get to the hallway, a feminine laugh followed by a deep chuckle, and my hackles go up instantaneously. What I expected to find: Taylor hunched over a washing machine, toiling away with sweat dripping down her brow, more grateful than ever that I've kept her on as an employee even though I should have fired her. What I actually find: Taylor taking advantage of my goodwill. She isn't alone, which explains why a task that should have taken her an hour to complete has filled up her entire morning.

"I can't believe you thought I was into *Mark Granger*." Taylor groans with mock disgust. "He's not my type at all."

"Well what else would explain why you broke up with me right before the homecoming dance—"

My presence in the doorway cuts off the guy's sentence. I don't know his name, but I recognize him as part of the new crew. He looks like he should be on a beach with his surfer-length hair and easy smile. That's right, he's smiling at me.

"Get back to work," I say, pointing him out the back door of the washroom.

His brows crinkle in confusion. I half expect him to reply with a stoned, *Aw, c'mon man, we were just havin' some fun.* Instead, he hops to it and walk-runs right out the door, leaving Taylor to fend for herself. Nice guy.

She keeps her back to me and continues to pull clothes out of the dryer.

"Why was he in here?"

"You'll have to ask him," she replies with a cold, even tone.

"I'm asking you."

She shrugs. "It was his lunch break. He saw me through the window and came in to say hi."

"Friend of yours?"

The edge of her mouth tips up in a private smirk. "You could say that."

I don't like the jealousy creeping through me like an invasive vine.

"How many guys on this crew are '*friends*' of yours?"

My meaning is clear, and finally, I've got her full attention. Her eyes cut to me and there's so much resentment and fury there, I know she's right on the cusp of losing her temper. Her cheeks are flooded with color. Her lips are parted. I can *feel* her anger. She takes a step toward me, about to say something, but then she reaches for my laundry, which is stacked neatly on the dryer, and with one clean sweep, tosses it all onto the floor.

"Your laundry is done."

Then she does an about-face and marches right out the door.

So you could say things are mellowing out nicely between us.

I know this is mostly my fault. I know I'm behaving like an ass. I know it and yet here I am, unable to help myself. To say she gets under my skin is an understatement. It's as if every bad character trait I possess—jealousy, anger, cruelty—is controlled by one button, and she's not only found that button, she's pressing down on it with her full weight and then some.

She doesn't come back by the trailer the rest of the afternoon, and I'm grateful for the reprieve. That's what I tell myself. I throw myself back into work and then around 4 PM, Hudson comes to get me so we can walk the site and check on progress. The stable has been completely demolished and the debris has been hauled to the dumpster. He needs me to check on the few trees that might need to be cleared before we can level the ground.

As I walk out of the trailer, I spot Taylor moving toward the construction site with a water bottle in hand. She looks determined to get somewhere fast, and I watch as she finds Robert and hands him the bottle. He nods in thanks and they start talking. I can't hear them from where I am, but he's pointing his hand out as if explaining something to her. They're still together after we walk the site. Now, they're hunched over the plans.

"What're they doing?" I ask Hudson, nodding over to Robert and Taylor.

"Uh…shouldn't you know? She's your assistant."

The glare I aim his way withers half the forest.

"I mean," he amends quickly, changing his tone, "let me check on that right away."

Ten minutes later, he walks into the trailer and shrugs. "Apparently she was curious about how the site runs. Now, she's headed to clean your cabin."

"She is?"

He narrows his eyes. "Should I tell her you want to see her?"

"No."

Absolutely not. The laundry was enough for one day.

CHAPTER FOURTEEN
TAYLOR

Well, okay, tossing laundry onto the floor was admittedly not my proudest moment. I'd rank it right after…oh, stealing Ethan's wallet, I suppose. So, he's had the privilege of seeing me not only at my worst, but also at my second worst. I keep coaching myself to stay calm, to put up an impenetrable force field where he's concerned and just let everything he says go in one ear and out the other. Unfortunately, when push comes to shove, that's easier said than done.

He deserved that little outburst. He'd be eating crow if he knew what I was up to all morning. I wasn't just twiddling my thumbs and flirting with his crew. First of all, I spent a solid hour trying to get that ancient washing machine up and running. I even had Jeremy take a quick look at it, but it was no use. The thing was toast. Even if it wasn't, we didn't have the necessary parts to fix it. I ended up having to hand-wash every piece of Ethan's clothing by hand in the sink, which shouldn't have taken too long, but there was mud caked on his jeans and some of his workout clothes were extra dirty. I didn't want to leave a single speck behind. No way was I going to give him ammunition against me. After I was done washing everything, I threw the stuff in the dryer, which thankfully still worked, but not well enough. It took twice as long to dry the clothes as it should have and by the time I started to fold, it was lunchtime, which was when Max came strolling by.

For the record, I didn't invite him in. He invited himself.

He had a few minutes left of his lunch break and wanted to say hi. Apparently, he finds my company enjoyable, unlike *some* people. In fact, Max likes me, maybe even a little more than he should. I was spot-on in my earlier assessment that Max would want to revisit our relationship if I gave him the green light. In fact, he steered the conversation toward that topic almost immediately.

"Why didn't you and I work out?" he asked, leaning one hip against the washing machine, watching me fold Ethan's clothes.

I shot him an amused smile. "Oh, I don't know. Does there have to be a reason? We were fifteen."

"So that's it? We were just young?"

I caught him giving me a once-over before his smiling gaze met mine again.

"*And* you were a flirt."

That's the problem with guys like Max. He soaks up attention like a sponge and doles out smiles and love to any and everyone, not at all discerning about who the recipients are. It's a good character trait, don't get me wrong—no one has a bad word to say about Max—but I'm just not sure I could date someone like him. I'd rather be one *in* a million than one *of* a million.

Still, a little time spent with him is good for the ego. I didn't even mind the flirting. It felt nice to laugh and smile.

Then Ethan showed up like a black cloud rolling right over our beach vacation.

"How many guys on this crew are 'friends' *of yours?"*

The memory of his words makes my hands fist with rage.

If I had his clothes in front of me, I'd fling them across the floor all over again. *No*—I'd carry them to the lake and toss them out into the water, watch them float away slowly with a crazed smile on my face.

After lunch, I didn't bother going back to ask Ethan for another task. I didn't trust myself to be in his vicinity just yet. Fortunately, Robert saw me walking by and politely asked if I could get him some water. I jumped at the chance. I wasn't doing anything important. When I handed it off to him, I asked how demolition was going. Maybe it was the pitiful way I sounded or the redness still burning my cheeks, but he took the time to walk me through the process while I listened intently.

Now, I'm off cleaning Ethan's cabin with cleaning supplies I grabbed in the mess hall. It was a stroke of genius on my part—the cabin needs a good scrub-down and it puts me very, *very* far away from him.

I worked as a maid in that roadside motel for the last year and though I never hoped that one day—*fingers crossed*—I'd grow up to clean someone else's toilets, I don't actually hate the work. It keeps me busy and moving. I focus on the shower and make it as spotless as thirty-year-old tile can be. I wipe down the sink and the mirror. I arrange Ethan's toothpaste and toothbrush so they're perfectly aligned in the cup.

His bed is already made, but not well, so I redo it, ensuring the corners are tucked in. If I had a little piece of chocolate, I'd leave it on the pillow. Then I remember whose bed I'm making and decide if I did have chocolate, I'd eat it all in one bite, spitefully.

Dinner has rolled around by the time I'm finished sweeping dust off the front porch, and I'm ready to collapse when I make it back to the mess hall. After sleeping on a pallet on the ground last night, I'm ready to fall asleep where I stand, but I need food first. The crew's already eating and

I feel their eyes on me when I walk in with the cleaning supplies I had to haul back. I know they're curious about me. It probably seems odd that I'm here, but I have no plans to leave any time soon, so they'll just have to get used to me. Jeremy and Max are in line to get food and Jeremy mouths that he'll get me a plate. When I'm done putting everything away, we head outside to eat.

I still haven't quite wrapped my head around this whole arrangement, the living in the forest thing. If not for the construction project and the awkward girl-to-guy ratio, it would feel like an adult summer camp. The weather in late spring is beautiful, the temperature hovering in the low 70s most days with sunshine overhead. The scenery is beautiful, and the food is a lot better than anything I make at home. Even now, we're outside eating lasagna on some lawn chairs under a canopy of pine trees. A guy a few feet away from us is strumming on a guitar he must have brought from home. All in all, it's not half bad, especially now that I'm among friends again.

I try to grab hold of the little things while I can, because as soon as Ethan walks toward the mess hall with Robert by his side, my mood immediately sours.

"He's looking at you," Jeremy says, nudging me with his elbow.

"Who cares?" I hiss, mopping up some marinara sauce with my breadstick. *Can't he see I'm busy?!*

"He's coming over here."

My heart drops right through the seat of my chair. *Please, God, no.* Not in front of Jeremy and Max. Not while I have a plate of lasagna. I'd like to eat my dinner, not throw it in his face when he says something rude and I fly off the handle again.

"Taylor, can I speak with you?" Ethan asks coldly.

Guitar guy stops strumming. Everyone within a five-yard radius turns to stare at me. I have to stand up.

"Sure," I say through gritted teeth before putting my plate of food on my seat and turning to let him lead the way. I figure we'll head around the side of the mess hall so there'll be no witnesses to our discussion, but we only walk a few paces, just far enough that we're out of earshot. Everyone can still see us, so I steel my shoulders and look up at him. That way, no one can accuse me of being a coward.

He's looking down at me with his head tilted an inch to the left, one eye sort of winked in thought. Then he props his hands on his hips, puffs out a breath, and speaks.

"I'd like to apologize for what I said this afternoon."

A record scratches.

"What?"

"It was uncalled for."

I'm slack-jawed from shock. "Oh, okay. Well, thank you, and…" My right hand catches my left elbow and I realize I'm shuffling my feet. I immediately stop. "I'm sorry for throwing your laundry on the ground. In hindsight, it was pretty childish of me."

He nods, turns, and walks away.

I stand there watching until he disappears inside with Robert.

Huh. That went…well?

Jeremy and Max hound me about the encounter for ten minutes. To them, it seemed like an odd exchange, definitely not a casual employer-employee conversation.

"You looked petrified," Jeremy points out. "Like Bambi in headlights."

Max agrees.

Seriously?! I thought I looked like a badass. I even met his gaze. My chin was raised!

"He didn't exactly look happy either," Max adds. "Though maybe that's just how he is? He was a total dick when he found me talking to you earlier."

Thankfully, Jeremy doesn't ask him to elaborate, and we all go right back to eating our lasagna. After, we sit out in front of the mess hall talking until the sun starts to set. Some of the guys wander off to shower and attempt to call home. A few of them start up a poker game. We stay right where we are, though, listening to the cicadas and the soft strumming of Mike's guitar. That's his name—I know because we invited him to join us. There's a big group sitting in a circle while he strums. Someone starts telling a story and we all listen, heads tipped back, staring up at the trees and the moon starting to overtake the sky. Most of us were born and raised around here. Even if we didn't go to the same schools and live in the same small towns, we all had similar upbringings. No one puts on airs. No one gets offended by the sound of someone spitting chewing tobacco or the smell of a cigarette burning beside them. Even if it's not my thing, it's still oddly comforting. We're all trailer trash, everyone one of us, and the thought makes me smile.

An hour later, I'm inside my new bedroom, AKA Jeremy's truck. It would work if he had a normal bench seat that stretched from one door to the other. If that were the case, I'd be catching so many z's right now, I'd have some to spare.

Unfortunately, Jeremy's truck is older than dirt and there's a massive gear shift in the center of the floor that breaks up the two seats, therefore preventing me from lying across it like a bed. My only option is to sleep upright in the passenger seat with my head angled against the window. Even with my pillow wedged between my ear and the door, it's no use. I'm a sleep-walking zombie in the morning.

I tell myself sleep is overrated. New parents don't sleep. Insomniacs don't sleep. People avoiding their bosses by sleeping in trucks don't sleep either. I greet the morning with enthusiasm, ignore the crick in my neck, and go into the day with a new attitude. Yesterday, I messed up. I let my guard down where Ethan is concerned. Even after his abrupt apology at dinner, it's still clear he's a coldhearted jerk. That's fine. I know that now, and I'll be better prepared going into today. I have to be. Ethan might not have any reason to be nice to me and help smooth over our rocky relationship, but I do. I need this job badly enough to swallow my pride, keep my temper in check, and get to work.

After I take a quick shower in the communal bathroom while Jeremy stands guard at the door, I throw on a pair of jeans and a white t-shirt then frown at my reflection in the mirror. The V-neck isn't necessarily encroaching on dangerous territory, but when you're top-heavy, if you give your boobs an inch, they'll take a mile. I adjust the neckline so it sits a little higher and then spray my hair so it'll air-dry with beachy waves, and that's that. I'm ready to tackle the day!

I think ahead and bring two hot coffees out to where Ethan's finishing up a meeting with some of the subcontractors. They're standing in front of the demolished meeting hall. All the lumber has been hauled off and the dirt that's left is uneven and rocky. Still, now that the building is gone, there's a straight shot all the way from here to the lake, and the view is breathtaking. Much better than staring at a truck dashboard at 3:30 in the morning.

The meeting breaks up a few minutes after I arrive and I rush forward, seizing the opportunity. I look like the aide to a president on a sitcom. Ethan starts walking and I have no choice but to match his pace if I want to keep up.

"Do you like coffee?" I ask genially.

"Who doesn't like coffee?"

"Some people."

Our conversation dies a quick death. I have no choice but to revive it.

"Well, would you like some?" I hold both coffees out to him, which—due to the fact that I'm having to take five steps for every one of his—makes it so there's spillage over the sides and onto my hand.

He reaches over and takes a cup, and afterward I realize he's left me the one without cream and sugar. There's no way he did that intentionally. There's no way he likes sugar in his coffee. He's got no-frills straight-black-coffee-drinker written all over his perfectly honed features. He must not have been paying attention.

A small nod is the only thanks I get, but I eat it up and continuing walking.

"Should we discuss what happened last week—"

He cuts me off. "I don't have time."

"Right. Okay." I match his no-nonsense tone. "Let's focus on work. I couldn't agree more. In fact, I'd like to learn more about the construction side of things."

I'm not even sucking up right now. It's the truth. Yesterday, Robert barely skimmed the surface. I want to be useful, want to know what's going on. I'd like to see a blueprint and have some inkling of what it is I'm looking at. *Is that a bathroom or an elevator? No idea.*

"Not on this project."

His rejection stings, but I move along. It's called picking your battles, and it's how I'm going to win this war.

"Okay, no problem. Why don't you just give me a list of tasks you'd like me to complete today and I'll get to work."

"First, I want you out of my hair."

I stop walking. He continues, then realizes I'm not beside him.

He turns back to find me.

"How's this?" I ask, half shouting.

His eyes squeeze closed and he tilts his head to the sky, praying for patience.

Laugh, dammit!

He regains his composure and shakes his head. "I wasn't lying when I said I didn't have enough work for a personal assistant."

Crap. I thought he was just saying that in the heat of the moment as a way to get me to quit. I have a mini panic attack. He can't fire me. He needs me. No, I *need* him. *I need this job!*

"But you're the boss," I point out, dumbly. "You're a busy guy. Busy guys need assistants."

He arches a brow.

"I did your laundry." I'm desperately trying to prove my usefulness.

"Yes, and look how well that turned out."

Point taken.

"What did you think of your cabin last night?" I goad. "Spotless, right?"

"*Our* cabin."

"What?"

He looks away. Sips his coffee. "It was fine. I liked how you arranged my toothbrush and toothpaste."

Of course he did because he's a neurotic control freak. It's probably the reason he makes a good manager on building projects like this.

"Okay, well, that just goes to show that maybe there *are* things I could do to help you around here, but you don't have time to micromanage me. So, here's the solution: I'll come up with ways to be useful, and I'll try hard not to pester you while I do it."

"You're pestering me right now."

I nearly smile, because I swear he's teasing me—I mean, no one is *this* rude—but his beautifully arrogant mask doesn't crack even a bit.

This guy.

I swear.

"Noted. No more pestering." I start walking backward and he stands there, watching me. Then I throw up a salute, turn, and head in the direction of the mess hall so I can start brainstorming ways to be useful.

CHAPTER FIFTEEN
ETHAN

An hour after we part ways, Taylor walks into the trailer while I'm on a conference call with my partners and, without saying a word, she picks up the coffee cup on my desk and replaces it with a new one, its contents still steaming. Then she reaches for the trashcan under my desk and carries it outside. A few minutes later, she replaces it, empty.

I sit there, watching her as Grant drones on about one thing or another. He likes the sound of his own voice, which is why these calls always take thirty minutes longer than they should.

Taylor walks over to the desk Robert and Hudson share and tidies it up, wiping away dust before carrying their trashcan out to be emptied as well.

When she comes back inside, she moves quickly and quietly, keeping her gaze on the ground. It's like she's trying to blend in with the wall, which is absolutely impossible for someone like her.

Most of the time she wears her hair up in a ponytail, hidden. Today, it's down and longer than I thought it'd be. Not Amish-girl-wearing-a-denim-dress long, but long enough that it catches my attention. It's pretty. *Pretty!* Jesus. It's brown, but to call it that would be like calling a tree plain ol' green. There are other colors in there too, chestnut and honey, and right then, she glances over her shoulder, apparently aware of the attention I'm paying her.

I look up at the ceiling and recline in my chair.

“Grant, can you wrap this up?” Steven says, making me chuckle under my breath. “This could have been condensed into a two-sentence email.”

“You guys never read my emails!” he argues.

It’s the truth, but he only has himself to blame for that. Too many forwarded memes means he basically has to mark something URGENTLY URGENT in all caps before any of us bother.

Grant rushes to finish his rambling diatribe about nothing all that important and my gaze skates right back to Taylor as she finishes tidying up the other desk.

In jeans and her work boots, she shouldn’t be all that noteworthy. I’ve never heard a guy beg to see his girlfriend in a pair of boots versus a sky-high pair of heels, but maybe I’ve been stuck in the middle of the woods for too long because Taylor in a simple outfit of boots and a t-shirt has me nearly enraptured. The shirt pulls a little too tight over her chest. Her jeans are too big on her, but that just means they hang loose on her small waist, allowing a sliver of skin to show when she leans over. She tugs them back up and puffs a piece of hair away from her face as she surveys the space. Short of bringing in a vacuum and mop, she’s done all she can. She smiles to herself and then leaves.

I sit there with my phone pressed to my ear, unaware that the call ended five minutes ago. Everyone else has already hung up.

“Where’d you find Taylor?” Robert asks later that afternoon while we’re walking the site.

I peer at him out of the corner of my eye.

“How I find any of my employees—she came to the recruiting event.”

His brows perk up. Apparently, that wasn’t the answer he was expecting. “You didn’t know her before all this?”

My silence serves as a placeholder for my reply. I’d rather not lie to Robert. We’ve worked together for years, and I know from seeing him deal with my crew that I’d be hard-pressed to regain his respect if I lost it.

Our boots hit the dirt. Silence stretches on until he fills it.

“She reminds me a little of my daughter.” Then he snorts. “Nah, I take that back. My daughter’s a girly girl through and through. She’s never once asked me a question about a jobsite. Maybe I just mean that Taylor brings out some kind of paternal instinct in me.”

“Robert, are you going soft on me?” I smirk as we near the edge of the lake. We have soil engineers out here performing a secondary analysis before we continue leveling the ground.

He waves away my joke. “No, no, nothing like that. I don’t know.” He turns to study me. “She just seems a little…I don’t know, like a wounded bird. Don’t you think?”

I want to tell him it’s an act, that anything having to do with Taylor is a facade she erects for her own benefit. I saw that firsthand the night we met. She was the wounded bird then, too, and I wanted to be the one to rescue her. Turns out, I was the one who could’ve used a little rescuing.

I’m on the phone with Isla later that evening when Taylor peeks her head in the trailer and asks if I’d like her to bring me dinner since they're about to shut down the kitchen. I didn't realize it was so late.

"Yeah, I'll be working for another hour or so."

She nods and closes the door right before Isla nearly shouts, "That sounded like a woman!"

"It was."

"Not just a woman, but a young *pretty* one!"

"How can you tell what someone looks like just from hearing their voice?" I mock, glad she can't see my scowl.

"It's a gift. Tell me I'm wrong."

"This conversation is pointless."

"Oh my god, I'm right! *I knew it.* Why didn't you tell me there was a pretty woman working with you? Is she part of the crew?"

"She's my assistant."

"Oh, I see."

I roll my eyes. "You see nothing."

"What a scandalous turn of events," she continues, grabbing hold of this stupid idea she's gotten into her head.

"Goodbye, Isla."

"Have fun with your new assistant!"

As soon as I hang up, Taylor returns balancing two plates and a can of Coke.

"They made tacos tonight and I wasn't sure how you liked them, so I just put all the toppings on the side. Lots of guacamole, that's a given. Some sour cream, lettuce, tomatoes. I didn't go heavy on the hot sauce, but I can get more if you need it."

She sets the plates down on my desk, careful not to put the food too close to the plans stretched out beside my keyboard.

Then she moves to leave.

"Taylor—"

Her name is tossed between us like a grenade. Silence follows. Then, I remind myself that usually when someone addresses another person, there's a reason. I'm supposed to follow her name with something. *Taylor, can you get me some water? Taylor, thanks for the tacos. Taylor, hi.*

In truth, I said her name because I want to ask where she's been sleeping the last two nights, but I stopped myself because I'm unsure I want to know the answer. It could be with that Max guy.

And if it is?

The thought doesn't sit well with me. I wish I could say it's because I'm worried about Max's safety or wellbeing, but there's no mistaking this twisting feeling in my gut.

"Did you need something?" she asks, brows raised with hope.

I look down at the food she carefully arranged for me. "No. That's all."

CHAPTER SIXTEEN
TAYLOR

I've found that by making me prove my own usefulness, Ethan has likely turned me into a better employee than I ever would have been otherwise. I'm so determined to work hard and make him *aware* of how hard I'm working, I barely stop moving during the second week at the camp. If I'm not straightening up the trailer or cleaning the cabin, I'm making sure Ethan's coffee is topped off (he *does* like it with sugar!) or that he hasn't missed lunch or dinner. I run messages back and forth between Robert and Hudson and Ethan.

I don't wait for him to tell me he needs his laundry washed again. I take the initiative and make sure it's folded and back in his drawers when it's all clean.

When Ethan has to go out and walk the property, I stay back and answer the central office cell phone. It rarely rings since most people who'd need to call have Ethan's personal number, but when it does, I take thorough messages and leave them neatly on his desk for him.

I learn how to use the scanner and have Hudson walk me through their preferred filing system. There's apparently a ridiculous amount of paperwork involved in building projects. Ethan has started to leave me items he'd like scanned and filed on Lockwood's online database. Since most of the time I have no idea what I'm looking at, he usually jots down where he wants me to store it. It's a win-win for everyone because it gives me one more task and frees Hudson up to be out on the site more.

On top of being as useful as possible to Ethan, I try to do the same for everyone else at the camp as well. The catering team—a husband and wife duo they brought in from Austin—mostly keep to themselves, but I make sure to come early for meals and help with setup, and if they're in the trenches during a lunch rush, they put me to work doling out food. Last night, I offered to help wash dishes, and I think I saw genuine tears in their eyes.

The subcontractors and crew have started to realize that the quickest way to get information to Ethan is through me, so I start to get waylaid with messages for him. It works well because Ethan wants me out of his hair so badly he's quick to give me a response for them. They're always grateful for the fast turnaround since time is money on a project like this.

Robert gets his own special treatment because I happen to like him. I've been sneaking him snacks from the mess hall in the afternoons and in exchange he updates me about what they're doing on the site that day.

Basically, my goal is to become an asset to everyone I come across, that way when Ethan finally decides he's had enough of me, maybe they'll all revolt and demand justice on my behalf.

The only hiccup in my master plan is that I'm still sleeping in Jeremy's truck at night. I've added a pillow and blanket I stripped from my bunk in Ethan's cabin on top of what I brought from home in an effort to make it semi-comfortable, but let's call a spade a spade. It sucks and I don't think I will last much longer.

By Friday morning, I'm so happy about the prospect of going home. Not only will I get a decent night's sleep, I'll also have a break from incessantly attempting to please a man who is apparently un-pleasable.

I get the sense he's not going to forgive me for my perceived grievances against him any time soon, and maybe I'm not all that angry about it because deep down, I know I deserve his anger. I did steal from him. I did use him. Just because I didn't take the cash doesn't mean I didn't do anything wrong.

I thought perhaps he'd start to be charmed by my hardworking enthusiasm, but no.

It'd be different if I were making progress, if I saw a hint of a smile peek out from beneath his moody exterior, if even one kind word had been uttered in my direction, even *once*. Don't get me wrong, we do talk, but it's only if it pertains to work, and there's no fluff around it, no blooming comradery among coworkers.

I watch him carefully whenever he interacts with other people to try to determine if I'm reading too much into his treatment of me. Like Max said, it could just be his personality. My findings are as follows: he's not chummy with the crew, though that's not all that surprising—no one wants to hang out with their boss after hours. With Robert and a few of the subcontractors, though, he's relaxed and—*dare I say*—good-natured. Last night, he ate dinner outside with them and I saw him smile. The glorious sight threw me for such a loop that I tripped over my own foot and pitched forward onto the dirt. Fortunately, Max helped me scramble back to my feet and I brushed my jeans off quickly. When I peered back over in Ethan's direction, he was back to scowling. *Ah yes, that's more like it.*

But honestly…DIMPLES. I saw them!

Mr. I'd-rather-die-than-smile-in-your-vicinity has dimples!

If that's not injustice, I don't know what is.

I'm still thinking of that smile at quitting time on Friday. Truth be told, I've been carrying it around with me all day like it's my little reward for a week of hard work. *Why*, you might ask? *Why* do I care at all about Ethan's smile? *Why*, after everything we've been through, do I still think of him incessantly? Oh, it's simple: despite his cold demeanor and bad attitude, I can't seem to stop myself from wanting his attention. I know it's purely physical. I know his muscular build and perfect jawline are catnip to my libido. I know, I know, I know, and yet I want, I want, I want.

I can't turn it off. I can't help the memories of our kiss that flood my mind.

Because that's the thing I cannot quite comprehend: I KISSED THIS MAN.

At one point, this arrogant boss of mine wanted me so badly he followed me into a public bathroom and hauled me up onto the sink and kissed me like I was the sweetest damn thing he'd ever tasted. I get a tingle down my spine just thinking of it.

I wonder if he thinks about it too…

I shake the thought from my head when I spot Jeremy in the distance. I've been leaning against his truck for the past hour, expecting him to show up any minute. All my stuff is already tucked away inside due to the fact that the truck has been my bedroom for most of the week. All we gotta do is start 'er up and head home.

I can't wait to get a tight hug from McKenna. I can't wait to see my mom smile, happier than ever because we're all three together again. Without a doubt, there's a stack of pancakes in my future, and my stomach grumbles just thinking about it.

"Where've you been?" I ask as Jeremy nears.

It's later than I was planning on leaving. All but a few cars have gone. Even Ethan already headed back home for the weekend—not that I noticed him driving off in his truck or the fact that he didn't even wave as he passed me by.

That's when I see Jeremy's face and notice it doesn't shine with happiness at the prospect of being reunited with his beloved Khloe in just a couple of hours. In fact, he looks shocked. His hair is standing on end like he's been tugging his hands through it. His eyes are wide and red-rimmed.

"What's going on?" I ask, right before he reaches out and pulls me into a hug so tight I can barely breathe.

"Taylor…I'm…" He laughs and sounds absolutely deranged. Did someone slip him something during lunch?

"What? What's wrong?!"

"I'm going to be a dad," he finally forces out, barely above a whisper.

I jerk back, hands flying to cup either side of my face. "What?!"

What is he talking about? We were just at work. Dad? What? How? *Who did he impregnate?*

He claps a hand over his mouth and shakes his head. His eyes are welling with tears, and now the redness makes sense. He's been crying.

From joy.

"Jeremy, that's…" My voice breaks. "That's really great news."

More than anything, I want Jeremy to be happy, and he *is* happy right now. He's over the moon about this news, news that is going to absolutely turn his world upside down.

"I can't even believe it. I just got off the phone with Khloe. She's been trying to reach me all day. She's already six months along."

"Six months?! Hasn't she been showing?"

My heart races trying to catch up with all this news.

He nods, more tears running down his cheeks before he wipes them away. “She’s always been curvy and I guess I should have been paying more attention, but it doesn’t matter now. She says we’re having a little girl and she wants to name her Jacqueline after her grandmother. She was keeping it a secret because she wasn’t sure how I’d take it. That’s why she called me here instead of just waiting until I got home. She was nervous I’d want nothing to do with her or the baby.”

I can’t wrap my head around this. Jeremy had goals. He wanted to get out of debt and start building up a nest egg. I’m so happy for him—*I am*—I just…

What happens now?

Apparently, what happens now is that Jeremy is moving.

Khloe has family in San Antonio, an aunt and an uncle who want to help her out. Her uncle has work for Jeremy at a car dealership he manages.

“It’s a good opportunity for us.”

“Better than this?” I ask, feeling like a jerk for even bringing it up. I’m just still in shock.

His eyes find mine and pity settles there. I feel terrible. He should be getting to enjoy this moment, but how can he with me standing here like a joy-sucking leech?

“Khloe’s dead set on going to San Antonio, and I can’t abandon her. I have to do what’s best for my family.”

Family.

That’s right.

Khloe and Jacqueline are Jeremy’s family now, and just like that my safety net is gone, because if Jeremy is quitting, I can’t leave with him and drive back to Oak Dale. I’d have no way of getting back here on Monday. Max would be an option if Max had a car, but Jeremy says he’s been catching a ride with another guy. He isn't sure on the details and he doesn't even have Max's current number and I feel like I'm on the brink of tears, but I can't cry in front of Jeremy. I can't cry and ruin his moment more than I probably already have.

"Hey, why don't I just drive you back here on Monday?" Jeremy offers, but I shake my head.

"No, that's silly. You've got a lot to do with...*everything*, and I don't mind staying here. I just need to grab my stuff out of your truck."

He frowns. "Where are you going to sleep? You can have my bunk now."

I could, but I'd rather not have to sleep in the bunkhouse and use the communal shower without Jeremy there to stand guard.

I guess it's probably time to head back to Rose Cabin.

The camp is a ghost town. Everyone's left. The cars that were parked beside Jeremy's drove away soon after he did. Now it's just me...me and a deer munching on some grass a couple yards away. I try to get it to come closer, but it gets spooked and flees. So yeah, it's just me. I didn't really think my plan through. I'm not even sure we're allowed to stay at the camp on the weekends, though if no one is here, who's going to report me?

I haul my stuff back through camp and out to Rose Cabin. It reminds me of the first day I arrived, quiet and secluded. The door creaks and I glance down at Ethan's bunk, still perfectly made from when I tidied up the cabin earlier this morning. He didn't take all of his things with him. There's a baseball cap on the dresser and some clothes still in the drawers. I unpack my duffle bag—for good this time—and then try to call my mom. Three attempts and no successes have me ready to throw my phone clear across the forest. I curse phone carriers and their lack of forethought in putting cell towers out here in the middle of nowhere.

Then when that doesn't soothe my anger enough, I storm out of the cabin, haul butt down the stairs, and let out a soul-on-fire, life-cannot-be-this-unfair scream. Birds shoot up out of the surrounding trees, apparently terrified of me. I would be too.

There's such a thing as too much crap.

One person can only handle so much. I have a breaking point, and apparently, I've reached it.

That first scream felt so good, I release another.

There.

That's for our car falling to pieces and the zero dollars in my bank account and the bleak state of my future job prospects if things go south with Lockwood Construction. That's for the loser guys I've dated and the loser man who cared enough to get my mom pregnant but not enough to stick around. That's for Mr. Harris and his leering stares at the motel. That's for Jeremy leaving. That's for Ethan being in that bar the night I was at my most desperate. That's for me choosing him over every other man. That's for the fact that I wish I could hate him as much as he hates me.

I pull in oxygen like I've been held under water for hours. My lungs swell and then empty while my heart pounds against my ribs.

I feel better.

Those screams were good for my soul.

I look down at my phone in my hand and don't even bother. I don't want to talk to anyone. I have things to do. I'm going to turn this cabin into a home, and I'm going to start by picking wildflowers. There are a million around me, more than I've ever seen. I go for the big fat yellow ones and pluck up as many as I can hold in one hand, then I start in on some tiny white ones that look like miniature daisies. There's a bucket in the mess hall I fill with water and carry back to the cabin. Once it's overflowing with flowers, I plop it down in the center of the desk.

I arrange my toiletries in the bathroom, claiming half the counter space on the sink and making it perfectly obvious that I've returned and belong here. I might as well have drawn a lipstick heart on the mirror.

My bed is made with clean linens and looks so inviting, and because I have nothing better to do and haven't had a decent night of sleep in what feels like years, I climb up onto that bunk, close my eyes, and am dead to the world in a matter of moments.

I sleep hard and wake up so early Saturday morning, it's still dark outside. All the troubles I ran from last night come rushing right back, so I have no choice but to get moving in the hopes that they can't keep up. I turn on the lantern, make my bed, shower, and head toward the mess hall. From helping out around mealtime, I know how to find what I'm looking for. There's some cereal and milk and I pour myself a small bowl, feeling guilty for taking any at all. Surely they won't mind, right?

I eat it outside while the sun starts to rise.

Then, I try to call home once more, and it connects and starts ringing! But then, no one answers, and hope slips right through my fingers. How dare they sleep at a time like this?! So what if it's ungodly early?!

When it goes to voicemail, I leave a message.

"Hey Mom, I'm not sure if you've talked to Jeremy yet. He said he was going to call you once he got back to Oak

Dale since cell service is so bad out here. He and Khloe are moving to San Antonio. Khloe's pregnant. It's…yeah…he'll do a better job of explaining everything. He's going to be a dad. Did I already say that? Anyway, I'm calling because I won't be coming home this weekend. I didn't want to be stranded in Oak Dale on Monday morning and miss work, so I thought it was better to stay. Anyway…" I look down at the ground, brows furrowed. "I miss you guys."

The voicemail cuts me off, and it's just as well because I was already starting to ramble, the feeling of homesickness brewing up inside of me not something I want to indulge. It's a glorious Saturday and I have absolutely nothing on my agenda. I can do whatever I want! Well, I can do whatever I want while stranded in the middle of the forest.

In a pure stroke of genius, I tromp back to Rose Cabin and grab a fresh towel and some clothes I don't mind getting wet. I'm headed back out the door when my attention catches on Ethan's paperback, a book by Brandon Sanderson. Without a second thought, I snatch it off his bed and carry it out to the lake with me. I stay out there most of the day, reading and lying out in the sun. When I'm feeling my bravest, I creep toward the edge of the lake and dip my toes in. It's freezing, but after sitting in the sun for so long, it's refreshing and the water is so clear and inviting, I can't resist. I dive in and swim until my limbs start to ache. Then I head back to shore, towel off, read, and repeat the same process until my stomach is aching with hunger. In the mess hall, I fix myself a sandwich then take my book outside to sit where we've been gathering after dinner the last few days. Usually Mike plays his guitar and we get a nice flame going in the firepit.

Now, the fire pit sits empty and the camp is quiet, but this book is way better than I thought it would be, and I actually don't mind having tons of time to sit and read alone.

The next day, I repeat the same schedule through most of the morning, except I take a longer swim and follow it with an extra-long nap while partially concealed by the canopy of pine trees. When I stir, I realize it's because there's a group of deer nearby, chomping on some plants only a few yards away from me. I hold perfectly still, watching two white-freckled fawns as they stick close to their mom, stealing sips of milk when they get the chance. They're tiny and clumsy, both greedy for food. I laugh when one of them nudges the other out of the way, and the doe's head perks up at the sound before she darts away, her offspring following quickly after her. The three of them remind me of my family, and the thought doesn't fill me with sadness like I thought it would. I feel hope. I'm doing the right thing for my mom and McKenna. Being here means making more money than I ever could back in Oak Dale. Just because Jeremy is gone doesn't mean anything bad will happen. I've made friends with a few of the guys, and I'm beginning to find a place of my own among the crew.

With that thought, I shed my towel and dip back into the lake, going for a second swim before I trudge back to camp, soaking wet.

In late spring, the temperature isn't quite hot enough to warm me, and I'm still shivering by the time I make it back to the cabin. I change and eat a late lunch before sitting out on the porch, reading. I'm nearing the end of the paperback and the suspense is killing me. The author has been building toward an epic battle and I know I need to read quickly if I want to finish it before Ethan gets back.

The wind picks up and I shiver, unsure of the time. I was too hungry to rinse off earlier, but when I walk back into the cabin to escape the cool wind, my eyes catch on the aluminum tub in the corner. There's a drain on one side. I know it could be used as a bath, and it's clean thanks to my sweep of the cabin this week. The showers around the camp don't get hot water. They get whatever the hell water they pull up from the wells, and usually that means quick freezing-cold showers taken with chattering teeth and goose bumps covering my entire body.

A hot bath sounds like an indulgence I can't pass up, even if it means boiling water in the mess hall and lugging it back to Rose Cabin over and over again. My arms are shaky from exertion by the time I'm done, but when I put my hand down into the half-filled tub, I nearly groan with pleasure. The water has cooled down enough that it doesn't scald my skin, but it's still hot enough to relieve my aching muscles after I strip off my clothes and step in.

I lather up my arms and legs then spend extra time on my hair, letting the conditioner sink in while I lie back and close my eyes. The scent of my floral body wash hangs heavy in the air. I could stay here forever, but I pry my eyes open and finish washing so I can reach for the paperback and rush to finish the last few pages. Before Ethan gets back, I'll have to put it right back where I found it so he doesn't know I've borrowed it all weekend.

My fingers and toes turn to prunes and the water cools another few degrees as I turn pages, hungry for resolution.

I'm so caught up in the fast-paced ending that I don't notice the creak of the cabin stairs or the sound of the door opening. All I know is one minute, I'm alone in that cabin, reading, and the next, I glance up just as Ethan freezes in the doorway, staring straight at me in the tub.

I scream and his paperback flies out of my hand, landing in the water with a heavy *thunk*. My eyes widen and I don't give a crap that I'm so exposed because I WAS TWO PAGES AWAY FROM FINISHING and now—NOW the book is sopping wet.

"No, no, no!" I scramble to pull it up out of the water and shake it quickly. Water flies into my eye, but who cares?!

I lurch over the side of the tub and lay the book out on my towel, patting it dry.

"I'm so, so sorry!"

I didn't want him to know I read his book. Now not only does he know I read it without asking him, I've ruined it too.

The words bleed together and when I flip to the end, the thin pages rip clean from the binding, all but disintegrating in my hands.

"Jesus," Ethan groans, stomping forward. "What are you going on about?" He yanks the towel out from underneath the book and throws it onto me.

Ah yes, I'm nude.

Oh so nude.

My eyes fly up to his, and he's looking down at the book, his hands on his hips, his face pulled into tight angry lines.

"Sorry," I mutter, though the word sounds weak and useless.

CHAPTER SEVENTEEN

ETHAN

Let's get one thing perfectly clear: I don't give a shit about that book. I couldn't recall the name of it right now if my life depended on it.

She's going on and on about it as she stands up and wraps the towel around herself, and though she didn't ask me to, I whip around and give her my back. I'd expect her to be embarrassed to have been caught naked in the tub. Instead, she keeps apologizing for ruining my book. Who cares about the book? I walked into the cabin, expecting to find it empty, and instead, I found Taylor, sitting there with her hot curves on full display. Instead of walking right back out the door like a gentleman and giving her privacy, I stood there dumbstruck, lost, utterly enraptured by a woman who is nothing short of a fantasy with her tantalizing breasts, narrow waist, and long wet hair.

I am so ridiculously hard right now, I'm actually glad Taylor is babbling about the book because if she weren't, she'd realize I'm making a complete fool of myself.

I've seen naked women before!

I've had plenty of sex!

Good sex with hot women, and sure, it's been a couple months, but I've been busy, and I'm good at taking care of my needs in the shower, with my hand, while picturing this very woman with her small hands wrapped around me and her wet hair tickling my chest. I jerk myself away from those thoughts as I realize Taylor is kneeling in her towel, flipping through the book.

"Don't worry about it," I insist, tone hard and clear.

She's mumbling under her breath. "Borrowed it without asking…ruined it…let me just see if I can dry it out and…"

She's acting like I'm about to attack her for ruining my book. Is she really so scared of me?

I reach down and grab her bicep, easily lifting her up to her feet. Her skin is wet and warm. She keeps the towel closed with one hand and her big brown eyes find mine. She looks doe-eyed and innocent.

"The book doesn't matter."

"But you already hate me."

I don't refute that.

Right now, I hate what she's doing to me. I hate how I'm reacting to her. There's a lot of hate tangling with lust and it's hard to separate one feeling from another. Maybe I do hate her. Or maybe it's the exact opposite.

"I'll buy you a new one," she insists, nodding along with the idea. "Yes, that's what I'll do."

I don't point out that we're about three hours from the nearest bookstore and I don't think Amazon ships to cabins in the middle of the woods.

Her attention falls to my hand on her arm and I should drop it, but I don't. Instead, my gaze moves over her, up from her bare feet and shapely calves right to the point where her white towel cuts across her bare thighs. A drop of water runs down them and I'm seconds from doing something very bad.

"You look deeply disapproving right now," she says, actually sounding amused. "Like everything about me offends you."

I try to relax my features, but it's no use.

"Did you stay here all weekend?"

There's a long pause before she replies diplomatically, "Will I get in trouble if I say yes?"

"I don't know."

Her eyes are suddenly lit with an inner twinkle of mischief. "Then…I don't know."

Paired with her long dark lashes and high cheekbones, her teasing words make it impossible to suppress the lazy smile spreading across my lips.

Her gaze catches there, and that's the moment I step away and release her arm. I know what it looks like when a woman wants a man, and Taylor and I are not here in this cabin for that reason.

The warring emotions inside of me yank my heart in different directions as I head for the door.

"Let me know when you're dressed," I say gruffly, tugging a hand through my hair and slamming the door open harder than necessary. It bangs against the side of the cabin, the sound too loud and too sharp, making it look as if I can't control my temper. I've never had an issue until now.

I sit on the top stair and train my eyes on the forest, cooling off, thinking of my grandma and baseball. When that doesn't work, I think of my grandma *playing* baseball, and when Taylor walks out a few minutes later, I don't even feel the effect she has on me. Not at all. Dressed in loose jeans and a t-shirt, she's still barefoot. I'm looking at her pink-polished toes when she speaks up.

"I've decided to come back and sleep in the cabin. I know you won't exactly love having me here, but I don't really see another option unless there's another vacant cabin somewhere else."

I look back out along the trail, giving her my profile. "It's fine." I don't ask where she's been sleeping. Chances are, I won't like the answer anyway. "However, I don't want you staying here on the weekends again."

It's not safe for her to stay out here alone, not only from a liability standpoint for the company, but for her own wellbeing.

Still, she bristles at the brusque order, turns around, and heads right back into the cabin only to return a few minutes later with her shoes on and her damp hair thrown up in a ponytail. She brushes past me on the stairs without another word and walks down the trail back to camp.

When I stand and reenter the cabin, I'm met with a heavy scent of her body wash. It's like the entire place has been steeped in it. On the window sill, propped up and fanned out to dry, sits my paperback. Below it, wildflowers sit in a bucket on the desk.

It suddenly hits me that I'm doing something I've never done before: living with a woman.

Of course I've had girlfriends stay over at my house in Austin and leave their things behind, a jacket here, an earring there. In my last relationship, we were together a few months. She wanted commitment and promises and a ten-year plan. I wanted nothing of the sort.

Suddenly, the tables are now flipped, and I know how it feels to want someone who seems just out of reach at all times.

Taylor is elusive and wild, a clever little cat. I couldn't predict her next move if there were a million dollars on the line.

I'm glad she left when she did because otherwise, she'd see me right now, touching the flowers she picked with utter bewilderment, like I've never seen flowers before in my entire life. Because, the thing is, deep down, I'm not at all mad that she moved back into the cabin. I've wanted her here with me since the beginning. It's why I had them assign bunkhouses in the first place.

After unpacking my clothes and getting prepared for the week ahead, I go on a long run. Taylor's back in the cabin when I return, sitting up on the top bunk, cursing her phone before launching it halfway across the room. I reach out and catch it before it collides with the wall.

"Bad reception?" I ask with an arched brow.

Her cheeks are flushed with fury from having been caught during her little outburst of anger.

"Yes. This entire cabin is a dead zone—no, this entire *camp*! Sometimes I'm able to pick up a signal near the mess hall, but even that's not reliable. How do you get service all the time?"

"Well for one, my cell phone is from this century," I say, handing hers back. "And I also bought a signal booster. It's necessary out here in the woods."

Her eyes widen with approval. "Oh. I hadn't thought of that."

My phone burns like a beacon across the room. I know what I should do in this moment. She's obviously trying desperately to get in contact with someone.

She mistakes my hesitation for something it's not. "Don't worry, I won't ask to borrow your phone. I know you don't trust me, though it's a little silly. What do you think I'm going to do? Hack into your bank accounts?" She groans and moves to the ladder. "You know what? I'll just ask one of the guys to borrow—"

My phone hits her pillow and then I turn for the bathroom.

"I'm showering. You have until I'm finished."

Truth be told, I actually *don't* trust Taylor with my phone. Why would I? A month and a half ago, she stole my wallet and all the cash that was inside of it. I'd be a fool to think I could trust her. An absolute fool.

When I'm done showering, she's still talking on my phone. I hear her laughter, light and carefree through the bathroom door.

"I miss you too," she says sweetly. My stomach twists into a knot as I brush my teeth hunched over the sink, scowling like the grump she's turned me into.

After I change into some lounge pants, I walk over and hold out my hand.

Her eyes lock with mine and she keeps talking.

I motion for her to hang up.

She holds up her finger and points to the phone, clearly hoping to continue her conversation.

I reach out, take the phone, and hang up. She can call her boyfriend back later, sometime when I'm not here listening to her flirt with him.

"Ever the gentleman," she says with a snide glare.

"You're welcome for allowing you to use my cell phone."

She rolls her eyes and starts down the ladder. "You know I keep telling myself to take the high road, but with you I find it absolutely impossible. Why do you have to be so rude all the time? Are you like this with everyone in your life?"

"Just people who try to take advantage of others."

My comment is very clearly referring to the time she took my wallet and we both know it. She grinds her teeth and is about to let out a string of words sure to send me into an equally annoyed rage, but then she turns on her heel, storms into the bathroom, and slams the door behind her. The whole cabin shakes.

"I'd like to be reassigned to a new cabin!" she shouts through the wood. "If I'm going to have to deal with you all day, I need a break at night."

"Too bad."

"What?" she shouts.

I raise my voice so she can hear me through the door. "Too bad!"

The door flings open and she stands there with her toothbrush in her mouth, white suds foaming at the corners. "Why do you even want me in here with you anyway? I know you don't like me any more than I like you."

With the toothbrush in the way, her words come out warbled, but I still understand her perfectly.

"Keep your enemies close," is the only response I deign to give her before I flop back on my bed. I'd grab my paperback and start reading, but, well, that's not an option. Instead, I fold my hands behind my head and stare up at the bottom of her bunk.

She spits out her toothpaste in the sink, the faucet runs for a few seconds, and then she's back out here. This cabin feels as confining as a jail cell when we're both in it, like two caged animals.

My eyes go to her—as they always do when she enters a room—and I watch as she stalks over and leans down, her head dipping beneath the bunk. Her hair grazes my bare chest. Blood rushes south without my consent.

"Just to be clear, anything that happens in this cabin is outside of work. Is that clear? From dusk till dawn, I'll be sweet and doting, will fulfill your every need—but when we're in this cabin, don't expect me to treat you like my boss."

I can't help the snide smirk that curls the edge of my mouth. "See, that's where you're wrong. As long as you're on this property, I'm always your boss."

Yes, *Ethan*, you're always her boss, so stop trying to sneak glances down the top of her shirt.

She fists her hands by her sides, swallows whatever retort was forming on her tongue, and hurries up the ladder, apparently ready to be done with me.

I have no choice but to stand to turn the lamp off. The cabin's plunged into complete darkness. I have no clue what time it is. I don't even feel tired, but there's nothing else for us to do out here unless we want to kiss and make up, and right now we're probably closer to biting than kissing.

"Oh, and I wasn't going to mention it because I knew you'd only accuse me of snooping, but what does it matter now? Your opinion of me can't get any worse—"

"Just say it," I snap.

I can sense her desire to strangle me as she speaks with a clipped tone. "A woman named Isla texted you while I was on the phone. I didn't try to read it, but it popped up, and well…she's wondering where you've been."

"So you read my text messages?" I ask, sounding pissed.

"Like I said, I couldn't help it. Also, I was a little curious. Who would possibly want to text you? Finding out it was a woman wanting to know where you were was shocking to say the least. She should count her blessings that she can't find you. I'd *love* to be in that predicament."

I'm grinning now, utterly annoyed and yet entertained nonetheless.

"Trying to get rid of me, Taylor?"

"A girl can dream."

"Then why'd you come back to the cabin?"

“It wasn’t by choice. In fact, last week, I slept in an old truck instead of bunking here with you. That’s how desperate I am.”

In a truck? That’s where she’s been?!

I turn onto my side and stare at the wall. Cicadas fill the quiet until Taylor speaks up again.

“And just for the record, if I still had the option, I’d be in that truck right now.”

“Are you going to keep doing that all night?”

“What?”

“Talking.”

She growls and her sheets rustle as she turns over, probably facing the wall too, probably wondering how she can pull off killing me in my sleep.

CHAPTER EIGHTEEN
TAYLOR

Isla...Isla...Isla... Who is she and why is she texting Ethan? If she were in my shoes, she'd know better. He's not worthy of a text. He's not worthy of a polite greeting at this point! He's under my skin and going nowhere, and even when we're not together, my annoyance and hatred of him seem to fester. He's just so...so *arrogant*! And rude! And coldhearted! I cannot believe he hung up on my mom. It was my first phone call with her in two weeks where I could actually hear her clearly. All our previous calls were more like poor parodies of those old Sprint commercials. *"Can you hear me now?"*

I truly thought he'd comply with my wish for a cabin change. He cannot want me sleeping above him every night, but then of course he does. He obviously finds happiness in tormenting me, and it makes sense. He thinks I stole money from him, and this is his way of punishing me.

I want to text this Isla person and tell her to run for the hills. I want to ask her what she possibly wants with Ethan and also...yes, fine, I would also like to know more about her. What she looks like, what kind of personality she has, what her hobbies are. Purely for curiosity's sake, I need to know what sort of woman Ethan finds attractive. Who could possibly thaw that frozen heart of his?

Truthfully, I'm not sure it's possible.

The following week is proof of that. I wake up and get to work bright and early. I do my job insanely well—bringing Ethan his breakfast and lunch, tidying up around the cabin and the trailer, faxing, scanning, filing, taking messages, running notes to Robert and the subcontractors. After this, there's only two more weeks of preparation before the concrete trucks arrive, so the crew works tirelessly to level the ground and prepare the site for foundation work. Robert walks me through all the steps and I'm grateful. If it weren't for him, I'd have no idea that Ethan will be extra stressed this week and next. Concrete pours are time sensitive and extremely tricky, especially in a location like this. Concrete can't sit in trucks more than a few hours or it won't pour right and they'll have to tear everything out and start over. The concrete also can't be poured if it's raining outside or if it's too hot or too cold. The list goes on…

Fortunately, that shouldn't be a problem. Outside, it's still a perfect 70 degrees most days and the crew works happily, soaking in the sun that breaks through the canopy of pine trees. I soak it up myself as I run from one task to another, building a killer tan and also a thin sheen of sweat. Not that it matters—everyone's sweaty here. Compared to the guys, I smell like a rose.

It's weird without Jeremy, especially when lunch rolls around. Normally, we'd meet in line and share anecdotes about our morning (read: I'd complain about Ethan and things pertaining to Ethan) but now that he's gone, it's just me, in line, nodding hello at people, hoping I don't stick out like a sore thumb.

Max saves me when I run into him at lunch on Tuesday and he insists I sit with him even though Jeremy's gone. I have reservations considering Max hasn't exactly been shy about flirting with me and I don't want him to get the wrong idea. I'm not looking to pick up where we left off all those years ago. Fortunately, he addresses that.

"I know without Jeremy here, you need a friend now more than ever. No strings, I swear."

So, I give in, and we eat lunch together the rest of the week. He and his friends are who I sit with at dinner too, and it's nice, a little family of sweaty construction workers chowing down.

I even work up the courage to ask Max how he's been getting to and from the jobsite.

"Oh, I ride out with Nolan. He's got a truck, so there are like five of us who pile in."

Ah, that was the answer I was afraid of. Squeezing myself in as a sixth passenger doesn't sound all that appealing, but I need to find a solution soon because Ethan made it perfectly clear that he doesn't want me staying here on the weekends. More than that, I'd like to go home and see my mom and McKenna sometime soon.

Though I thought he would, Ethan doesn't avoid the cabin all week. Neither do I—on principle. If he can survive in that tiny room, I can too. It's a game we've unknowingly agreed to: Who Can Seem Less Affected. To hide out at the camp and slink in at midnight would be on par with admitting you have an issue with the other person. *Not happening.* We both return to the cabin right after dinner, when the sun is still up and there's plenty of time left for annoying, passive aggressive behavior.

He likes to take his sweet time putting on his workout clothes so I'm forced to avert my eyes for as long as possible. Because no, he never goes into the bathroom to change. He wants me to *ask* him to go into the bathroom. He wants me to admit I'm bothered by his naked torso. BUT I AM NOT.

I take extra-long showers and steam up the whole cabin, ensuring my body wash is a lingering scent that clogs his nose for hours afterward.

I bring in more wildflowers and set them up in jars around the room. That way, wherever he looks, he sees them and therefore has to think of me. It's beautifully evil.

Tuesday night, Ethan starts chatting on the phone precisely when I'm slipping off into dreamland. He proceeds to continue talking for what feels like hours but is probably only five minutes. I can't tell who he's talking to—it could be just a friend, but I bet it's Isla, which is the only reason I lean over the side of the bunk and not-so-politely ask him to hang up the call so I can go to sleep.

The next night, I borrow Mike's guitar and strum a few chords, acting as if I'm teaching myself how to play. In reality, I produce nails-on-a-chalkboard level screeches for exactly one hour. Ethan doesn't utter one complaint. I'm forced to give up because one of my fingers is about to blister.

The bathroom is an easy place for friction since both of us have bedtime rituals we can't forego. Brushing our teeth has turned into a shoulder-to-shoulder standoff, our arms moving quickly, toothbrushes swirling over teeth. We floss and brush like we have dentist appointments in an hour and we're trying to prove we've kept up with our oral hygiene since the last time we lied about flossing. Our strokes are hard, aggressive, like we're buffing away years of gunk. In reality, our smiles are pearly white. We take turns leaning over and spitting then rinsing. I dab my mouth with a towel and he does the same.

That's when I usually start to wash my face, but he doesn't give me space. Of course he doesn't, because I don't give him space in the morning when he's trying to shave. He crowds me, acting as though he still has reason to be in the bathroom.

It's infuriating.

All of it.

I can't crack first. I refuse to tell him again how much I loathe rooming with him.

Not only because it would give him untold pleasure, but also because it's a flat-out lie. In reality, I would never, *ever* switch rooms. There is one part of life in this cabin that feels like a tiny gift, like the universe is trying to make amends with me. This is it: if I happen to wake up in the middle of the night and need to pee, I get to see Ethan asleep, quiet, nice, tucked in the bottom bunk, cast in moonlight. A bare-chested god, the planes of his hard face relaxed in sleep, he seems somewhat less intimidating but no less handsome. I'm beginning to think my body is waking me up to use the bathroom just so I can spy on him while he's sleeping, but don't worry—I'm not trying to get caught watching him like a creepy child in a horror film, so I cut my obsessive perusal of him down to the time it takes me to pass slowly from the bathroom to the ladder on our bunk bed. That way I never officially stop moving, maintaining plausible deniability if he happens to wake up. I'll be mid-step. The explanation is obvious: *Oh, just heading back from the bathroom, that's all.* So what if there's drool on my chin? That could be from sleep. And my heavy breaths? Just had a night terror.

Friday can't come soon enough, though I'm no closer to solving my issue about my ride home. Max confirms again that he's carpooling with a group of guys and it's a full house. I could try to ask around, but I'm not *that* friendly with anyone else. They're all proving to be pretty nice and welcoming, but asking them to drive hours out of their way to drop me off at home is just not something I'm comfortable with. I could look into a taxi if I had cell service or an internet connection, but it's probably for the best because I can't exactly afford to pay for a taxi.

We did get paid today and my check was the full amount. My hands shook as I opened it up. It's more money than I've ever earned in a single paycheck before. It might even be enough to cover the car repairs so my mom can get it out of the shop. I'm sure she and McKenna are both sick of asking people for rides.

I pop the check in an envelope and address it. Max promised he'd drop it in the mail so my mom can deposit it in our joint account.

Everything is settled except for my ride, and unfortunately, Ethan is suspicious.

"When are you leaving?" he asks Friday evening in the cabin. He's grabbing the last of the things he's taking with him for the weekend and I'm pretending to do the same. *Ah yes, one sock, can't forget that.*

"Oh, my ride will be here any minute."

"How do you know? You have no cell reception."

I cast a tight, your-arrogance-has-no-effect-on-me smile over my shoulder. "Call it a hunch."

"Then I'll wait for you," he says, straightening to his full height, which is annoyingly large.

"No need. I wouldn't want to keep you from Is—*your weekend plans*."

I nearly said Isla, and he still smirks, fully aware of where my thoughts were headed.

"You're right. I do have plans I'd like to get to. Have a good weekend."

Once that door slams closed behind him and I know he's a good distance away, I lie back on the bottom bunk and heave a deep breath. Truthfully, I'm tempted to let out a barrage of expletives that outlines every single feeling I have toward Ethan. I want to shout every single word I've had to keep bottled up all week so that by the end, the walls would blush, but I just don't have the energy.

Being around him zaps it right out of me. I have to be *on*, aware, and mentally present at all times. He keeps me on my toes, and my toes are tired, and I should not have collapsed onto this bunk because it smells like Ethan. It's a smell I can't quite categorize. Normally scents are either good or bad. Some thrust you right back to a favorite memory, like freshly sharpened pencils and elementary school. Ethan's scent—masculine, woodsy, fresh—makes my stomach flip over and my chest ache right near my heart.

I roll off his bunk and step away, scared of what that smell could do to me if I let it linger.

Then I realize I'm stuck here, all alone. Again.

The fact is, I have no ride home, and even though Ethan told me not to, I'm going to have to stay here over the weekend. I'll just have to be careful. No long leisurely baths on Sunday afternoon. In fact, no baths *ever*. Also, I should probably make it look as if I return to camp after him, just so he doesn't think even for one second that I might have disobeyed him.

Plotting out how to do that eats up the first half of my Saturday at the lake, the second half of my day consumed by reading. Oh yes, I found another book. This one was tucked in one of the mess hall cupboards, and I found it while I was cleaning this week. It's a well-worn romance from the 70s. The pages are so yellowed they're nearly brown, but I tear through that puppy and enjoy every delicious glance, every teasing innuendo and playful conversation between the hero and heroine. It gets my loins burning and I'm forced to swim in the lake as a reprieve because there is no man in sight to soothe this ache—no man in the whole entire state, it seems.

I walk back out of the water and shake my limbs, flinging water everywhere. Then I lie back down on my towel and pick up the book.

Though I wish I didn't, I think of Ethan with Isla. I imagine her just like how the author describes the heroine in my book: tall, blonde, effervescent. What a word. Can a woman wearing oversized jeans and work boots even attempt effervescence? I hate Isla on principle.

I glance down and take in my wet t-shirt clinging to my curves. My underwear peeks out just below the hem, and I think of when Ethan accidentally walked in on me bathing last week, how there was no time for me to register my nakedness because I was too preoccupied with getting caught reading his book.

Now, I indulge the memory, twisting it into a create-your-own-adventure story in my mind. I imagine that in another world, Ethan strolls in and loses himself at the sight of me, lounging there, breasts barely visible over the top of the water. Maybe in this world, we're friends, more than friends. Maybe in this world, he strolls over and uses his hands—the hands I've only seen doing busy important *boss* things—to pick up my soap and washcloth and start to bathe me. I tuck my knees up against my chest, rest my cheek on my knee, and sit patiently while he starts on my lower back. The towel drags up my spine and I groan with pleasure in the simple act of him touching me with reverence and awe. No one's touched me like that before. Gently, beautifully.

Even in this other world, though, Ethan isn't the perfect gentleman, and what starts out as an innocent bath tips toward something more playful when he tugs on my shoulders and forces me to recline, legs stretched in front of me.

He kneels down behind me, outside of the tub, and uses his hands to soap and lather my chest, creating a wake of bubbles between my breasts and down across my stomach. My head tips back against the lip of the tub, my eyes flutter closed, and he continues south. His mouth slants over my neck and his lips press against my pulse point just as his hand slides between my thighs.

Oh, Ethan.

OH, ETHAN!

I snap back to reality and fling the book away from me like it's a hot potato, realizing what I'm doing: fantasizing about him! A man I loathe! A man who brings out the worst, most childish side of me. Even this line of thought seems like another mark added against him, though rationally I know he had nothing to do with it. *But didn't he?* He's the one who sleeps in our cabin without a shirt on. He's the one who purposefully walks out of the bathroom with a low-slung towel around his hips.

Of course, it would be best to handle this as an adult and tell him I'm not comfortable with the lengths he's resorting to in an effort to get a reaction out of me.

Instead, I wonder if two can play his game.

CHAPTER NINETEEN
TAYLOR

Sunday evening, I kill two birds with one stone. I carry all of my clothes to the mess hall and hide out in there doing my laundry, that way when Ethan arrives back at the cabin it'll look like I'm still gone for the weekend.

My plan works flawlessly until he strolls by the window and sees me sitting up on the washing machine, finishing my book.

I hear his voice before I see him.

"When did you get back?"

I jerk out of my reading haze and slam the book closed, glancing up in time to see him lean his tall frame against the doorjamb. He's wearing jeans and a white cotton t-shirt. Somehow, it's the best he's ever looked.

"Not long ago," I say with a casual shrug.

"Huh."

His eyes are narrowed, but his mouth is edging toward an amused smirk.

"What?" I snap, my good mood wiped clean in five seconds flat.

He tips his head toward the dryer. "It just seems odd. I watched you pack all your stuff on Friday before you left."

I glance down at the machine currently filled with my clothes, tumbling them dry.

"So?"

"So…you lugged everything home only to repack it and bring it all back here to wash?"

I won't admit defeat so easily.

I arch a sardonic brow. "Are you always this obsessed with other people's laundry habits?"

His smile stretches. His dimple pops. He seems to be enjoying this far too much. And well, of course he is. He's caught me. "Did I not make myself perfectly clear when I told you no one is allowed to stay here on the weekends unless you get prior approval?"

"From who?"

"Me."

My laugh is short and sarcastic. "You'd never give me approval for anything. In fact, I think you go out of your way to make my life difficult."

His brow arches. "So then we both agree that's what we've been doing."

Making each other miserable, he means.

I bite down on my bottom lip and shrug. "Let's just say I never had any interest in learning how to play guitar before last week."

He grins then and my stomach clenches tight. I can't help but remember what I did yesterday morning down by the lake—what I imagined him doing to me—and my cheeks burn with heated embarrassment. Fortunately, his next question thrusts me right back into the present moment.

"Why do you want to stay here on the weekends?"

He assumes I *want* to?

Well, it's probably good that he does. I'd rather not correct him. It would only open me up to another line of questioning, and I think a common rule of war is that you don't give your enemy more information than is totally necessary.

"It's nice, quiet without you here tormenting me," I say with a bored tone.

"So you're going to continue to do it even though I've asked you not to?"

He doesn't seem so against it now.

I tip my head to the side, assessing him. "I don't know. If it were no longer forbidden, maybe I'd suddenly lose interest."

He chuckles as he shakes his head, finally pushing off the doorway and turning away, leaving me there with my heart and mind racing after him.

Neither of us relents the following week. If anything, we escalate.

Oh, don't get me wrong—during the day, you'd only ever hear Ethan speaking to me in the same curt, professional tone he uses for everyone. I don't talk back or utter a single word that could be misinterpreted as insolent. In fact, I'm even better at my job than I was in previous weeks because I'm starting to get the hang of the construction site. In short, I'm flourishing, and Ethan would be crazy to let me go. Even Hudson, Ethan's loyal sidekick, informs me that it's much better with me around, though I think that's just because I keep his and Robert's desk tidy.

But all that prim-and-properness all day just means we have more energy for antics after quitting time.

Ethan has begun doing leisurely workouts in the center of the cabin. Push-ups, sit-ups, anything and everything that works up a sweat and produces low grunts that remind me of sex every time I hear them.

"You know there's a whole wide world outside that cabin door," I say, airing out my shirt while I lie on my bunk. "You can work out wherever you'd like."

"I'm fine right here," he says, bringing his t-shirt up to wipe his brow.

Rock-hard abs greet me, and I flush deeper before returning to my book.

It belongs to Ethan. Thankfully, he brought back half a dozen paperbacks with him from Austin. Slightly overkill, but it was probably out of fear that I'd accidentally drown a few of them. He lined them up on the desk Sunday night and I perused them while he showered, proceeding to borrow the one that looked most interesting, a psychological crime thriller. He never officially offered to let me read it and I never asked, and yet when he sees me up here flipping pages, he doesn't say a word.

Brought on by his antics last week as well as his new fondness for cabin-calisthenics, I've decided it's probably time to start burning him up with desire too. I shouldn't be the only one having to splash cool water on my face every time he finishes a workout. And so, we slide into an even more vicious cycle.

If before our game was to try to appear unaffected by the other person, now it's morphed into Who Can Turn the Other On the Most. I "accidentally" leave the shower door open when I rinse off on Tuesday night. The door isn't cracked so much that he can see me, just enough that the steam wafts out into the cabin and the sound carries easily: hands lathering skin from head to toe, water splashing against the tiled floor. It's no surprise that when I cut the water and stroll out in a towel a few minutes later, he's pacing like a lion.

When I arch a brow, he turns and slaps his hand against the front door so it swings open. Heavy footsteps pound on the porch stairs and then he's gone for the next hour. It's the best hour of my entire life, alone in that cabin, smiling fondly at having bested him.

The next day, I take scissors to a pair of jeans. It's the pair that were too long on me anyway. Now, they're denim cutoffs, and I'm every country boy's fantasy come to life when I stroll around the cabin later. I wouldn't dare wear them around the site. Outside these four walls, my goal is to assimilate. Here, though, in this cabin, I want Ethan dying a slow death.

"Do you like them?" I ask as I turn in a circle in the center of the room, trying to catch sight of myself in the bathroom mirror. "I can't tell. Are they too short?"

He's on his bunk, shirtless, reading. One arm is folded behind his head, the other holding the paperback up on his hard stomach.

"That depends. Who're you trying to attract?"

His lazy words drip with disinterest and seem to hint that the "who" in that question definitely won't be him.

I roll my eyes and head for the door, needing air. I seem to be starved for it lately.

Just before I step out onto the porch, Ethan's voice cuts through the air.

"Don't wear those shorts around the camp," he says sharply, like the authoritative tyrant he is.

I'm just going for a short walk nearby, but he doesn't need to know that.

I smile as the door claps closed behind me.

The following evening, I ask politely to borrow Ethan's phone. I haven't reached McKenna or my mom since the last time he let me borrow it and I'd like to make sure my mom got the check I mailed home. Again, Ethan says I can use it, but I only have as long as it takes him to shower. Truly, he wouldn't know chivalry if it bit him in the ass.

"Fine, but make sure to wash every nook and cranny," I say sweetly.

He grumbles something I can't hear and then shuts the door. Thank God. If he started doing what I do, leaving that door cracked even an inch…well, a girl only has so much willpower.

I don't dillydally once he's in the bathroom. I sit down at the desk and call my mom, knees bouncing while it rings. She answers and I nearly explode with longing to be there with her.

"Mom, it's me, Taylor," I say, unsure if she saved Ethan's number to her phone the last time I called.

"Taylor!" She leans away and shouts, "McKenna! Taylor's on the phone!" Then she's talking to me again. "How are you? I tried calling you all day yesterday but it never went through. I hate that I can hardly get in touch with you while you're out there. It makes me worry."

"Did you tell her we got the check?" McKenna asks in the background.

Relief floods through me. "So you got it then?"

"Put it in the bank on Monday. Couldn't have come at a better time. I wasn't sure how we were going to buy groceries this week."

Guilt cuts like a knife. Here, in the mess hall, I have more food than I know what to do with most of the time. I feel bad that I can't send some back to them.

"Good. So you bought some groceries and stuff? Was there much left over? Any for the car?"

"Well, there would have been had there not been a stack of overdue bills. I figured I better pay the electric and water company before they shut off service. Then there was health insurance, and McKenna's doctor has her on a new prescription—"

"I told you I didn't need it! My old inhaler worked fine," McKenna protests, never one to be a burden.

"No, Mom, that's fine. Really." I don't let on how disappointed I am that we're no closer to getting the car out of the shop. "Her medicine is more important. I'll get another paycheck in two weeks and another after that."

"Are you liking it out there? Listen, I know it's good money, but I don't want you doing anything that makes you unhappy. From what Jeremy was telling us, it sounds like they've got you stuck out in the middle of nowhere. No hot water even!?"

I laugh. "Mom, it's really not bad, I swear."

She doesn't reply.

"I mean it!" I insist. "It's actually kind of nice."

Still no answer. I pull the phone away from my face and realize with a roll of my eyes that the call dropped.

Of course. Even with his signal booster, Ethan's phone isn't completely immune to the crappy cell reception out here.

Suddenly the phone rings in my hand and I answer it immediately, bringing it to my ear.

"Mom, sorry. The call dropped."

"Oh, hi!"

The voice that replies is much softer and more youthful than my mother's.

My eyes widen as I look down at the phone and realize I accidentally answered a call from Isla. ISLA.

Oh god. My finger hovers over the red END button but she speaks up again, nearly shouting.

"Please don't hang up on me! Hello?!"

I pause, completely paralyzed with indecision. I feel bad. I don't want to hang up on her, so I quickly explain, "Hi, sorry. This isn't Ethan, obviously. I'm just using his phone for a second."

She laughs and it's playful, not enraged. Odd considering if a strange woman answered my boyfriend's phone, my first reaction would not be light giggles.

"I know you're not Ethan. It might come as a surprise, but you sound nothing like him. I hope that doesn't disappoint you." I nearly smile as she continues. "I've been trying to get in touch with him all week. God, he's bad at answering his phone lately. Anyway, who are you?"

"Ethan's assistant."

"Of course! The pretty one!"

I frown, confused.

She hurries to continue, "Ethan hasn't told me what you look like or anything. Don't freak out. I just assumed you were pretty because of your voice. Are you? Pretty?"

I look down at my oversized t-shirt. "Uh…"

"And humble too! Oh, this just keeps getting better and better."

I stay perfectly silent, trying to figure out who this person could possibly be. I scratch out jealous lover.

"Are you two friends?" she continues.

"No!" I rush out. "*No*. Not really. In fact, I feel like he can hardly stand me most of the time, to tell you the truth." *Whoever you are.*

"And yet you're answering his phone. How…*intimate*."

I worry I might have been wrong. I don't want her getting the wrong idea.

"I swear it's not like that. You don't need to be upset with him over this."

"Upset?"

"Yes, because…well—"

"Oh! Oh, no no. You have the wrong idea. Totally wrong idea. I'm Ethan's sister—*twin* sister, in fact."

I'm floored by this information. Ethan has family! A sister! In a mere moment, my brain generates a million and one questions. I want to know every detail of his childhood. Who wronged him? Who flushed his head in a toilet or stuffed him into a locker in middle school? Who made him into the callous man he is today?

I'd get around to asking these questions if Ethan didn't walk out of the bathroom in that moment wearing only a pair of workout shorts and towel-drying his hair with a rough hand.

"Give me my phone," he says brusquely.

I swear the man takes the world's fastest showers. He can't stand the idea of me using his phone. He doesn't trust me as far as he can throw me. No, that's inaccurate—with those toned arms and muscular shoulders, he could toss me halfway to Africa. Better to just say he doesn't trust me.

"Now," he bites out, stepping closer.

"Is that him?!" his sister asks, gleeful. "Oh good, put him on!"

"Okay, Mom," I deadpan. "Good talking to you too. I'll call you tomorrow. Bye!"

Then I hang up and toss him his phone, praying he won't check his call log.

CHAPTER TWENTY
ETHAN

"I talked to your lovebird last night."

"Excuse me?"

Isla chuckles. "I called your cell phone trying to reach you and your assistant answered instead. You can imagine how excited I was to—"

I hang up on Isla, suddenly furious.

A second later, a text pops up.

Isla: Did you just hang up on me or did the call drop? Either way, I didn't get a chance to say we're planning a Memorial Day Weekend trip to the campgrounds to visit you and see what you've been working on! Everyone's in: Jace and Alice, Brody and Liv, Tanner...maybe Camille. I knew you'd say no if I asked you first, which is why I'm not asking. We'll barbecue and camp out. It'll be tons of fun!

Ethan: No campout. No visit.

Isla: Yes campout. Yes visit. Invite your assistant. She's a lot nicer than you these days.

Obviously, I'm getting nowhere with her, so I chuck my phone across my desk and stand. This week's been crazy because we're prepping for the foundation pour. There've already been a few hiccups, but Robert and Hudson have stayed on top of things and it should be smooth sailing into the weekend with no major issues to resolve before Monday.

Well, other than the brunette currently acting like a thorn in my side.

She's outside with Robert and a few of the guys. She's wearing a hard hat and a neon safety vest—the items I took from her on her first day, ones she apparently stole back.

Robert says something and nudges her with his elbow, and she throws her head back and laughs. Every single man in that group stops what they're doing and watches her, dumbstruck, half in love already. Even Hudson is a simpering fool around her these days. Robert's the only one who treats her normally, and that's because he's three times her age and thinks of her as a daughter.

I stomp down the steps of the trailer and make it halfway to them before Taylor notices me. Her smile fades and her eyes narrow with suspicion.

When I reach the group, my booming voice makes three guys jump out of their boots.

"I need a word," I say, effectively parting the group in half.

I don't take my eyes off her as the guys slink away quickly, more than happy to find that my ire isn't directed at them.

Robert stays beside her. "Uh oh, what have you done this time?" he quips, shooting a teasing smirk at Taylor.

She returns it with one that sends my heart into overdrive. "Oh, who knows. It could be anything. Yesterday, he found a pair of my underwear accidentally mixed in with his laundry, and you should have seen his reaction. It's like he's never seen a pair of panties before."

I was taken aback, that's all. Can't a man put away his laundry without having to come across a silky thong? So what if I stood motionless, holding it in my hand until Taylor walked out of the bathroom, saw me staring down at it, and quickly lunged over to snatch it out of my grasp.

Robert doesn't give me the benefit of the doubt though, whooping and hollering like he's never heard anything half as funny in his life.

I nail him to the ground with my gaze. "You done?"

He smirks, wiping tears from his eyes. "Oh, just about."

"Taylor, you're fired."

I have to try it, at least.

That makes Robert double over in laughter yet again before he finally walks away and gives us privacy.

Goddammit, what has happened to respecting the boss around here?!

Oh right, Taylor happened.

She's looking up at me, all big eyes and flushed cheeks beneath that ridiculous hard hat. There's a smile playing on her full lips. She didn't believe the *You're fired* line any more than Robert did.

"I thought you'd be happy with me this afternoon," she says, sounding sugary sweet. "I stole two cookies from the dessert counter at lunch for you. They had the most chocolate chips out of any ones I could find."

"You answered my phone last night and talked to Isla," I say, abrupt and curt.

Her smile drops, face pales, and she rushes to reply, "Not intentionally!"

"Right. I unintentionally answer someone else's phone and talk to the person on the other end all the time."

Her pleasant mood sours with my harsh accusation—and it is harsh, but then she deserves it for snooping into my personal life, for pushing my boundaries yet again. It seems we're always here: at each other's throats.

"I thought I made it clear: I let you borrow my phone so you could talk to *your* family, not mine. Find another phone to use from now on."

Her face turns into a mask of anger and I can tell her hand is itching to reach up and slap me. I wish she'd do it. Then I really could fire her.

"And I don't want you staying here over the weekend."

She stands there in silence, rage pluming off her like smoke.

Her anger isn't enough though. I want to make sure she's taken my words to heart. I want her assurance that she's going to obey me. For once.

I step closer. "Have I made myself clear?"

She whips the hard hat off her head and shoves it against my chest.

"Yes *sir*."

It's no surprise that Taylor avoids me the rest of the day yet still manages to complete her work with unfailing accuracy. She's not in the cabin by the time I'm getting ready to leave for Austin, and I get a wild idea that maybe I shouldn't leave. Maybe I should stay and ensure she follows my orders, but I have no choice. I need to get back to Lockwood's main office for a meeting I have in the morning with a prospective client. My partners have made it clear that I need to be present since I'm one of the main draws for them.

So, I'll just have to assume Taylor is complying with my command and leaving for the weekend. In fact, I should be focusing my attention elsewhere during the long drive home, and yet when I pull into my driveway and walk into my quiet house, I'm still thinking of her and wondering if I've been too hard, too unyielding where she's concerned.

I haven't ever been so heavy-handed with an employee before, but to call Taylor just an employee is a gross understatement. The fact is, I've never lived with an employee, which is the only explanation for why it feels like she's started to entwine herself so deeply in my life.

I've never thought of my house as being quiet before tonight. I've always loved it here. I purchased the 1960s bungalow a few years ago, back when you could still afford to buy property in Austin without breaking the bank. It's centrally located near downtown without being in the thick of it, the lot oversized and shaded with three sprawling live oak trees. The house itself needed a lot of work. I had Steven draw up the plans for the renovation and I oversaw it slowly, painstakingly, ensuring the historical details weren't wiped clean by the new, modern updates.

Compared to the cabin I've been living in, it might as well be a palatial mansion.

I wonder what Taylor would think of it, and then I yank that thought right out of my head and reach for my phone.

It's late and I have that meeting in the morning, but I can't just stay here. I know if I try to go to bed now, I'll just lie awake, thinking of her and the details of a week that seemed equal parts infuriating and addicting.

Isla texted me earlier that our friends were all heading over to Easy Tiger, so that's where I go after I rinse off and throw on a clean set of clothes. It feels good to walk into the bar and see my friends all crammed together in a booth, raising hell. When Brody sees me, he throws up his hands and they all turn, faces lighting up.

"Didn't think you'd show," he says, grabbing an extra chair from another table for me.

I take a seat, holding up a hand for the waiter. "Yeah, it's been a long week. I need a beer."

Jace and Alice are there too, nearly fused at the hip just as Isla forewarned they would be. Beside them, there's Brody and Liv, who've been married for the last few years. Isla sits opposite them, and beside her is Camille, a coworker of Liv's and a new addition to the group.

It's funny seeing her beside Isla. The two couldn't be more different. My sister has a row of freckles across her nose, shoulder-length brown hair, and an affinity for wearing clothes that should make absolutely no sense yet somehow blend together pretty well. Right now, she's wearing a pair of denim overalls over a white blouse with a little silk scarf tied around her neck. Her brown eyes—a pair that match my own—shine with happiness. Any ill will I felt toward her for chatting with Taylor doesn't stand a chance.

Camille, by contrast, is wearing a tight black top. Her black hair is long and straight, her bee-stung lips coated in a layer of red lipstick so bright there's not a guy in this bar who hasn't noticed them. Her eyes are what I notice most, though—they're clever, *shrewd*. She and Liv both work at a law firm downtown and Liv has boasted before that Camille rarely loses a case.

"Glad you showed up," she says with a flirtatious smile.

Isla catches my attention and barely contains her laughter. That's my sister—her smile seems to always take up every square inch of her face, even now when she's not so subtly laughing *at* Camille.

I throw her a reproachful glare. She needs to ease up on Camille. It's obvious to anyone who's been around our group for long that Camille is interested in me, but that's not what bothers Isla. She doesn't like Camille because when they were first introduced, Camille asked about Isla's job.

When Isla mentioned she works in advertising, Camille looked down her nose and snidely asked if she came up with "those little jingles for commercials". Isla took offense considering she'd just been promoted to senior art director at one of the largest ad agencies in the country. No, she doesn't come up with *jingles*. First and foremost, she's an artist and designer.

I thought they'd smoothed things over since then.

Apparently not.

"How's the project coming along?" Brody asks just before the waiter comes by to take our order. Everyone's due for another round, so I open a new tab.

"It's on schedule, which is all you can really hope for with these large-scale projects," I reply once the waiter leaves.

"Isla told us all about it." Camille smiles. "It sounds like it'll be amazing once it's complete."

"Can't wait to check it out," Jace says, throwing his arm around Alice's shoulders.

"Yeah, it'll be a fun weekend," Brody adds.

My gaze clashes with Isla's and her eyes beg me not to ruin the moment by telling everyone the trip is off. Memorial Day is two weeks away and the resort won't even be framed by then, much less welcome to guests.

I don't want to rain on everyone's parade, so I try for honesty instead. If they realize how shabby the camp actually is, I doubt they'll still want to come.

"It's not going to be a luxurious vacation. The camp is old and there's nowhere to stay. My crew is taking up the old bunkhouses."

"So we'll pitch tents!" Isla replies brightly.

The guys agree.

Camille wrinkles her nose at the idea, which only excites Isla more.

"And there's a lake, right? Can we swim in it?"

We had water samples taken when we were testing the soil, just to get our bearings as to what the bacteria levels looked like. It's actually cleaner than the water coming out of most people's tap owing to the fact that it's fed from an aquifer underground.

"You can, but it's freezing."

That doesn't faze them either.

It's no use.

Everyone's curious about the site and no one—except maybe Camille—minds the fact that they'll have to rough it in nature.

After drinks on Friday night, the weekend creeps forward like a slug. In fact, I'm not totally sure it isn't moving in reverse. The meeting on Saturday lasts hours and only holds half of my attention considering it's a very straightforward project based here in Austin. I've done ten just like it in the last five years. After that, I work, go to the gym, decline an invitation to have drinks with Camille, and snuff out each errant thought I have about Taylor like I'm pinching the wick of a candle.

It doesn't always work though. That flame still flickers, and every spare minute I have amidst the flurry of activity is spent debating whether or not I should head back to camp early. I nearly do it, too. I pack my stuff Saturday afternoon and catch myself just before I walk out the door.

What the fuck am I doing?

There's no good reason for me to go back to camp early except to see Taylor. Oh, sure, I try hard to mask it with another motive like wanting to check up on the jobsite or confirm that she followed my orders. That said, the fact is plain and simple and a hard pill to swallow: I'm actually anxious to see her, anxious to get back to that cabin.

Obviously, this infuriates me, so I double down and force myself to stay in Austin even longer than I would have otherwise. It's why I join my parents and Isla for dinner Sunday night.

My knee jostles under their table while my gaze flits to the clock every five minutes. My bag is already in my truck. I've got a full tank of gas. I plan on heading back to the camp straight from here.

"Seems like you have a lot on your mind," my mom says, nodding toward the untouched dessert plate in front of me. It's my favorite: warm apple pie with a dollop of melting ice cream beside it. I hadn't even noticed it was there.

Isla's grinning at me from across the table. I haven't brought up Taylor to her at all this weekend, but it doesn't matter. Isla knows me too well.

I narrow my eyes, and she gloats as she scoops up a big ol' bite of pie.

I wonder if it's too late to put her up for adoption. Being a single child sounds nice.

After dinner, Isla and I walk out to our cars together. I'm aiming for pleasant silence.

She has different plans. "You've really put in an A-plus effort this weekend. I kept expecting you to growl at me for talking to your assistant on the phone. What was her name again? I don't think you ever told me."

"I forget."

She chuckles. "Well anyway, I admit defeat. I clearly was trying to find feelings where none exist. It's obvious you want nothing to do with her."

I frown and turn to face her as we reach my truck. I know I shouldn't continue down this road and yet I still hear myself asking, "Why do you think that?"

"Oh, well, it's the only explanation for why you're still here, dawdling instead of heading back east. Tell me, is she completely hideous? Does she have a personality like Camille? If so, I don't blame you one bit for avoiding her."

Neither and neither.

She's so beautiful I'm tempted to take up writing poetry, something I'd be piss poor at. *Roses are red and violets are another color and I don't care, just please let me kiss you again.* And her personality is so enthralling, so unnervingly spirited that as much as I want to despise her, I can't seem to actually follow through with it.

Isla tips her head then, studying me. The long stretch of silence following her assessment proves her point for the both of us.

Without another word, I yank open my truck door and, instead of heading to the jobsite, I head home. It's a test of my willpower, a way to prove to myself yet again that I'm in no hurry to return to Taylor.

That night, I sleep at home, and I don't set out for the camp until the break of dawn the following morning. I arrive just in time to get to work.

When Taylor walks into the trailer with my cup of coffee, I can tell right away she hasn't forgiven me for Friday's argument. Her striking features are a study in cold aloofness, her chin raised, her shoulders pushed back. Her eyes stare at a point just over my head as she sets the mug down and then curtsies—*curtsies*—before politely mentioning that if I need her to get me anything else, she'd be happy to "obey". She stresses that word so heavily, there's no way for it to go over my head.

I wait until she's outside before I give in to the urge to laugh.

I swear I'll be gray-haired by the time this project is finished.

CHAPTER TWENTY-ONE
ETHAN

The next two weeks blend together in a flurry of activity as foundation work gives way to framing. The crew stays on longer, working right up until dinner. I give them the option to cut out early if they need to, but most guys are happy for the extra pay.

A sense of comradery has formed among them. They hang out together after dinner, some scattered in chairs around the fire pit. A few of them play cards or shoot darts on a board they've hung near the mess hall.

Taylor is always there, in the thick of it. I was nervous at first, careful to keep an eye on her considering the circumstances, but she's done well making a place for herself among a crew of construction workers most women would happily steer clear of.

In fact, she hasn't just made a place for herself—she's stepped right up onto the pedestal they've polished for her. If she happens to walk by the fire pit, at least five of them jump out of their seats, offering a chair. If she needs an extra napkin or a refill on her water at lunch, there's a slew of men waiting to do it. It's not out of the question for one or two of them to come knocking on the trailer door on their breaks wondering where she is. I ask what they need her for, and they always fumble with a reply.

"Oh…nothing, just wanted to thank her for saving me a plate at lunch…"

"She mentioned she'd never tried homemade pecan pie and I had my mom make some over the weekend…"

"She told me she just finished a good book and offered to let me borrow it…"

There's a line around the block for her attention, but Max seems to always be close at hand, the first to snag her if she ever has a spare moment. Last night, they played cards together during dinner, and I could hear her laughter clear across the mess hall.

Worst of all, though, is Hudson. His schoolboy crush on her has grown roots. He damn well thinks he's in love with her and drones on about it constantly, even though I've given no sign at all that I'd like him to continue talking. In fact, I've asked him to do the exact opposite, a request he can't seem to process.

"Please go outside if you're going to continue rambling," I say, forcing my attention back to my computer. "And shut the door behind you."

He's standing at the window, sighing. "I think half the crew is as in love with her as I am," he continues morosely. I can hear his heart splintering right down the middle.

Oh wait—that's the sound of the cheap blinds parting as he presses his nose to the glass.

"I could kill that Max guy," he says suddenly, whirling away from the window to start pacing. "I heard they used to date. He told me so himself—*gloated* about it."

I start typing louder, really pounding on the keys, sending a message that goes unnoticed.

"You know what, though? I'm not going to let that stop me. I think she's into me."

She's not.

"Last week, she brought me a cookie after lunch."

What?! That scheming…

She brought me one too!

Then I remember it's a chocolate chip cookie we're discussing here, which only serves to heighten my anger. I shouldn't care about this. It's silly.

"Hudson, get out."

"What?"

"You've been annoying me for the last ten minutes and I have work to do."

He rushes toward the door, making quick apologies.

That's not the last I see of him that day. Nope, as I round the curve of the trail heading to Rose Cabin after dinner, there's Hudson standing on the front porch with Taylor's hands clasped tightly in his. Her back is facing me, which means I'm treated to a full view of Hudson's pleading eyes.

I can't hear what he's saying to her over the hum of the forest, but she squeezes his hands and a moment later, he's flinging himself at her, mouth attached to hers like one of those algae-sucking fish.

She doesn't push him off right away like I assumed she would. She steps back slowly, shakes her head, and then reaches out to pat his arm.

I think Hudson's about to cry, but then he nods and forces a smile.

That's when I reach them.

"We'll still be friends, right? This won't change anything?" she asks.

Hudson nods. "Friends."

Then he catches sight of me and sobers, wasting no time in scrambling down the stairs.

"Evening," he says as he rushes by.

I glance after him for a moment before returning my attention to Taylor.

"I hope I didn't interrupt," I tell her, tone deceptively kind. "I can make myself scarce if you two need some alone time."

She crosses her arms and I'm momentarily lost in the sight of her standing there, bathed in the warm light of the sunset. The effect makes it so her eyes are bright amber. Her hair is shining chestnut and mahogany, curling loosely around her shoulders. Her lips are bright red and slightly swollen from Hudson's amateur attempt at courtship.

As I see her just like this, Hudson suddenly has my deepest sympathies. Maybe if I were a weaker man, I'd be in the same boat.

"If you must know, he asked me out to dinner and I told him no. Don't tease him about it," she pleads, scowling at me. "He means well."

I start up the stairs. My arm brushes her shoulder as I start to pass, but then I stop abruptly, glancing down at her.

"Be truthful—how many men have asked you out while you've been here?"

She shrugs and looks away, squinting toward the sunset.

I was expecting her to laugh me off.

"You shouldn't lead them on," I add dryly before continuing inside.

She catches me before I reach the door, hand shooting out to grab my forearm. "Lead them on?! What are you talking about?" She waves her other hand down her baggy clothes. "*Hardly!*"

"The clothes don't hide a thing."

She groans and pushes past me as if all of a sudden she's in a hurry to get into the cabin before me.

It's futile. Once we're both inside, we don't know what to do with ourselves.

She walks to the bathroom, drags a hand through her hair, and then turns back, scanning the room as if looking for something to throw at my head.

I stay by the door, lean back against the frame, and watch her, more amused than I'd ever care to admit.

"Are you going to start packing?" I ask with an inquisitive brow.

She stumbles mid-pace and glances up, her eyes flaying me. "Why would I pack? Are you trying to fire me again? Because—"

I smile, and my good humor only makes her angrier. "It's Memorial Day Weekend starting tomorrow after work. Everyone's off for three days."

A blush creeps up her cheeks, and there, *right there*, is my answer. She's not going anywhere. Isla will be so happy when she arrives to see Taylor will be spending the weekend with us.

Of course, Taylor doesn't know that.

Taylor thinks she'll have a few days to herself. She assumes I don't know she defies me and hides out here on the weekends, parceling off just enough food from the mess hall so she won't starve but not so much that someone would notice anything's been taken.

I've wondered why she doesn't leave. Any guy here would give her a lift home if she asked for one, and yet she doesn't ask. She doesn't impose. She stays here and she reads the books I keep bringing for her, titles I intentionally pick with her in mind.

I could save Taylor the embarrassment and confess that I'll be staying here this weekend as well along with a handful of my friends, but where's the fun in that?

I push off the doorframe and head to grab my workout clothes.

"Of course I'll be packing." She nods. "I'd completely forgotten with how busy this week has been."

"Oh, so you have big plans then?" I ask with my back turned toward her as I tug open the top drawer of the dresser.

She makes a noncommittal sound, like a soft moan followed by a clearing of her throat. "Yep. My family grills out every year. Potato salad, watermelon, fireworks—"

"For *Memorial Day*?"

"The whole nine yards."

I hum as if I'm interested in her lies. "Do you have a big family?"

"Why do you suddenly care?" I can hear the suspicion hardening her tone.

"It's a fair question. After all, you know about my family. You know I have a twin sister—"

"And parents?" she interrupts. "Do you have those, or were you just spawned from the underworld one day?"

I'm glad she can't see my smile.

"Ah yes, Rick and Judith. Been married thirty-five years this September. What about you?"

"Yup. Parents, in love, married forever."

"What're their names?" I ask, continuing the charade.

"You won't believe this, but *Rick* and *Judith*. What are the odds, right?"

She's trying to gain the upper hand with biting sarcasm, but she doesn't realize how transparent it is. By deflecting the questions, she answers them so plainly, and I'm left with a tightness in my chest.

Who gets defensive over simple questions about their family? Who turns abrasive when asked the names of their parents? It's obvious she didn't have a storybook childhood. It's clear there are parts of her life she's not proud of. I had my suspicions, but this confirms it.

With my workout clothes tossed on top of the dresser, I turn and glance at her over my shoulder. Her hands are propped on her hips, her eyes assessing me coldly. If she were a cat, her claws would be out.

I turn back around and start unbuttoning my work shirt.

"Sounds like you have quite a weekend ahead of you."

She hums in agreement.

There's only silence after this, a moment that stretches so long I have no choice but to cave and glance back at her again. She hasn't changed her pose at all, but her face has softened.

I arch a brow.

She tilts her head.

A little dimple starts to appear beside her lips as she fights off her smile.

"I don't suppose you ever believed I was leaving, not even for one second?"

"No."

"Why did you let me carry on like that for so long then?"

"It amuses me."

Her eyes narrow. "Would you believe that until I met you, I would have called myself an honest person? Something about you…" She waves her hands to encompass my body as if that's the root of our issues. "It's just—you're so damn difficult and stubborn and rude, and if I'm speaking frankly, which I guess I am because I've said too much already, I'd rather swallow my tongue than speak the truth to you, than share one piece of my life beyond the four walls of this cabin."

Her honesty stings more than she probably intended. I know we've pushed each other to our limits and likely crossed every line there is to cross, and yet I don't feel good about how far we've dragged each other through the mud. I didn't realize how dirty we'd gotten. In fact, I'm not even sure we'd ever find our way out of this war if we tried. The realization cuts as deep as a knife.

I yank off my shirt and replace it with a t-shirt before I speak again. "What a charming confession. If you'll excuse me, I'm going to work out."

I try to move around her, but she blocks my path, arms coming up to grip my biceps, or at least try to. She's too small to really do much.

"Did I…Did I just *hurt—*"

She cuts herself off as she studies my face intently, searching for something I won't reveal. Then she shakes her head in confirmation as if there's no possible way she could have hurt my feelings. To her, I have none.

When I don't speak, she takes a step closer. Her body is only an inch or two away from mine and even though I'm over six feet, a soft breeze could sway me in her direction and bring me right up against her. What would it feel like? Different than the first time? *Better?*

"The point I was trying to hint toward is: aren't you tired?" she asks, sounding exhausted. "*Of this?* Don't you think you and I could be friends if only we'd put down our weapons?"

"Do you always call your friends stubborn and rude?"

She hasn't picked up on the fact that she's bruised my ego. She still thinks we're playing a game. She aims a teasing smile up at me and my cold heart wants to thaw, but instead, I double down on my annoyance. I've seen that smile aimed at every man around the jobsite this week. She has so many of them wrapped around her finger and I refuse to add myself to the multitude jumping for the chance to vie for her attention.

"Only if they deserve it," she answers. "And *you*, Ethan, deserved to hear that more than any man I've ever met." Her smile widens. Her eyes glitter with good humor. "You should hear the names I've called you in my head. Stubborn and rude sound like glowing compliments compared to the rest, I assure you."

I glance over her head, trying hard to keep my dejection off my face. "Actually, now that you bring it up, I've found I'm all set in the friend department. I think you and I better just stick with the relationship we know best."

"Which is?" she asks, hopeful.

"Employer and employee," I say coldly.

She rears back, stricken, and I use the opportunity to push past her and leave the cabin.

CHAPTER TWENTY-TWO
TAYLOR

Well that went amazingly well. I tried to extend an olive branch, and Ethan broke it over his knee and tossed it in my face. I don't understand him—truly. Being around him is on par with traversing a minefield. I'm failing miserably.

Every time I try to push us in the direction of friendship and peace, he seems to want to do the exact opposite.

Sometimes I truly think this is who he is—a mean, spiteful man—but I know that's not the case. I've seen glimpses of another side of him, moments when he's on the phone with his sister or playing cards with Robert. There's an easygoing, charming side to him, a compelling, smiling, warmhearted man I'd really like to get to know.

Of course, I probably never will.

He stays out of the cabin the rest of the night, or at least until I'm asleep. When I wake up in the morning, I hear soft sounds coming from the bathroom: the ting of a toothbrush as it hits a cup, the sink running and then cutting off. I blink my eyes open and immediately search for him.

The bathroom door is cracked just enough that I can peer past the frame. I have a clear view of him and my lips part on impulse.

He's standing at the sink with a towel wrapped around his waist.

The air in the cabin is spiced with his body wash and I inhale deeply, filling my lungs as I watch him lean forward and drag his razor down the bottom of his cheek and jaw. The tan muscles in his back flex as his arm moves and I'm a spectator at a tennis match, my eyes flitting from one swoon-worthy part of him to another: wide shoulders, tapered waist, the smooth ridge of muscles across his shoulders and biceps.

But that's just the back of him. The mirror reflects his abs and chest too, and I want to kick off my blankets, suddenly overheated, but I can't. I'd draw attention to myself and the fact that I'm awake, lying here, worshiping him with my eyes without him realizing it.

His razor glides along another patch of his cheek and I watch, enraptured. I'd love to feel his skin there: the juxtaposition of his freshly shaved, smooth skin and hard jaw. He's more tan now than he was a few weeks ago from all the work we've been doing outside. It sets off his brown hair and brown eyes even more, one playing off of the other, making his eyes seem lighter, his hair darker.

He finishes shaving quickly, rinses off the excess cream, and then turns.

I jerk my eyes closed again.

His smooth-as-scotch voice is only heightened by my lack of sight. "I could feel you watching me. Don't pretend to sleep."

I wink one eye open to see he's over at the dresser, grabbing clothes.

"If you don't get up," he continues, "you'll be late for work."

"You were hogging the bathroom," I point out tartly, a little embarrassed to have been caught.

"Well it's free now."

I grind my molars and jerk the blankets off me, moving to the ladder. He doesn't move out of the way, and I don't bother asking him to. I start to climb down and the backs of my bare legs brush across his shoulder and arm. I've been sleeping in oversized t-shirts lately, foregoing the sweatpants. It's the only way to keep cool now that spring has given way to summer, at least temperature-wise.

I hurry the rest of the way down and he steps back, trying to give me space. It only makes the problem worse. We're fumbling in that tight corner, trying to get around each other. His warm skin seems to envelop me. His body wash is almost overpowering and yet *intoxicating*. My arm brushes his abs. Our feet dance around each other. I let out an exasperated laugh at the same time his hands lock onto my biceps. Then he plucks me up off the ground and deposits me in the bathroom, out of his way.

"Sorry," I squeak lamely.

He grunts and turns, leaving me frowning at his back.

We get ready in silence and he's about to head out the door before he speaks up again.

"This weekend, I have friends coming to visit. Since you'll be here, I thought you'd like to know."

I gulp.

He's not leaving?

The only thing getting me through the last few days was the knowledge that I'd soon have a three-day weekend without him, a few days to regroup and put a lid on this boiling pot of tension.

I have no choice. I have to leave. Scram. Hitchhike. Walk. Staying here at the camp this weekend with Ethan is not a scenario I want to play out. There would be no survivors.

I hurry to finish getting ready and then rush to find Max at breakfast. He's smack dab in the middle of a sea of guys, and every one of them greets me with a warm smile and a friendly wave.

"Taylor! You hungry? Want me to grab you a plate?"

I fend off their generous offers and nod my head toward the door.

"Max, do you have a second?"

Everyone's brows shoot up.

They're intrigued about why I'd need to speak with Max privately. No doubt they're reading too much into the situation, about to start singing *Max and Taylor sittin' in a tree*, but I don't have time to care because I need to speak with Max *now*.

"What's up?" he asks once we're outside. His blond hair has grown longer in the weeks we've been here. He looks more boyish than ever—the antithesis of my bunkmate.

I wring out my hands. "You've been catching a ride home on the weekends with Nolan, right?"

He nods.

"And his truck is full? Even this weekend?"

"Yeah, we've even got one more than normal…but if you need a ride, we can shuffle some people around, or maybe see—"

I cut him off, feeling uncomfortable enough as is. I don't want to be a burden and I don't want to take anyone else's spot. "No, no. Don't worry about that. I'm going to call and see if my mom can swing by and pick me up."

"All right, but let me know if she can't and we'll figure it out."

Throughout the day—as I run around working—I try to reach my mom. I don't want to ask Ethan to borrow his phone since he expressly told me I wasn't allowed to use it anymore. In fact, I'd rather use a carrier pigeon or some kind of smoke signal, but in the end, I don't have to because I finally reach her in the late afternoon.

Relief swells within me as soon as the call connects. I don't have time to chitchat though.

“Is there any chance you’ve been able to get the car out of the shop?” I ask, talking a mile a minute, scared our connection will be lost at any moment. “Like maybe the mechanic was wrong and the car doesn’t need any repairs? In fact, it’s in perfect working order and you can come pick me up here tonight?”

“What are you talking about? What’s wrong?” she asks, her voice concerned. “The car’s still in the shop, but if you need me, I’ll find a ride and come get you.” I squeeze my eyes shut as despair fills my veins. “McKenna has a little award ceremony tonight up at the high school for making honor roll, but I could ask Nancy if she’d be willing to let me borrow her car. We’ll have to pay for gas and I’ve already been borrowing it a lot lately—”

“No, no, Mom. It’s okay. Nothing is wrong or anything. I just miss you guys and was wanting to make it back this weekend. Don’t worry about it.”

She sighs as if she’s just as upset about the situation as I am. “We miss you too. I wish things were different.” Her voice picks up, as if she’s trying to have enough hope for the both of us. “And they will be soon. Once I finish up school and get licensed, I’ll make all this up to you. I promise.”

Her kind words are my undoing. Unshed tears burn my eyes and make my throat ache unbearably.

I know I need to go find Max and insist on a ride home. I’ll sit on someone’s lap. I’ll sprawl out in the bed of the truck the whole way home, whatever it takes to get me away from this place.

Unfortunately, it’s later in the afternoon than I realized, and I’m still back at Rose Cabin, getting it cleaned up for Ethan and his friends. I scrubbed the bathroom so it’s spotless and washed every piece of linen I could find in case they need a spare pillow or blanket. I even washed my own in case they want to borrow it. I won't be here, so it doesn't matter. After I finish adding water to the bucket of wildflowers on the desk, I make a mad dash back to the camp, heading straight to find Max.

At this time of day, there's usually still a flurry of activity. Right now, though, the place is deserted. I spot a guy from the crew heading back from the site.

"Hey! Where is everyone?"

He nods toward the entrance to the camp. "Ethan let everyone knock off a little early. They were anxious to get home for the long weekend."

WHAT?!

I panic and start to hurry away before I realize how rude I'm being and throw a "Thanks! Have a good weekend!" over my shoulder.

The bunkhouses are all but empty. A few stragglers are left, packing up last-minute belongings. I search for Max among them, asking if anyone's seen him. One guy finally has an answer.

"Nolan was in a rush to leave. They all set off about an hour ago."

My heart plummets. Max is already gone? He left without seeing if I had a ride or not? I guess I did insist I'd figure it out, but still…

I glance around, taking in the three stragglers I don't know all that well. I couldn't even tell you their names if push came to shove. Still, at the moment, they're my only option.

"Is there any chance you guys are heading west toward Oak Dale?"

The guy closest to me, the one who told me Nolan already left, shakes his head. "We're going to Louisiana."

In other words, they'll be going in the exact opposite direction.

It's for the best. I probably shouldn't get into a car with near strangers anyway, even if they are part of Ethan's crew. But for the record, I would have! I would have gone wherever the hell these guys were going—*Oh, wow, what a charming murder shack!*—if it meant escaping from here.

I thank them for the information and tell them to have a good weekend, and then I walk with slumped shoulders out of the cabin. I'm defeated. Squashed. It's the same way I felt that night at the bar—the night I first met Ethan. I'm so close to crying, one wrong glance could push me toward a complete meltdown.

Then voices and laughter carry over the sounds of chirping and humming from the surrounding forest. I glance up just in time to watch a group of people walk past the mess hall with backpacks and luggage. Ethan is among them.

His friends!

I watch them pause for a second and Ethan starts pointing out a few things, directing their attention down to the construction site and the lake, though neither is visible from where we are. He points to the trail that leads toward the cabins and then just before he turns toward the bunkhouses, I jump back inside and try to hide. It's poor timing, though, because the guys are finished packing and trying to leave. I bump into one of them, my elbow colliding with his stomach, and he grunts. I cringe, praying Ethan and his group haven't spotted us.

"*Sorry!* I'm sorry."

He shakes off my apology, unbothered, and then they're gone, leaving me there alone in the bunkhouse with my back pressed against the wall, my breathing completely erratic.

I'd just stay here all weekend if I could, but I have nothing with me: no clothes, no food, nothing to do to distract me for three long days. It's the food that would really end up forcing me out of hibernation. I could scavenge for berries behind the bunkhouses, but I don't know the first thing about which ones are edible or not. Chances are I'd end up poisoning myself. I'd hate to give Ethan the satisfaction.

I know I'll have to cave and show my face eventually, so I decide it's better to get it over with now.

I'll introduce myself and explain that the cabin is all theirs after I gather my things. On my way back to the bunkhouse, I'll grab some food then strip one of these beds, wash the linens, and hide out here all weekend.

It's fine.

It *will* be fine.

Just as soon as I get this awkward introduction over with.

CHAPTER TWENTY-THREE
TAYLOR

Walking out of that bunkhouse is on par with pulling myself up out of the trenches on a battlefield and walking toward enemy fire with no protection, no shield, nada. Ethan and his friends notice me walking toward them right away and I'm left to close the last several yards with eight pairs of eyes aimed straight at me.

I try to imagine what I look like to them: dusty and dirty from a long day of work. I'm wearing a Lockwood Construction t-shirt Hudson gave me a few weeks ago. I thought he was just being nice. Now, I realize it might have been his way of flirting. My jeans are ill-fitting. My work boots are scuffed and muddy. My hair is up in a high ponytail, and I haven't looked in a mirror all day so there's no telling how many wispy pieces have snuck out to curl at my temples, making me look childish. It's a shame because I want so badly to appear half as intimidating as they do.

I wish it made sense to apply a full face of makeup before a day on a construction site. I wish I were wearing a trendy outfit, just so that dark-haired girl with the red lipstick would stop staring at me like I'm raw sewage seeping up from the gutter.

She's the first one I spot, not only because of her sour expression but because she's standing closest to Ethan, her hand resting on his arm possessively. The sight is the final crushing blow to what has been an all-around terrible day. For some silly reason, I'd dismissed the idea of Ethan having a girlfriend. Once I found out who Isla really was, I just assumed there was no one else. It's not as if I've heard him talking to a girlfriend, but then we're not together all day, every day, even if it sometimes feels that way.

If he is dating her, it has to be a recent development considering what happened between us in that bar—either that or he cheated on her. I discard that thought immediately. While Ethan might have a list of bad qualities that could stretch a mile long, I don't think being a cheater is one of them.

"Taylor!" a feminine voice calls, and my attention flies to the woman on the other side of Ethan, the one not only waving me over but doing so with a giant smile on her face, a smile that looks eerily familiar. *His sister.* Isla. I blink fast, trying to reconcile how it's possible that she could look so much like her brother and yet completely feminine at the same time. I realize they share the same eyes and the same mouth, but her chin is heart-shaped and demure. Her hair—the same rich brown as his—is shoulder-length and curled. She's closer to my height than his and must have soaked up all the positive energy in their house growing up, because while her brother is a stormy raincloud, she's a ray of sunshine.

"I knew it was you the second I saw you," she says, coming forward and wrapping me up in a tight hug as if we're the closest of friends.

I freeze with my hands at my sides, completely taken aback, but if my nonresponse offends her, she doesn't let on. She steps back and her smile is still there, possibly even wider than before.

"You're even prettier than I imagined," she says, her voice so low no one else can hear. "No wonder he's been so angry lately."

I frown, trying to decipher what she means, but I don't get the chance.

The others are closing in now, demanding introductions. Now that Isla's given her stamp of approval, they're all eager to meet me. Well, other than the black-haired woman and Ethan. They hang back, and *yes*, her hand is still on his arm.

Is she incapable of standing upright without holding on to him for support?

Isla tugs me close to her as she starts the introductions.

"Guys, this is Taylor. Taylor, this is Tanner," she says, pointing to the guy closest to my left. He's handsome with shaggy honey-brown hair that barely touches the collar of his black shirt. He reaches out to shake my hand and his grip tightens as our eyes lock. The edge of his mouth curves into a seductive smile.

"Tanner works in the art department with me at the agency," Isla continues. "You should see his stuff—he's crazy talented."

I swear he blushes as he steps back and lets go of my hand.

"She's exaggerating," Tanner insists before Isla waves her hand toward a couple standing beside him.

"This is Brody and Liv."

Brody has tattoos running the length of his arms and a buzz cut. Liv is tall and delicate with a loose braid and yellow cotton dress. She looks like a librarian and he looks like the bad boy who skips class to go check out the librarian.

"They're married and boring," Isla continues. Brody protests and she laughs. "I'm *kidding*. Just don't expect them to stay awake past ten o'clock."

Beside them she points to another couple she introduces as Jace and Alice. Jace stands beside Alice with his arm wrapped around her shoulders. In fact, they're squashed so close together, you couldn't slip a piece of paper between them if you tried. Not only that, they almost *look* alike. Either they've coordinated on purpose or it's a subconscious thing, but they're both wearing thick black-framed glasses and worn Converse.

"As you can see, they're in that annoying new phase of a relationship," Tanner quips. "It's like if they stop touching, the other person might die."

Alice shoots him a sarcastic glare. Jace just flips him off.

I smile at how comfortable they all are with each other. They poke fun, but it feels like it comes from a place of love.

"And that's Camille. She and Liv work at the same law firm," Isla explains as she waves to the woman near Ethan.

I nod and toss a wave toward Camille. Ethan tries to step away from her, but she clings to his arm and offers him a rueful grin. "Sorry, I'm just scared I'm going to roll an ankle out here."

We all glance down at her shoes and I realize that, yes, she *is* going to roll an ankle, because wedge heels are about the dumbest type of footwear you could wear into the middle of the forest. The only thing worse would have been stilettos.

Ethan clears his throat and I can sense he's uncomfortable, but he doesn't argue and he doesn't leave her side. I guess he's ever the perfect gentleman as long as it has nothing to do with me.

"And well, you already know me, and you *definitely* know Ethan," Isla says, emphasizing that word enough to ensure everyone's ears perk up, intrigued by the insinuation.

"He's my boss," I say lightly, like it's nothing more, nothing less.

Camille's brow arches and her sly grin widens even more. "So you're a construction worker?"

She finds the idea so genuinely pleasing, she's practically frothing at the mouth.

"Oh, *I wish.* I did try to work with the crew," I say, shooting her a playful smile. "But Ethan stole my hard hat my first day on the site and forced me to take an office job instead."

The group laughs, Isla most of all, but it's clear by Camille's barely concealed sneer that she didn't like my answer. She wanted me to be embarrassed and flustered by her, but I steel my spine and prepare for more of her taunts. I wonder what she'd say if she knew that before this job, I worked as a motel maid. I doubt she'd even let me shake her hand for fear I'd get germs on her delicate, manicured fingers.

"Not very nice of you, Ethan," Tanner points out teasingly, coming to my defense. "Why'd you do that?"

I finally meet Ethan's eyes, surprised to see that the hatred I expected to find is absent. When our gazes meet, his expression softens, almost like he's pleased. *For once!*

"He was scared I'd be too good with a hammer," I answer for him, aiming a private smile his way. "Didn't want me intimidating the rest of the crew."

There's more laughter while Ethan raises his brow, making my stomach dip. That haughty, teasing expression paired with his ruggedly chiseled features makes me feel no steadier on my feet than Camille. Soon, I'll need to ask to lean on his other arm.

Isla claps her hands, drawing everyone's attention to her.

"Well, now that everyone knows everyone…Ethan, would you mind telling us where we should put our stuff? I want to freshen up before dinner."

Freshen up?

She looks adorable in her jean shorts and light blue blouse. I'm the one who needs to freshen up, and by freshen up, I mean scrub off the ten layers of dirt caked on my body.

"I told you there *is* no place to freshen up," Ethan says sharply. "That's why I had Brody and Jace bring their tents. You guys are camping."

I speak up quickly, wanting to be helpful. "You're welcome to use our cabin. It won't fit everyone, but—"

"No," Ethan says, cutting me off.

He probably doesn't want them sleeping on his bed, but he'll have to get over it.

"I washed the bedding today so at least two people can sleep in there, maybe more…" I cast a quick glance to Jace and Alice. If they're going to stay fused like that all night, they could easily share one bunk.

"Perfect!" Isla says, grinning. "I'll stay in the cabin with Taylor, and—"

I shake my head. "Oh no!" I realize I'm protesting too vehemently and drawing curious stares. My tone softens as I continue, "I'd just rather someone else have my bunk."

"Great. I'll take it," Camille says quickly, sounding very relieved to be escaping a night spent in a pitched tent.

Isla's smile fades momentarily, but then she's back to playing hostess again. "Well, that works out. Taylor, Camille, and I will stay in the cabin. Everyone else will camp."

I don't know why she's trying to include me here. Now that introductions are complete, I should be hurrying away to grab my things. I still need to strip a bed in one of the bunkhouses and wash the sheets. I'd rather not be doing laundry in the middle of the night.

The group splits apart as the couples and Tanner go to grab their tents so they can set them up in the clearing by the fire pit. Ethan tries to step away from Camille, having forgotten his oh-so-important duty as her crutch, but she emits a little helpless whine, like a small pampered pet.

Isla groans and stomps over to grab Camille's other arm, throwing it over her shoulder like she's a wounded soldier. "There, now, lean on me. As soon as we get to the cabin, you're taking off those shoes."

Not exactly in a position to protest, Camille gives in and allows Isla to lead her away.

I'm left standing a few yards from Ethan, suppressing the ridiculous urge I have to apologize for encroaching on his weekend.

"You were so eager to give up your bunk, now you don't have anywhere to sleep," he says with a deep frown.

I force an unaffected shrug. "It doesn't matter. I know you just want me out of your hair for the weekend. I promise I'll make myself scarce."

"That's not…or rather, I don't—"

Isla comes up then and hooks her elbow through mine, cutting him off. "Let's go, Taylor! I have a dress I brought that you'd look amazing in. You'll have to try it on just to humor me."

I shake my head, trying to come up with a polite way to tell her to leave me alone, but it's no use. Ethan's sister is a force of nature. She drags me all the way to the cabin even as I offer up protests about this weekend, telling her it makes more sense if I hang out by myself, insisting I really don't want to intrude or make anyone feel awkward.

Camille stays perfectly silent, probably hoping I'll make good on my promise to disappear. Meanwhile, Isla acts as though she hasn't heard a single word I've said. She just keeps dragging us along like two pieces of luggage she's hauling through an airport.

As we round the corner and Rose Cabin comes into view, Camille steps away from Isla and frowns.

"This is it?" she asks, visibly disappointed. "When you said cabin, I pictured something bigger."

"Like what?" Isla asks mockingly. "A resort?"

She shrugs and starts walking toward the steps, more than steady on her feet all of a sudden. *It's a miracle!*

Isla and I look toward each other at the exact same moment—thinking the exact same thing—and we both lose it in a fit of laughter.

Still, I force myself to sober up. This is no good. I don't want to like Isla. It's an inconvenience to click so well with Ethan's sister. If anything, my life would be much simpler if she turned sullen and grouchy like her brother. Now *there's* a personality I'm accustomed to dealing with.

Isla nods her head toward the cabin and we finish walking up the steps. She pushes open the door and takes off her backpack, dropping it in the corner, out of the way.

"My things are back in the car. I thought one of the guys was going to grab it for me." Camille frowns, hovering in the doorway, inspecting the space from ceiling to floor as if she's never seen a piece of architecture like this ever before.

And what's this charming thing called?

Ah, a log.

"All right, well, we'll be here when you get back," Isla says cheerfully, kicking off her sandals and walking over to test out the bottom bunk. The mattress bounces underneath her and she grins.

Camille puffs air out of her nose like a disgruntled bull—a dainty disgruntled bull—and then she's gone.

Finally.

"Finally!" Isla says, throwing herself back on the mattress.

I suppress a smile. "I take it you and Camille aren't the best of friends?"

"What gave it away? My snarl or my glare? Truth be told, I wish we'd left her back in Austin, but Liv insisted she come. She's new to the city and doesn't have many friends which means we have to try to like her, but between you and me, she's proving very hard to like. Did you see those shoes?! We're in the middle of the woods for God's sake!"

I mash my lips together in an effort to keep my opinions to myself. I don't feel like it's my place to gossip about Ethan's friends. I know he wouldn't like it.

"So are they dating?" I ask, scratching my wrist then propping my hands on my hips, looking intently at the desk as if hunting for a speck of dirt.

"Who? Jace and Alice?"

"No, uh…Ethan and Camille."

She jerks back up to a sitting position like someone who's just been zapped in the chest with defibrillator paddles. Her forehead nearly collides with the bottom of the bunk. "*WHAT?!* Are you kidding?"

Thank God.

I can't hide my smile, so I turn away.

"Why would you ever think that?"

"Oh…" I shrug, sounding casual. "Just the way she was holding on to him, and…well, she *is* beautiful. And delicate, like a china doll."

"Beautifully *annoying*. A *delicate* pain in my ass."

My smile has turned into a full-fledged grin.

"Besides, she's not Ethan's type."

I whirl around. "What is his type?" My eyes go wide with the realization that I all but shouted the question and I shake my head quickly, stepping back. "No, never mind. Don't answer that. It's none of my business."

She's the Cheshire Cat with that grin of hers.

"Oh, I'd say spunky brunettes in work boots are more his speed these days."

My cheeks flame. "We aren't dating. Not even close."

"I know."

"He doesn't even like me."

"Really?"

"Yes! And it's getting absolutely ridiculous. There has to be some kind of explanation for it. I mean, you could say we did get off to a...*rocky* start, but he should have gotten over that by now! He really knows how to hold a grudge. What was his childhood like? Terrible? Haunting?"

Her face turns solemn then and she casts her eyes toward the ground. I immediately feel like an ass for prying, but not so much that I'm prepared to backtrack. I want to know what makes Ethan tick. I want to know all his secrets.

"This is usually where people say, 'It isn't my story to tell.'"

My heart plummets, but I understand. She's obviously going to be more loyal to her brother than to a perfect stranger.

But then her gaze sweeps up and crashes with mine as she continues, "So if I tell you, you cannot say a word to him under penalty of death."

"*Death?*"

"Yes. Are you prepared for the consequences?"

She's being perfectly serious. Her face is a mask of earnest sincerity. Then, suddenly, it's not. Her eyes pinch closed and her hand hits her chest and she's really laughing now, completely surrendering to a fit of giggles. She wipes tears from her eyes before she speaks. "Oh my gosh, sorry. *Sorry*. That was mean—terrible, really. I was totally kidding. '*Penalty of death*'...oh it's too good. Really, I've just always wanted to say something like that and I couldn't resist." She clears her throat. "But getting back to your question…honestly, no. Ethan had a great childhood."

"That can't be. Surely he was dropped on his head too many times when he was young?"

She smiles mockingly. "I'm sure we would have noticed a scar or two."

"Jilted by a woman?"

"Unfortunately, that doesn't happen to men like Ethan, though I would love if it did. He deserves to be brought down a peg or two."

I can't give up. I start to pace while I brainstorm. Then I stop on a dime and whirl around to face her, eyes bright with another idea. "Oh! Maybe your parents had a bad marriage? Lots of fighting? It's tainted the idea of love for him permanently?"

"Our parents have been married for thirty-five years this September." That's right. I'd forgotten. "In fact, my dad still calls my mom Honeybuns and she pretends to hate it. It's a whole routine they do."

I'm shaking my head now, in full disbelief about what she's saying.

She tilts her head, unable to conceal her smile any longer. "What makes you think he doesn't like you?"

"Oh, his surly personality, constant glares, menacing presence—that sort of thing."

"Huh, how odd. He's usually pretty charming."

"Charming?! You're joking."

"I think in our senior year of high school he won best personality *and* dream date. There was a fuss because usually you're only allowed to win one superlative—"

"Was your school very small? Maybe he was the only boy in your class?"

"Oh no. My graduating class had over 800 people."

So then that proves it once and for all.

Isla comes to the same conclusion.

"Hate to break it to you, but I think you're right…he must just not like you."

CHAPTER TWENTY-FOUR
ETHAN

I'm annoyed with Taylor for offering up our cabin to my friends. Oh, sure, as a doting brother, I should want Isla to take my bunk rather than forcing her to sleep on the ground, but y'know what? Isla is nothing if not resourceful. She brought an inflatable mattress and a four-person tent just for herself. Even if she hadn't come equipped, she would have had no issue finding a nice bear den, scaring the bear off, and settling in for the night.

Not to mention *she* was the one to force this weekend even after I told her there was nowhere for people to sleep. It's just like her to finagle a nice, comfy cabin for herself while kicking me to the curb, although I guess technically Taylor's the reason I'll be sleeping on the ground tonight, not Isla.

Taylor.

The woman currently sitting across from me at the other end of the table, trying to blend into her surroundings. I know she doesn't want to be here. She hasn't said a word to me since she reappeared from the cabin with Camille and Isla. In the time the rest of us were out here setting up tents and unrolling sleeping bags, the three of them were "freshening up". Isla and Camille both look like they're dressed for a garden party rather than dinner in a camp mess hall. Taylor showered and changed, but Isla must not have won the dress battle because she's still wearing jeans and a simple white blouse. She's fresh-faced, with a pink tinge of color on her tan cheeks. Her dark chestnut hair is starting to softly curl as it air-dries.

Tanner wasted no time going over to chat with her when they rejoined us at the center of camp. Meanwhile, I struggled with the tent Isla brought—a large, ridiculous contraption that would take a whole crew an entire day to set up. Tanner made the girls laugh, and I nearly threw a metal pole at a tree. As a longtime friend of Isla's, I know he's a good guy, which is precisely why I don't think it was a good idea that Isla invited him here this weekend. He's had a crush on her for years and she's dangled him on a string. Now, maybe he's sick of waiting around, because he's made it perfectly obvious he's into Taylor.

He asked me about her while we set up.

"So she works for you? That must be interesting."

"Why would it be interesting?" I asked blankly, focusing on the forty-five-page instruction manual that came with Isla's tent. It might as well have been in Chinese. I work in construction and still had no idea what I was doing.

"Oh just because, I mean…she's obviously attractive."

"It hasn't been an issue. Hand me that stake, will you?"

A few minutes passed before he steered the conversation back to her. "So is she dating anyone?"

"Why would I know the answer to that?"

"I thought you two were friends."

I could tell from the break in his voice that I was making the guy sweat, so I decided to ease up. "She's my employee, Tanner. If you're curious about her relationship status, you'll have to ask her."

That must be exactly what he planned to do because after Brody and I finished grilling chicken for dinner, Tanner snatched up the seat beside Taylor at the table in the mess hall. Right now, they're at one end and I'm at the other.

We're all digging into our meals. Conversation flows around the table, except for near me.

Brody passes me a beer and I give him a thankful nod while I pop the tab and take a long drink. When I go to set it back down, I look up just in time to see Taylor unleash a devastating smile aimed at Tanner. He leans closer to say something. She blushes and shakes her head and then Isla joins in, laughing alongside them.

The aluminum crinkles in my hand and I immediately loosen my grip when I get a few curious stares. I'm quickly encroaching on Hulk territory.

"I'd love to take a tour of the jobsite after we finish dinner, Ethan," Camille says with a seductive lilt. I glance down beneath the table, notice she's still wearing those ridiculous shoes, and shake my head.

"My partners would kill me if I let you guys get near the site without wearing closed-toe shoes, not to mention it's already dark. There's nothing to see."

She pouts and goes back to pushing potato salad around on her plate. "Maybe tomorrow morning then."

"Oh, actually…" Isla says, loudly enough to catch everyone's attention. "I was thinking it'd be fun to spend the day at the lake tomorrow. The weather's supposed to be really warm and Brody brought some speakers so we can set up music. Plus I have a volleyball net if we want to play."

"It's not a good idea," I protest with a sharp tone. It's best to take a firm stance when dealing with Isla. "It's too close to the site."

A small voice speaks up from the other end of the table, a voice I've come to know all too well. "It's actually totally safe if we stay on the right side, closer to the edge of the clearing near the forest. All the framing supplies are piled up neatly on the other side of the lake and there—"

“There could still be debris scattered around there.”

I expect that to be the end of the conversation, but then she continues, “I’ve never seen anything like that when I go—”

“Go where?” I ask with a bite to my tone, my gaze crashing into hers across the table. She swallows past a lump in her throat, and for one brief second I don’t think she has the courage to continue down this path in front of everyone. Then she surprises me by lifting her chin and speaking clearly.

“To swim.”

“*Swim?* On the weekends when you’re not even supposed to stay here, you mean?”

She shrugs in an act of defiance. “Don’t pretend to be angry with me now. You already know I stay here.”

Her cavalier expression only heightens my anger.

“Yes, but I wrongly assumed you had enough sense to stay away from the site. What would happen if you stepped on a nail or some other piece of scrap metal lying around? Your phone doesn’t even work!”

My voice is nearly booming now as I imagine her out here all alone, bleeding. A nail in the foot might not seem so bad, but if she were out here for two days by herself with no way to see a doctor or get stitches…

Camille’s hand hits my arm and I realize then that everyone has turned to look at me with wide eyes, slightly unnerved by my reaction, but no one is brave enough to say a damn word except for Taylor.

“Yes, well, it’s too late to go back and erase what I’ve already done,” she says in a steely manner. “The fact is, I’ve never come close to injuring myself, and if you’re intent on ensuring everyone’s safety, well then, there’s a solution. We’ll all put on boots first thing in the morning and make sure the area is clear. With there being so many of us, it shouldn't take long."

"I don't have any boots," Camille protests weakly.

Taylor's gaze practically flays her. "Well then you can just stay back and sleep in. How's that?"

"Sounds good!" Isla answers for me.

She's the only one at the table in good spirits. In fact, she's smiling like a fool, asking Brody to pass her the potato salad.

It takes the second half of the meal to recover the mood. Even then, I can feel my friends glancing back and forth between Taylor and me, waiting to see when round two will begin.

As soon as we're done eating, Taylor stands and makes excuses so she can head to bed even though it's still early.

Everyone protests, Tanner most of all. "C'mon, the night's young. I promise to protect you if Ethan decides to go all caveman again."

There are a few quiet laughs as everyone looks to me. It's clear I should be the one inviting Taylor to stay since I'm the one who made her feel so uncomfortable in the first place.

Instead, I raise my beer. "Good night."

Taylor's gaze is full of amber fire when she glares at me before turning and storming out of the room.

"Well good job, big brother, you successfully scared her off. Now what are you going to do? Pick a fight with a baby bunny? Maybe harass a little fawn?"

We stay in the mess hall as night falls, swapping our dinner plates for a deck of cards. The atmosphere isn't so fraught with tension now that Taylor's gone, but still, no one tries to drag me out of my surly mood, which is just as well because they wouldn't succeed. We pair up and play cards well past everyone's bedtime. Having Camille as a partner is more ideal than I first thought it would be because having to carry the team means I'm distracted for a few hours, which is exactly what I needed. Brody and Liv are the first to peel off. Camille is next. Then Jace and Alice. Tanner volunteers to walk Isla back to the cabin and I'm left there to toss the beer cans in the recycling bin and close up the snacks.

I have no idea what time it is when I'm done. I could collapse on the spot, but then I realize grumpily that everything I need is back in the cabin, a toothbrush being the top priority. I carry a lantern out into the woods and use it to light the path back to the cabin, careful to skip the stair that creaks on my way up to the porch. At the door, I set the lantern down so it casts just enough light into the cabin that I can see where I'm stepping but not so much that I'll wake anybody up.

Inside, I spot Taylor asleep on the ground and frown as I sweep my gaze up to her bunk, finding Camille dozing peacefully beneath a black silk sleep mask.

If it wouldn't cause a scene, I'd wake her up and demand she get out of Taylor's bed. It's a silly impulse, and yet something in me stirs when I glance back down to Taylor there on the ground. She has a blanket underneath her, but that's hardly enough to soften the wood floor. She shivers in her sleep and rolls over, tugging up the thin sheet covering her, but then her feet peek out at the bottom.

I know it's her own damn fault for conceding her bunk to Camille in the first place, but I still yank a sweatshirt out of the dresser drawer and use it to cover the bottom half of her legs.

My feelings toward Taylor are nothing short of a conundrum. Even now, I know if she woke up, she'd fling off my sweatshirt and claim she doesn't need it, and I wouldn't blame her. Not after the curt goodbye I offered her at dinner.

I know I'm behaving like an ass, and I wish I could go back to the version of myself I was before Taylor. I can't remember ever having a difficult time reining in my emotions around a woman. If anything, my issue was having any emotions *to* rein in.

If you asked any of my past girlfriends if I was coldhearted, they would have laughed and said, *Ethan? Ethan was perfectly nice.*

And I was.

Our relationships didn't fizzle because of my inability to treat them well. They fizzled for all the other reasons: lost interest, stagnant feelings, incompatibility.

Taylor and I? We'd have entirely different issues…starting with her smart mouth.

In the beginning, I hated her for what she did to me. I painted her out as a monster and never gave her the chance to prove otherwise. Any time she was vulnerable, I assumed she was pretending, acting like a damsel in distress to serve her own malicious intent. Each time another man fell over himself trying to please her, I figured it was because she craved the attention.

It occurs to me now that painting her in that light was a defense mechanism, my way to heal a bruised ego. I got hurt and wanted to safeguard against it happening again, so I made her small, because otherwise, I'd be a simpering fool, chasing after the woman who lured me into a bathroom so she could steal my wallet. It seemed pathetic to forgive her so easily for her transgressions, and yet now I realize, somewhere along the way, I *did* forgive her. Deep down, I know she's just a young woman with few options who was pushed into a corner, one who made a mistake and has more than atoned for it.

In fact, I don't just forgive her for what she's done; I trust her. I trust that she's here for the right reasons, that deep down she's not malicious or cruel. She's a fighter. A survivor. Someone I've actually come to admire.

Our game of tit for tat these last few weeks was never truly about mutual hatred. We've been needling each other because we both secretly like it, because the button-pushing banter and teasing remarks are the only ways we've allowed ourselves to reveal our true feelings.

I realize I'm still standing in the cabin, dragging my hand through my hair and behaving like a perfect creep just staring down at her on the ground. With an inward groan, I snatch my toothbrush and some clothes for tomorrow and then I leave, wondering where she and I could possibly go from here.

CHAPTER TWENTY-FIVE
TAYLOR

"It looks AMAZING," Isla exclaims, stepping back with wide eyes and a hand covering her mouth.

"No. Absolutely not. I'm not wearing this."

"What? C'mon. It's a one-piece. You're *practically* fully clothed."

Isla is totally out of her mind. The bathing suit she insisted I try on *is* a one-piece, but it's a one-piece that looks like it belongs on the set of *Baywatch.* It's bright red with a plunging scoop neck.

"It's the same style as the one I have on!" she protests, waving down her body.

Maybe that's true, but I am much more endowed than Isla, and what looks tasteful and demure on her looks wholly scandalous on me. My boobs and butt are too big. I need like four more bathing suits layered over this one if I'm ever going to leave this cabin.

Camille is wearing a white two-piece with a yellow sarong knotted at her hip, and yet again, it looks tasteful because she's lithe and tall.

It's like I'm the only one of us who's gone through puberty.

"Camille, tell her she looks great."

She scrunches her nose like a little chipmunk. "The red is very bright, but yeah, it does look really good."

Camille's decided to play nice this morning, which I appreciate considering I currently have very little patience for her. I had a terrible night of sleep. My neck is sore and my back aches and I woke up in the middle of the night hugging a random sweatshirt that smelled an awful lot like Ethan, which is disconcerting on so many levels. When I realized what I was doing, I flung it away, but only so far that I could still reach out and bring it right back since it was kind of nice to have the extra padding under my head, and well, the man smells divine. I can't fault him there.

I think the scent actually rubbed off on me. Even now, I can still smell it. I'd jump straight in the shower but we're about to go down to the lake and there's no point in rinsing off beforehand.

"Just throw something on over it and let's go," Isla says, tossing me the sweatshirt. I have no idea how it came to be in my possession last night, but I'm definitely not wearing it out of the cabin. Can you imagine what Ethan would do if I showed up to breakfast in his clothes?

I don't want to find out.

I fold it neatly, set it on the dresser, and then find the only set of clothing I have that make sense for a day at the lake: a white t-shirt and those denim cutoffs I was teasing Ethan with the other week. Who would have thought they'd actually come in handy? Isla lets me borrow a pair of her sandals so I don't have to wear my work boots, and then we're off.

The guys took pity on us this morning and went down to the lake for cleanup duty without us. I was still sleeping when Isla waltzed in with three coffees, letting the cabin door slam closed behind her.

"Good news, sleepyheads! The site is cleared, the volleyball net is being hung, and Brody's already frying up bacon, so you two need to get up because I'm one of those people who gets really affected by FOMO, and even now, I wonder if everyone's down there having fun without us."

We walk toward the lake together, and I feel silly for the anxiety building up inside of me. This morning, again, I tried to tell Isla it was a bad idea for me to come along and spend the day with them. She saw the way Ethan treated me last night. There can be no confusion over the fact that he doesn't want me hanging around. I'm just his employee. To which she replied, "Well, screw that! You're my invited guest. How's that?"

Even Camille nodded in agreement. "It's going to be a pretty day. Don't you want to swim?"

I think her opinion of me has cooled now that she knows I'm in no way competing for Ethan's attention. She was at that table. She saw how he spoke to me, saw she has no reason to be jealous.

I'm grateful for that, at least, because I'd prefer to only have one enemy at the lake today. Especially because when we arrive at the spot where the trees give way to a sandy, pebbled beach, my gaze seeks him out right away. A sucker punch would be less painful than the reaction I have seeing him standing there in his swim trunks without his shirt. All the guys are dressed the same. It's a warm morning and the sun is already high in the sky. They're standing around a grill, laughing as they make breakfast. There's sausage and bacon arranged on plates sitting on a cheap card table they must have hauled down from the mess hall.

Behind them, closer to the water, they've set up canvas chairs in a semi-circle. I count them quickly and realize there are only eight. Panic fills my veins. Maybe Ethan really didn't want me here. I stop short, knowing they haven't seen us yet. I could still turn around and avoid the inevitable embarrassment, but then Isla whistles and catches their attention, thereby announcing our presence to the whole damn forest.

Ethan's gaze sweeps over to us. He didn't shave this morning, and his slight stubble only makes his ruggedly chiseled features more seductive. I hold my breath, waiting for him to continue what we started last night and order me to leave, but what he does instead is somehow worse. He doesn't smile or nod, but he also doesn't glare angrily. In fact, his brown eyes are so sultry and warm, I could melt. That confused frown he's wearing probably matches my own. It seems neither one of us knows how to proceed.

My stomach fills with dread, but Isla's hand clamps down on my arm as if she knows I'm about to bolt.

Then Tanner rushes over like the happy camper he is, gifting each of us a big smile and a hug. He immediately takes the beach bag Isla toted from the cabin then throws a conspiratorial wink my way.

"Glad you didn't let Mr. Grump keep you from coming today."

I don't trust my voice so I offer a tight nod and trail behind the rest of them as we make our way to the group.

It really is a fun setup. They've thought of everything we'll need: coolers filled with drinks, bags of snacks, a portable speaker currently playing Twenty-One Pilots. And though I know they had no control over it, it looks like it's going to be a beautiful day, unseasonably warm, which will make it perfect for long stretches of sunbathing followed by dips in the lake to cool off.

Isla and Camille peel off to say hi to the guys and I wander over to the chairs, dropping my things on the ground behind one of them. I'm more glad than ever that I thought to bring a paperback. Chances are I'll be spending most of the day reading and steering clear of Ethan.

I kick off my sandals and then nearly jump out of my skin as a red Solo cup hits my arm.

"Sorry." Tanner laughs. "Didn't mean to sneak up on you."

I smile and shake my head. "You're fine. I was just in my own world."

Tanner's honey-brown hair is playfully disheveled this morning, and while he's not as toned as Ethan, he's not exactly scrawny either. His blue swim trunks have a wild pattern on them and there's a tattoo stretched across the left side of his chest, an intricate abstract design. I immediately wonder if he drew it himself.

"Here, take the cup then laugh wildly as if I've said something really funny."

I frown. "What?"

He forces the cup into my grasp and chuckles loud enough for everyone to hear. Then he leans closer. "You're not very good at this."

"At what?" I frown, looking down at the drink.

"It's a mimosa. I figured you could use some alcohol."

He's not wrong. I take a long sip and then level him with a glare.

He's nothing but smiles as he turns me slightly so my back is to the group. Now they only see him, and he looks as if he's having the time of his life over here talking to me.

"The way I see it, we can be mutually beneficial to each other."

"How?" I ask, still skeptical.

"You're new to the group and clearly feel like you don't belong, right? Especially because of Ethan?"

"Oh, I—"

"And it's probably obvious that I'm in love with Isla." My eyes widen as he continues. "Ah, you didn't know? Yeah, well, to make a long story short, when I first started working at the agency with her, I had a girlfriend. Isla and I became good friends—*only* friends—but one day she worked up the courage to tell me she had feelings for me, feelings that went beyond friendship. But, you see, I was still with Britt and we'd been together a long time. I couldn't just end things on a whim like that. I owed it to her to really put in an effort. We stayed together for a few more months—the worst months of my entire life, I'll have you know. By the time I finally realized what a fool I was being and broke it off with Britt for good, Isla wanted nothing to do with me beyond our friendship. I'd hurt her, you know? She really put herself out there telling me how she felt."

"It was a brave thing to do."

He nods, agreeing. "I also think Isla feels like she doesn't want me to rush from one relationship to another. She wants me to really have my head on straight if we're ever going to date."

"So how long has it been since you ended things with Britt?"

"Two years."

"TWO YEARS?!"

He laughs again, and I can feel everyone's attention on us.

"So now you see why I'm desperate. I've given her time. Jesus, I've declared my love for her dozens of times. A man only has so much patience, so I think it's time for a different tactic."

My brows furrow. "What kind of tactic?"

"Isla knows how I feel about her, and I think she's comfortable with the way things are because I've made it too easy for her. So, I'm asking for your help today." His smile unfurls into a sinister smirk. "I want to make her jealous."

Admittedly, I don't feel completely comfortable with this arrangement, especially considering how nice Isla has been to me. I feel like an adult conversation where we all sit down around the campfire and discuss our feelings would be the mature thing to do, and yet it's totally out of the question once Tanner fills me in on all the details from the last couple of years while I finish my drink.

They've had stolen kisses, heated arguments. He's done the grand gestures and subtle sweet clues.

I feel bad for the guy, especially when he shrugs and looks out at the lake. "I guess a part of me realizes I'm coming to the end of the line. If we aren't meant to be, we aren't meant to be. I just want to make sure I've done every possible thing I can do to get her attention and force her to make a decision, even if it's childish."

My heart shatters for him in that moment, so I stand, retrieve a bottle of sunscreen from a chair beside ours, and slap it into his palm.

"Fine. I'll play along, but only because I think you and Isla would be really cute together. Also, I can't exactly put sunscreen on my own back, so if anything, I'm just killing two birds with one stone."

I've left off the other crucial detail about why I've agreed to go through with this: I don't want to spend the day moping by myself. These are Ethan's friends, which means they're going to follow Ethan's lead. I really don't want to sit around alone while they all have fun. This way, Tanner acts as a buffer, one I'm happy to use.

I know if I think too hard, I'll find a million reasons to keep my clothes on, walk right back to the cabin, and hide out there all day. So, before common sense can set in, I stand and tug off my t-shirt, leaving the denim cutoffs on for now.

Then I sit in a chair in front of Tanner, gather my hair in my hand, and tip my head down so he can start lathering me up. The cool lotion makes me shiver and I close my eyes, finding myself wishing his hands were someone else's.

"By the way, what's the deal with you and Ethan?" he asks, as if reading my thoughts.

"What do you mean?"

"Are you a thing?"

"No. Not at all. What makes you ask?"

"Oh, just because he's currently looking over here like he wants to rip my head from my body. I would stop immediately because the dude could probably accomplish the task, but Isla's standing right by him, glaring too."

"Well then, don't stop now. Actually, while you're back there, would you mind rubbing my neck, right here?" I ask, pointing to the spot that's tight from sleeping on the floor. He immediately obliges, pressing down hard and soothing the ache there. I practically swoon with relief. I don't even have to fake this for Isla's sake. I really needed someone to work the tension out of my neck and back.

"Tanner!" Isla shouts suddenly, coming over. "Hey, Ethan said he needed some help with breakfast."

"It looks like he's got it—"

"He doesn't. Here, I'll finish up Taylor's sunscreen since I'll need her to return the favor anyway."

I want to thrust my fist triumphantly into the air for Tanner's sake, but I keep myself perfectly composed as I glance over my shoulder and aim a sweet smile his way. "Thanks for helping."

Then he's gone and Isla takes his spot behind me, rubbing sunscreen onto my skin with short, angry swipes. In fact, it kind of hurts.

"You okay?" I ask, unable to hide the amusement in my tone.

"Peachy!" she says, her voice shrill. She tosses the bottle aside. "All done."

I glance over my shoulder and laugh. "Isla, it's not even rubbed in."

"What do you expect? I'm not a professional sunscreen applier!"

Through the second half of the morning, the tension around the lake is so thick I can barely breathe. Everyone's aware of it. I aim furtive glances at Ethan every five minutes, Camille follows him everywhere he goes, Tanner hovers near me, Isla grumbles near the drinks, and Ethan pays no mind to anyone at all. In fact, I'd be hard-pressed to get his attention even if I suddenly went up in flames while bouncing on a pogo stick *and* playing the harmonica. Brody, Liv, Jace, and Alice seem to be enjoying it all from a distance while they sip their drinks, which I actually can't blame them for. I'd be doing the same thing if I were them.

"Come hang out with me," Tanner says, nodding his head toward the lake's edge. It's flat enough to spread two towels out beside one another, and the ground isn't so pebbly that it's uncomfortable.

I grab my book and lie down on my stomach, prepared to read, but that goes out the window once Tanner starts rambling on about Isla. To an outsider, it looks like we're sharing an intimate moment, sunbathing together barely a foot apart. In reality, I'm trying to concentrate on my book and Tanner is yammering nonstop. I read the same paragraph four times and am actually relieved when a shadow eclipses my page. I glance up to find Ethan standing there, a veritable giant from this perspective. My gaze drags up his toned legs and abs, hitching on the subtle details: the veins on his forearms, the groove of his Adonis V just above his black swim trunks, the dark scowl he's aiming at Tanner.

Only in the confines of my mind do I actually admit that he's something to behold. So toned and yet not someone who *lives* for the gym, he's someone who clearly uses his body for physical labor. It's enough to make my mouth water, enough to make me lose track of my objective concerning him. Do I hate him for his arrogance or want him more because of it? Are we on track to kill each other or are we working toward an entirely different conclusion? One that promises *slightly* more pleasurable results?

This is the closest we've been all morning, and I'm acutely aware that I'm lying here in nothing but denim shorts and a bathing suit. It's more skin than he's ever seen—outside of the bath incident—but he's not technically *seeing* anything, because his gaze isn't on me at all. To him, I'm a ghost.

"Tanner, we're playing volleyball. You in?" he asks. "Isla needs a partner."

Tanner, having heard her name spoken in relation to himself, jumps to his feet like a well-trained puppy, and I'm left there on the towel, forgotten. I push up to sit, tucking my legs underneath me. Not surprisingly, my invitation to join never comes. Even more interesting, Ethan stays right where he is, hands propped up on his hips.

I know someone more diplomatic would offer a smile or maybe even an appreciative remark for allowing me to crash his weekend with his friends. I'd shrivel up and die before doing either.

"I know you're probably itching to invite me to play as well," I say with a teasing smirk, "but I'm happy right here."

I hold up my book. It's one of his, of course.

He narrows his eyes, seemingly on the precipice of saying something before he shakes his head and turns away.

I smile and go right back to reading—at least that's what I appear to do. In reality, I watch that volleyball game with the careful attention of someone who's going to have to write a dissertation about it afterward. I have every serve and point memorized. Ethan plays with all the finesse of an Olympic athlete, and Camille is pretty good too. Worse, she's taken off her sarong and is hopping around the makeshift court in a bikini. Any man would be drooling at the sight of her.

Tanner and Isla are laughably terrible. Tanner isn't the most athletic and Isla apparently isn't either because between the two of them, they've only scored one point, and that one was swiftly ruled out of bounds by Brody, who's serving as the volunteer referee.

Ethan serves and scores another point, sending Camille rushing over for another round of high fives, and my breakfast sours in my stomach. There can only be one explanation: they fed us expired bacon.

Then it occurs me that there could be another reason for the pit in my stomach, a seven-letter word I'd rather not name. I've never seen Ethan around other women. For the last few weeks, we've been living on a site where the male-to-female ratio is hilariously uneven. I've had it easy, and I never even realized.

Startled by the disturbing revelation, I turn back to my book and start reading with gusto.

In twenty minutes, I manage one page.

I can hear Camille's laughter and flirty comments, Ethan's taunting barbs to Isla and Tanner. The sun hovers high overhead, and I grow uncomfortably warm.

When the game ends, I glance up as Ethan walks over to grab some water from a nearby cooler. A bead of sweat rolls down his abs and I follow its descent with unwavering concentration.

I'm practically salivating.

Then my gaze shifts higher and, with a start, I realize he's caught me watching him.

My cheeks flush with heat just as Tanner walks over, yanking his shirt off and throwing it on the towel beside me.

"C'mon, let's swim."

He doesn't have to ask me twice.

I've been sunbathing all morning and my skin is hot and covered in a sheen of sweat. I strip off my shorts and toss them on top of my stuff, and together, we wade in slowly. The cold water shocks my system, but I don't give it the chance to overpower me. I dive in and start swimming toward the center of the lake with Tanner hot on my heels. We laugh as we race, stopping only because we're out of breath.

We tread water and he grins. "My plan is working."

"Oh yeah?"

"I've never seen Isla so grouchy."

I laugh. "You're playing with fire, you know. There's an equal chance she'll hate you for this."

"Maybe," he says with a cocky grin before he swims closer and our legs brush underwater. His hand touches my chin and he lifts it gently. My breath catches. *He's going to kiss me!* My body tries to get me to flee. I don't want Tanner to kiss me and yet I'd feel so bad if I ruined his plan. I squash my panic and brace myself, but then he grins, glances over my shoulder, and backs away quickly.

"She turned away."

"What?"

His smile spreads from ear to ear. "She turned away. She didn't want to see us kiss. C'mon, let's go dry off."

I feel exhausted by the time we make it back to shore.

I can't keep up with all the games. Even without them, my head is a swirling mess of restrained desire and confusing feelings. I don't want Ethan. And yet I do. I should flirt with Tanner, but I'd rather not. Camille shouldn't inspire jealousy, and yet when I look at her it feels like fire blazing through my veins.

The afternoon drags on and I go through the motions, swimming and sunbathing and sitting with the group while they all laugh and talk and I sit perfectly quiet. Tanner dotes on me with drinks and snacks, but the food goes untouched and the drinks get downed too quickly.

The day takes on a dreamlike state. My skin is so warm and flushed, especially around Ethan. We don't say a word to each other, and yet I know where he is at all times. I'm aware of his every movement. We brush shoulders accidentally on the shore of the lake. His hand catches my waist when we're at the drink table and we step back to walk away at the same time. His eyes catch mine when Tanner is leaning close, whispering something in my ear. I force a smile, but it's tight across my cheeks as Ethan's gaze smolders.

"You want another drink?" Tanner asks.

I shake my head tightly and then bolt right back to the safety of my chair.

I want Ethan to talk to me. I want his eyes to meet mine so I can see if he's feeling what I'm feeling. Maybe I've had one too many drinks or maybe I should take another dip in the water. Or maybe the ache I feel can't be washed away with a quick swim.

After they fire up the grill to start dinner, Jace and Brody start a small campfire in the center of our circle. As the sun starts to set, everyone carries their drinks over, and I'm so desperate for Ethan to claim the seat beside mine. My body is practically humming with nervous energy at the idea that he might, but he sits directly across from me instead. Camille is quick to snatch the chair next to him. They've been thick as thieves all day, and I overheard Liv betting Brody they'd make things official before the weekend was up.

"I've never seen him act like this around anyone," Liv whispered, not realizing I could hear her.

Now, I wonder if she was right, if Ethan will soon be off the market.

It's no surprise my stomach protests every sip of my drink.

"You okay?" Tanner asks from the chair on my left—the one he dragged from camp so we'd each have one.

I smile. "Yeah, just tired."

He frowns, not quite buying it. Then he slings his arm across the back of my chair and I feel everyone's eyes on us, Isla's most of all. I hate that Tanner dragged me into this game of his and suddenly, I'm done playing. I set down my drink and shoot to my feet. Everyone looks up, waiting for me to say something, and I nod toward the lake's edge.

"Going to cool off."

Tanner doesn't follow me, which is for the best. I've been pretending all day and it feels nice to just stand here, looking out at the dark water and wondering where the hell I go from here.

"You know, it's interesting seeing it firsthand," a deep voice says behind me.

I'm so shocked by the sound of it that it takes me a moment to realize I'm supposed to respond.

"Seeing what?"

"The way men fall at your feet," Ethan replies, stepping up until his shoulder brushes mine. I go perfectly still, scared he'll move and cut off the contact.

"I have no idea what you're talking about."

"I know you have no interest in Tanner, so what's your goal?"

His tone isn't as steely as usual. In fact, it nearly sounds drugged with desire.

I keep my gaze trained on the water while his eyes drag down my profile.

"How do you know I have no interest in him?" I ask, dredging up what little energy I have left for verbal swordplay. "Maybe Tanner's just the guy for me, sunny and happy all the time."

He laughs mockingly, finishing his lazy perusal of my body before he flicks his attention back to my face. "And yet you've seemed bored all day." I turn to walk away and his hand wraps around my elbow, keeping me near him. "I only meant it's obvious you and Tanner aren't going anywhere. Not only is he in love with my sister, you're interested in someone else as well."

"Oh really?"

His hand loosens enough that it feels more like a caress than anything else. His touch is hot. Searing. His thumb drags slowly down the inside of my forearm, inching toward my wrist.

I stand there with my head tipped back and my icy gaze frozen on his, waiting for a continued attack, waiting for the shots to be fired so I can pretend they've missed their mark and carry on with my day as best as possible.

But then he steps closer and his thigh hits mine. My breasts brush against his chest and only my thin swimsuit separates our skin. I gather a deep breath.

"You asked me the other day if I was tired," he says, using his other hand to life my chin, bringing our faces closer. "Do you remember that?"

I say nothing. In fact, I don't even move, so he continues.

"You wondered what it would be like if we put our weapons down. At the time, you mentioned friendship, which is why I rebuffed your offer. Friendship is for someone like Tanner, someone who is willing to sit around for two years and wait for the person he loves to make up her damn mind. Unfortunately, I don't have Tanner's patience. So again, you asked me if I was tired…" His sultry gaze is narrowed on my mouth as he says, "I'm fucking exhausted, so no more games. No more pretending I don't love the way you look in this red bathing suit. No more pretending I don't hunt for you every time you enter a room. No more pretending your wit and smart mouth aren't the perfect match for mine."

His words have the effect of warm lips dragging down my body. My insides clench tight and I feel as if I'm swaying on my feet.

"Taylor, you hungry?" Tanner asks suddenly, a few feet behind us.

It seems dinner is ready.

Ethan smirks then, stepping back to release me. It's a miracle I remain standing.

"She's starved."

CHAPTER TWENTY-SIX
TAYLOR

It's late and I can't sleep. Isla and Camille are both nestled nicely on the bunk beds. I took the floor again even though they both offered to swap with me. It just seemed easier this way, especially now when I sit up and push the thin sheet off my legs. I know I won't be able to sleep any time soon. My body is buzzing with nervous energy. I feel like I chugged four Red Bulls and then chased them with three espresso shots.

I glance down at my oversized t-shirt and consider grabbing pants, but I don't want to wake either of them up by rustling through my drawer. Also, I wouldn't mind feeling the cool night air on my bare legs. Maybe it's just what I need.

I slip on the pair of Isla's sandals she lent me all day and am careful to close the door behind me gently enough that it doesn't make a sound.

With a small lantern in tow, I set off down the path. The forest is awake with me, owls and crickets and cicadas reminding me I'm not alone as I head toward the camp.

I have no destination in mind.

I just had to do something.

I couldn't lie on that floor for another second, replaying Ethan's words in my mind, dissecting every part. I talked myself in circles: maybe he was drunk, maybe he was still playing a vicious game, maybe he wanted to teach me a lesson…or maybe he was telling the truth.

I pass the row of tents and wonder if he's inside one of them. I could go over and see, but I'd be mortified if I stumbled upon one of the couples instead. So, I follow the trail down to the lake and freeze when I spot a low fire burning through the trees.

Everyone went to bed a while ago. I'm not sure who was in charge of dousing the campfire, but I worry they might have forgotten until I continue down the path and spot Ethan sitting on a blanket, alone, with the lake at his back.

He's lost in thought, his arms wrapped around his knees and a beer seemingly forgotten in his hands.

I walk until I'm on the other side of the fire and when he looks up, I realize he must have spotted me a while back because he doesn't look surprised. His possessive gaze eats me up from head to toe as if he's saying, *Those legs belong to me, so why are you standing all the way over there?*

"Couldn't sleep?" I ask gently, unsure of what we are now. Friends? Enemies? Should I back away slowly or step around this fire?

"I was waiting," he says, and the words aren't teasing or seductive. They're heartfelt and earnest. "For you," he continues, shaking his head and finishing off his beer before setting it down on the grass beside the blanket.

My stomach flips as I tip my head to the side and smile. "We were together all day, you know."

His attention is on the fire now. When he speaks again, he sounds as if he's speaking straight from the heart. "No. You were off in your own world."

"And you were with Camille."

There. The jealousy has been given a voice, and it feels good to let him know—so good, in fact, I continue, "You smiled at her so much today."

"Smiled?"

I wrap my arms around my waist self-consciously. "Yes. You *enjoyed* yourself, something that doesn't happen very often when you're in my company."

He grins, then a soft chuckle escapes him. "If you think I haven't enjoyed the last few weeks, you're wrong." His gaze flicks back to my shirt. "Dead wrong."

The fire crackles between us, but it's dying down. Soon, it'll be nothing but embers.

I frown down at my loose t-shirt, wishing I'd planned my outfit a little better, but when I glance up from beneath my lashes, Ethan doesn't seem to give a damn about what I'm wearing.

His eyes are stormy black and his jaw is locked tight.

"Did you mean what you said earlier?" I ask, finally picking up where he left off, wanting answers once and for all.

He frowns at the fire. "If you're just hoping I'll repeat it again for your amusement, I won't."

"I was hoping you'd repeat it again for my pleasure," I reply, a wicked little smile on my lips.

Tension sparks between us as our gazes catch. We stare so long, my heart hammers in my chest and my stomach clenches tight. I look away first, back down at the ground.

"Y'know, it's funny," he begins. "I knew why Tanner was all over you today and yet I couldn't seem to rationalize how angry it made me. Maybe it's because I know there are a million men just like him, swarming around you for reasons that have nothing to do with making another woman jealous." His eyes meet mine. "I won't stand in line, waiting for my turn."

I wet my lips and wait for words, but words don't seem good enough anymore. He made the first move earlier, so it's my turn now. I won't let this rare confessional lead to another dead end. I won't wake up frustrated and hot in that cabin, alone and angry about it.

I walk around the fire as he watches me and when I reach the edge of his blanket, I kick off my sandals and continue up onto the soft fabric until I'm standing right in front of him. With the fire behind me, I cast him in shadow.

I've come to him willingly, all but on hands and knees, and I know from the smolder in his gaze that he's going to reward me for it. His hand reaches out and wraps around my left ankle then he slowly drags his palm up around my calf, behind my knee, and then higher, spanning the back of my thigh. Goose bumps bloom across my skin. I reach down to trace the contours of his jaw and cheek, letting my fingers glide into his thick hair just as his catch on the outer edge of my panties.

His thumb hooks inside them and he tugs them higher, revealing the bottom curve of my butt before he smooths his hand around and across my hip bone. Again, the material of my panties bunches up under his firm grasp, but he leaves it there, hiked up so it covers me—*barely*—as he continues his exploration of my body.

He gathers my t-shirt like a drape and pushes it up, revealing my taut stomach, which is quivering under his heavy gaze. I will myself to calm down, to stop shaking, but he's seeing so much of me, even more as he pushes my shirt higher and reveals the bottom curves of my full breasts.

There's too much to feel at once: the warmth of the fire behind me, the cool breeze blowing off the lake, the rough possessive way his hands heat my skin.

We're still in a safe zone. Nothing has been revealed beyond what he'd see if I were in a skimpy bikini, but I'm scared of where we'll go from here, scared to be on display so openly while he's still cloaked in shadow. That's when I realize he's staying down there on purpose, as if kneeling before me, showing me rather than telling me he's surrendering.

His hand curves around my ribcage so reverently my knees buckle, and it's just as well because I want to be down there with him. I want to feel his broad tan chest, still bare from a day at the lake. His swim trunks are long dry and their cool material brushes against my panties as I nestle myself down onto his lap. I'm barely there for a moment before his hand slides around my back and he brings me in for a hug.

A hug.

An embrace that crushes me against him so tightly I think his toned arms might break me in two.

My eyes squeeze closed as I bury my face in the crook of his neck and breathe him in like I'm trying to absorb him through the air, but it's not enough. I need more. I press a chaste kiss to his neck then one below his smooth jaw, and I'm about to press another kiss to his cheek when a growl escapes from deep in his chest and he yanks me back, sealing our mouths together.

A kiss that starts out hard and heavy only grows hotter. Scorching. His mouth slants over mine and I'm a hungry little minx—clawing at his skin, biting his lip, writhing against him.

His tongue touches mine and my entire body seems to clench in response.

Our kiss is unending and I can feel his hard length underneath me and I don't sit still like I should. I brush back and forth along him as if I'm giving him a seductive lap dance. It works me up, moving on him like this, finally giving in to the urge to touch him like I've wanted to for all these weeks.

My hands are everywhere, roving over the ridge of hard muscle along his shoulders, sliding down his toned arms until our hands meet, warm palm against warm palm, our fingers entwining. He kisses me deeper as he squeezes once and then he lets go so his strong hands can move over my body, feeling my curves with greedy possession.

A ripple of pleasure runs through me as he gathers the sides of my t-shirt and yanks it up over my head. He flings it aside and for all I know it's kindling now, but what do I care because his hands cover my bare breasts—*finally*—and he palms their heavy weight almost angrily, like he's been waiting ages to have them in his grasp and his patience is all used up. I feel him grow harder, feel the resulting shudder as I reach between us and brush my hand across his length. Even with his swim trunks on, the thick ridge feels large and intimidating in my small hand.

I stroke him tentatively, imagining what it'll feel like when he slides inside me, stretching and filling me. Our kisses start to burn hotter as his hands grow more and more impatient, toying with me.

I work my hand faster, stroking him lazily back and forth, and then suddenly he picks me up off him and sets me down on the blanket so he can crawl over me, covering my warm skin with his. His hands are on either side of my head and he keeps his weight off me just enough that I won't be crushed but not so much that his chest isn't brushing against my breasts, teasing me. He dips down to kiss my lips and then leans back so the breeze cools my flushed skin. Then his lips fall to my neck and I lift my chin and tangle my fingers in his hair. Down he goes, his lips caressing my collarbone and shoulder. Then they touch the tip of my breast and he delivers a gentle kiss there as well. I arch up off the blanket, yanking him back down, wanting more. His mouth covers me hungrily, eating me up, switching to the other side and bestowing the same sucking, teasing, hot kisses there as well.

I'm going to shatter apart if we continue, and yet the word "stop" no longer belongs in my vocabulary. There is only yes, please, and keep going.

We started this so long ago in that bathroom at the bar, and tonight, we're going to finish it. There's frantic talk of logistics like condoms and birth control and I've never been so worked up, so in a frenzy, so close to breaking into pieces that I think I'll die if we stop now. I think my heart will explode inside of me and I'll cease to exist.

Thank God he agrees we can't wait. Thank God his fingers are dipping past the hem of my panties, over my wetness, and he swirls once…again…one last time before he pushes lower and sinks a long finger inside me. My eyes squeeze closed and my hands are in his hair as he pumps in and out.

Words leave my lips, but they're nothing I hear. They're pleas for him to continue, protests when he pulls out and leaves me longing.

He chuckles and then his hands are on either side of my panties. I almost expect him to rip them to shreds with an angry growl, but he sits up on his knees and tugs them down so achingly slow that I know his attention is caught between my legs even if I'm too shy to look and confirm it.

My eyes are still squeezed shut as his lips press against the inside of my thigh.

"Sweetest thing," he murmurs before his mouth moves higher and he licks. My toes curl and my hips buck up off the blanket and he clamps me back in place with his arm, making it so even when I try to rock forward to meet his lips, I can barely move.

He has a mouth made for sin as evidenced by how skillfully he laps me up. He stays right there between my thighs until I gather the courage to open my eyes, until I look down and meet his gaze. With our eyes locked, his hands grip my thighs and he presses gently, parting me even more as his tongue swirls in a tight circle over and over and over. It's that combination of movements that has me catapulting toward an orgasm I'm helpless to fend off, a release that feels like it's been in the works for half my life.

I roll my hips against him, soaking up every bit of pleasure I can wring out for myself, and still, he's relentless. My oversensitive skin begs for a reprieve. My body shakes as if unsure of how to continue, but Ethan takes the reins for the both of us. He leans back so he's hovering over me again. One of his fingers slides into me slowly, replacing his mouth. Then another. The pair of them is nearly too much, but I don't dare tell him to stop.

My first orgasm was nothing but a small promise of what's to come. I feel hungrier than ever as I watch him sit back and untie his swim trunks just enough to pull himself out and pump his fist up and down slowly. He's encased by the faint glow of the fire, like a demon come to life. *No—an angel.* His gaze is between my legs as he strokes himself with one hand and continues pumping two fingers inside of me with the other. It's timed perfectly and as our eyes meet again, a silent question passes between us.

Should we continue?

My hand glides down my stomach. My skin is flushed and warm and smooth. All the while, he stares, enraptured, until I reach between my parted thighs and take him in my hand. Silky hardness, veined and thick. I'm the one doing the touching now. His fingers leave me empty as I brush him back and forth across me, teasing, working us up, making us shiver. He stares down with hooded eyes, nearly lost to the sight of my legs spread before him. It's only when his fingers dig into my thigh, when a deep impatient rumble breaks free of him that I start to guide him into me the smallest bit. My eyes roll back as he starts to stretch me. He goes slow, but not because he's unsteady or nervous. No. I'm being filled by a man who knows what a woman needs, whose bold confidence never wavers.

Ethan takes it from there, capturing my knees in his hands and pushing himself inside me inch by inch until we fit together like a lock and key. Deep and full. It's utterly unnerving, this all-consuming feeling of contentment. There's a rightness to the moment. This is an inevitable outcome we've been hurtling toward for months on end. He and I are as close as two people could ever be and I'm trying to desperately quell an overwhelming urge to cry as he stays buried inside me, unmoving. I force down the feelings, aware of how silly I'd look. Even so, tears still burn the edges of my eyes as my throat tightens, and Ethan sees. He sees me and, mortified, I turn away, focusing on the edge of the dark forest.

His fingers brush against my cheek and then he cups it in his hand, using it to guide my attention back to him. That's when I realize these feelings surging through me are surging through him too. He's as consumed by it as I am. He might not have tears rolling down his cheeks, but his eyes are the darkest shade of brown, a compelling mix of longing and adoration. It's like even now, he's not fully satisfied, as if being buried this deep isn't even enough. This one time won't sate him.

I pick his hand up off my cheek and kiss the center of his palm before guiding it down to my breast. It's my signal to him that I want this to continue, my signal that we're in this together.

His draws himself out of me slowly and pumps back in. A shudder racks through me. One hand moves down to grip my waist as he slides out and back in, filling me up until it's a hair's breadth away from being painful. My hands grip his biceps, holding on to him as if he's all that's keeping me rooted to the earth. Slow pumps give way to hard thrusts. Soon, we have a rhythm. Soon, there are no tears, only hips rocking together, backs arching, hands dragging down chests. My nails bite into his skin and he drops down to kiss me, sweeping his tongue across mine as his finger swirls circles between my parted thighs. My second orgasm chases the first and this time I come with him lying on top of me, pumping and thrusting and making love until he can't stand it for another second and he pulls out, fists his length, and comes with such force across my stomach and chest that I'm completely captivated.

He kisses my mouth and cheek and hair while we catch our breath, but we're only there for a moment before he scoops me up off the ground and carries me into the dark lake behind us.

The cold water soothes my overly heated skin and he keeps me against him, carried like a child in his arms. My arms wrap around his neck and I bury my head in the groove just below his chin. His palm drags down my chest, rinsing me off, and I feel like I'm dreaming, barely able to keep my eyes open after a long day and longer night. None of this feels quite real, which is probably why I feel compelled to pour out my soul, letting him hear the truth I've been so careful to hide.

"I once pushed my classmate Becky off the swings in the third grade because she told me my French braids looked stupid," I say, my lips pressing against his skin with every syllable.

He stills, obviously confused by my abrupt revelation.

"I drank before I was twenty-one," I continue, quickening my pace in the hopes he'll let me finish. "I cheated on a geography test and never got caught. I used to wish I'd been born into a different family—a *wealthy* family—so I'd never have to live in a trailer park ever again.

"One time, in the bathroom of a bar, I stole a man's wallet. I was at the lowest point of my life. My mom relied on me to help bring in money for the family and I couldn't ever seem to earn enough for us to make ends meet. The car needed repairs and my sister needed her prescription and we had bills and...well, I felt like I had no other choice. So, I took his wallet, but I didn't take his money. I chickened out and gave it back to the bartender so that when the man came back looking for it, he'd just assume he'd accidentally dropped it."

"Taylor—"

I shake my head against his chest. "I swear I didn't take your money. I just confessed to you the bad things I've done in my life and I'm sure if you gave me time, I'd think of a dozen more. Like—*oh!* I just remembered I smeared the frosting on McKenna's birthday cake when she was five because I was so jealous of the Barbie my mom gave her."

He laughs and then his hand comes up to cup my cheek. Our eyes meet and there's such tender affection in his gaze, it gives me hope.

"I'm not perfect, Ethan, but I'm not a bad person either. The truth is, I thought you were the most handsome man I'd ever seen *before* I thought of my harebrained idea. I *wanted* you, and not as some potential target. You have to know that.

I don't blame you if you never forgive me or if you never fully trust me, but at least now you've heard my side."

"I forgive you," he says, his brows furrowed angrily. "Taylor, of course I forgive you."

"And you don't think I took your money, right? You believe me about that as well?" I ask, knowing this is my chance to clear this up.

"The money was gone when I got my wallet back."

I go rigid in his arms. "I didn't take it! I swear to—"

He silences me with a kiss.

"I believe you. It was probably the bartender."

"Of course!" I say, slapping his chest with the realization.

That jerk!

"Take me back to shore and give me your keys. I have a bone to pick with that guy."

"It's the middle of the night," he says, wading back. "We're going to sleep."

My eyes go wide. "Together?"

"Together," he confirms, carrying me up and out of the lake. "I have Isla's tent. There's even an air mattress."

"Sounds like the Four Seasons. What the hell are we waiting for?"

CHAPTER TWENTY-SEVEN
ETHAN

Taylor and I race back to that tent with the blanket wrapped around us and her t-shirt and underwear clutched to her chest. We could have gotten dressed back at the lake, but I wouldn't let us. I want her again, and as soon as that zipper hits the ground, I toss her back onto the air mattress and climb on top of her.

She laughs and then immediately covers her mouth, realizing we're surrounded by my friends on all sides.

"Be as quiet as you can," I taunt, yanking her t-shirt away and throwing it behind us. Her full breasts beg to be licked, so I lean down and take one in my mouth, stifling a groan.

Her hands wrap around my neck and this time, in the tent, it's rough and fast and I come in my swim trunks because I still don't have a condom, but that doesn't stop us. We sneak off to the bathroom to clean up as best we can, but we weren't fooling anyone. Our whispered laughter is not whispered at all.

"Will you two keep it down?! We're trying to sleep!" Jace shouts sometime near dawn.

It's no surprise that Taylor tries to slink out of the tent as soon as the sun starts to rise.

I catch her arm, my eyes still closed. "Where are you going?"

"To the cabin, so I can pretend I was there all night."

"No."

"But I should be there before Isla wakes up, that way—"

"No," I say, dragging her back against me and snaking my hand up under her t-shirt. *Fuck.* She feels good. Her curves are ridiculous. Unending. Heavy in my palm. I'm hard again and it's getting a little embarrassing at this point. I had more control as a horny fourteen-year-old than I do now around a bra-less Taylor.

"*Ethan*," she groans, but it's halfhearted and tinged with lust.

She's putty in my hands, and it's not shocking that we're the last ones to breakfast in the mess hall.

When we walk in after showering back at the cabin, everyone stares at us expectantly.

"Where have y'all been!? We all went out on a hike this morning," Isla says, frowning.

"Oh, uh…" Taylor's voice dwindles as she realizes she has no good excuse.

"And Taylor," Isla continues, sounding eerily similar to our mother, "I woke up in the middle of the night and you weren't in the cabin—where'd you sleep?"

"With me," I reply, knowing it'll be easiest if we just get it all out in the open.

Taylor's cheeks are bright red as she nudges her elbow into my side. Then she rushes to add, "It's just that Ethan was scared of sleeping alone in his tent, so he wanted me to stay with him. Something about monsters."

I shoot her a narrowed glare.

"Don't let Isla fool you—that was just a ploy to get you both to confess. She wasn't in the cabin last night either," Camille reveals with a proud smirk.

Isla throws a half-peeled orange at her, but Camille ducks out of the way just in time.

Tanner's face is bright red as he glances down at his bowl of cereal. "Oh…uhh…"

"Tanner was scared of monsters too," Isla mutters, and now it seems everyone's private business is out on the table.

Brody and Jace find it all hilarious, and I'm pretty happy myself.

"Want some eggs?" I ask, directing Taylor to the seat beside Isla.

"Oh, um, yes please. And some toast if you can manage!"

"You know what? I bet I can," I say mockingly before I head for the kitchen.

Just before I turn, I see Isla and Taylor smile at one another. Apparently, the tension from the beginning of the weekend is long gone now.

Sunday passes in a blink. We're at the lake again, swimming and grilling just like yesterday, but this time Taylor is by my side, delivering lazy smiles, teasing me with her seductive beauty. I keep my hands on her whenever I can. We read beside each other and when she rolls over onto her back, I dip down and give in to the urge to give her a slow, unending, drugging kiss right up until someone shouts at us to stop. That red bathing suit is going to send me to an early grave, and all day I envision what it will look like when I finally peel it off her. That night, in the tent, I take my sweet time, savoring every moment before I lose myself inside her sensuous body. I keep expecting my desire for her to diminish, but it only grows hotter, more demanding.

Monday morning, the tents are broken down, bags are packed, and the grill and coolers are loaded back into cars.

The crew is due back today and because we slept in so late and took our time with lunch, we don't have much longer before they start to arrive.

I can tell Taylor is nervous. At breakfast, she played with her food more than she ate it, and when I tried to pull her aside to talk after everyone left, she begged off, claiming she had work to do before the crew returned to camp.

That work is apparently washing the linens from our cabin and remaking our beds.

I find her in there in the late afternoon, sitting on my bunk, her gaze intently focused on the floor at her feet.

"Taylor?"

She looks up and smiles wistfully. The expression doesn't quite reach her eyes.

"What are you doing?"

"Waiting for you, actually." She pushes off the bed. "Would it be okay if I used your phone? I haven't talked to my family all weekend."

I hand it off and she goes outside to sit on the porch. I try not to listen, but her voice carries easily. The topics don't sit well with me—car repair payment and overdue bills—especially considering what she revealed to me last night in the lake.

Then her mom must ask how things are going here.

"It's good…fine. I really enjoy the work, actually." There's another pause, and then she continues, "I'm not sure. Hopefully a few months. I'm not exactly an essential part of the crew or anything."

My gut clenches, and I make myself busy so I don't look so fucking guilty when she walks in a few minutes later.

"Thanks," she says, walking over to pass me my phone.

Our fingers brush, her eyes sweep up to mine, and there are two conflicting emotions warring there: desire and reservation.

"I heard your conversation."

She shrugs and looks away, brows furrowed. "I should have walked farther down the path, I guess."

"How much money do you need to get your mom's car out of the shop?" I ask, apparently wanting to cut right to the chase.

Color blooms across her neck. "No, Ethan." She steps back. "No. We aren't doing this, okay? You and I are—"

"What? What are we? I've tried to talk to you about it all day and you've blown me off."

"We're having sex."

"Obviously."

"And we care for each other."

She's doing a good job talking in circles, but I like to be a little more direct.

"We're in a relationship," I say definitively.

Her eyes widen.

"What? Do you expect me to say I'm fine with no strings? I'm not that guy, and I'd rather you not pretend that's what you want."

Her smile is squashed down as best as possible.

She wants to be in a relationship with me, even if she's not quite ready to admit it.

She turns away and shakes her head. "It's a terrible idea. I need this job, and I need the guys on the crew to respect me. I don't want them talking about us like that."

"I'll fire anyone who so much as whispers about us."

She glances back with a smirk before rolling her eyes. "Very heroic of you, but it's human nature to be curious. They'll all talk and soon you'll have no crew left at all."

I shrug. "So I'll build the resort myself."

Her laugh is tinged with annoyance. "Can't you be serious? This isn't a joke to me."

I walk toward her, grip her hips, and turn her around so I can bring her right up against me. We're a perfect fit.

"Tell me what you need then."

"No favors."

"Define a favor," I say, tone laced with desire.

She groans. "*Ethan*."

"Fine. No favors."

"That means I get paid the same amount, on the same day as everyone else. No more talk about money. After everything we've been through, I don't want that to be a part of our relationship."

Her attention is on my chest as if she doesn't quite have the courage to meet my eyes. She obviously still feels guilty about the incident in the bar.

"Fair enough. Next."

"I don't want the crew to know we're dating."

I drag in a deep breath, trying to cool my urge to argue with her. That's going to be a problem, but for now, I'm willing to concede that point if she thinks it's for the best.

"Fine. Anything else?"

"I don't know," she says, her attention sliding up to my mouth. "I could probably come up with another fifty things but I'd really like to kiss you right now, and would you please stop doing that?"

She's talking about how my hands are working up the bottom of her shirt so I can slide my palms up around her waist.

"I listened to your demands," I taunt, leaning down so my lips barely hover over hers. "Now I think you should listen to mine."

"So you probably saw what happened last week when I asked Taylor out to dinner."

I'm at my desk, trying to catch up on work. I have a million emails to read and respond to and I'm supposed to have a conference call with my partners in fifteen minutes.

"Hudson, I have work to do."

"I know, I was just wondering, since you talked to Taylor right after I left…do you think she's interested in me but just doesn't want to make things complicated at work?"

Jesus Christ. If Taylor didn't want to make things complicated at work, she'd let me tell everyone she's off the market.

"You know what? I think you're better off just focusing on the project. How's that?"

He groans and turns back to his computer, temporarily silenced.

A few minutes later, Taylor comes in with my coffee and aims a warm smile at Hudson. "Hey Hudson! Did you have a good weekend?"

His eyes widen as he takes her in. She's wearing jeans and her work boots. Her t-shirt shouldn't be all that sexy, but it is. She has her hair pulled up in a wavy ponytail, making her feminine features shine. The guy has L-O-V-E written across his forehead in fat Sharpie.

"It was good. Yeah. Okay…well, honestly not all that exciting. Did you have a good weekend?"

A sweet little blush creeps up as her gaze sweeps over to me. "Yeah, it was really great."

I arch a brow and accept my coffee, more than happy to listen to her describe her weekend to Hudson.

"Why don't you tell him your favorite part?" I goad.

Sure, I have shit to do, but this beats the hell out of checking emails.

"Oh, well, I really liked swimming," she says with a shy smile.

"Swimming?"

"Yes, swimming at night," she continues, eyes on me.

"That's dangerous," Hudson says with a frown.

"I was careful," she teases.

"Probably not careful enough," I respond.

Jesus, my voice is husky, and I'm seconds away from sweeping everything off my desk and dragging her down onto it.

Hudson is completely oblivious. "Ethan's right. I hope you don't do that often. Truly, it's much safer to swim during the day."

After assuring Hudson she'll be much more careful in the future, she turns to leave without any more private smiles in my direction. I'm left…wanting.

It gets worse at lunch, when I walk into the mess hall with Robert and find her sitting at a table with some of the crew. Her little puppy Max is in the seat beside her.

I remember what Hudson said about them—that they used to date way back when—and it has me tempted to make a fool of myself. I've never been a jealous monster, but then I've also never had to keep a secret like this. The fact is when the crew left on Friday, Taylor was fair game. Now, she's not, and I'd prefer they all know that.

I feel her gaze on me as I walk across the cafeteria, but I keep my attention on Robert and the story he's telling. If

Taylor wants me to hide our relationship, it's probably better I keep a safe distance in a room with so many spectators.

In the afternoon, she comes into the trailer to do some work. I'm on the phone with our client, discussing the progress of the project.

"The concrete pour went well. Did you get the photos we sent?"

Taylor finds the papers I left for her on Hudson's desk and starts flipping through them. I move my gaze down her slowly as the client asks about the next steps.

"We'll begin framing this week, so you'll be able to see the progress during your site visit in two weeks. Soon after, we'll install the air barriers."

Taylor frowns at a piece of paper and then carries it over, mouthing her question.

"Does this need to be filed?"

I nod and she turns to leave, but I catch her wrist, keeping her there beside me. My thumb brushes her pulse point and I lean back in my chair, looking up at her, appreciating this quiet moment after a hectic morning.

The client asks more about the site check and I confirm that my partners will be here as well. "Steven will walk you through the framed building so you and your team can confirm everything has been placed in accordance with the blueprints, even if it's still in progress."

Taylor smiles down at me and I tug her closer, bringing her down onto my lap.

She protests, but I shake my head, knowing she'll do as I say while I'm on the phone. She's nothing if not a dutiful employee.

I wrap my arm around her waist. She sits perfectly quiet with her head against my chest. A sudden warmth takes hold of me and I realize I'd want her to stay here like this all day if it were possible.

"While I've got you here, I got a call from our interiors coordinator in Austin and she mentioned that your team was still wavering on window selections for the patio on the west elevation. We'll need to put in that order soon if you don't want delays."

The client assures me they'll confer with the Austin office and make their decision soon, and then the call ends.

Taylor is still on my lap, but when I set my phone back down on my desk, she attempts to stand.

"Someone is going to walk in." She frowns as I pull her back down onto me. "Ethan…"

I silence her protests with a soft kiss, my hand wrapping around the back of her neck. She doesn't give in to it right away; in fact, she sits perfectly still while I tease her mouth, parting her lips. She smiles and leans against me and I tilt my head, finally kissing her deeply. Her hand flattens over my heart and she softens, accepting my advances and meeting them with desires of her own. Our tongues touch and her moan is hot wax dripping down my skin. I pull her up higher on my lap and slip my hand between her jean-clad thighs.

The door to the trailer opens and Taylor flies off me, the back of her hand flat against her mouth as Robert walks in with Hudson. They're talking animatedly about a basketball game when Robert's gaze catches on Taylor's back. He frowns and glances to me, but my steely gaze warns him not to say a word. Hudson is, again, completely oblivious.

"If you wouldn't mind scanning that," I say, picking up the paper Taylor brought over earlier and adding another sheet on top of it that outlines the notes from my phone call with our client.

She nods silently and rushes back over to the desk.

I feel guilty for what could have just happened, and I'm not surprised when Taylor leaves a few moments later without meeting my eyes.

CHAPTER TWENTY-EIGHT
TAYLOR

Ethan's in the shower when I make it back to the cabin later that night. I purposely stayed away after dinner, trying to cool my temper, but it didn't work, and when I pull that door open and step into the steaming bathroom, I'm still annoyed with him. What if Robert and Hudson had seen us!? What if they *did* see us and just decided to keep their lewd comments to themselves?!

Ethan is rinsing his hair, his tall, toned body on full display. He turns and spots me, and there's not even a hint of embarrassment on his face. The man is too arrogant for his own good.

"You nearly got us caught today," I accuse, my voice harder than I thought it'd be.

I'm glad. I don't want him knowing how close I am to pouncing on him.

He soaps up his palms and lathers his chest and arms.

"I take full responsibility," he says, a smile barely visible on his lips.

He's not taking this seriously, and that only annoys me more. I step under the stream, fully clothed, and push him back against the wall. Within seconds, I'm drenched. My t-shirt clings to my skin and my hair hangs heavy down my back.

"Don't do it again. When you kiss me like that, I…"

He brushes the hair off my face and tilts my chin up so our eyes meet. His eyes sweep back and forth between mine as if trying to ensure I'm really listening to him when he speaks.

"I won't let anything happen to you."

His voice is so sincere and resolute, I believe him.

Which is a relief, because now that I've let him have it, I'd really like to take advantage of him in this bathroom. And I do. I slink down to my knees, glad for the denim that softens the bite of the tile floor.

Ethan's mischievous grin makes him look like a devil in disguise. "Is this part of my punishment?"

"No," I tease. "That'll come later, in bed."

Two weeks pass like this and it's equal parts blissful and maddening. All day, Ethan and I wear our employer-employee hats. We carefully avoid touching one another. There's very little playful banter and absolutely no kissing, mostly because we're hardly ever given the opportunity. Hudson always seems to be around, and if he's not, Robert is, or one of the crew has a question or I'm off working *or…*

I still eat lunch with the crew, which I now realize really annoys Ethan. He takes it out on me at night, on that small bottom bunk. Every bit of jealousy he feels during the day gets poured into his lovemaking and I'm starved for more. I'm losing my head, which wouldn't be so concerning except that my heart is already long lost. I'm not sure when exactly that happened, but it's too late to turn back now. Putting up MISSING posters around camp wouldn't help because I know the man who stole it and I don't think he has any interest in giving it back to me. There is no point in trying to cap these feelings, no denying the love I feel toward a man I used to think I despised with every fiber of my being.

We stay together at the camp on the weekends and those days are so lazy and sweet, like a summer romance in a fairytale. We have nowhere to be and no one to answer to. We make love by the lake and swim until we're exhausted from it. He grills us chicken and burgers and hotdogs and he tugs me down onto his lap while we share our food.

He lies back on his towel, his eyes closed, and I brush my fingers over his chest, reading a book aloud. I think he's fallen asleep, and I pause, but then one eye peeks open and he insists I continue. With a smile, I pick up right where I left off.

After long days, we fill up that bathtub in the cabin and he washes me off just like I fantasized he would, his hands moving over my soapy, slick skin, his lips on my neck.

A part of me feels guilty for how happy I am. I know how much my mom is struggling and when I get paid again, it feels good to mail home that check, knowing how much she needs it. I insist she keep every penny for herself and for McKenna. I call home a couple times a week, always glad when McKenna updates me with good news about school. Summer will start soon, and she, Lilian, and Brittany have all been accepted to attend a six-week robotics and engineering camp at the University of Texas put on solely for young women. Better still, the camp is completely free to attendees thanks to a generous donation from Michael Dell.

I tell Ethan about it after I hang up the call and he grins, happy for her.

"But wait, why do you look like that?" he asks.

"Like what?"

"Annoyed?"

I immediately ease my expression. "If I looked annoyed, it's just because I'm hungry."

His eyes narrow as he studies me. "Do you not want her to go to the camp? Are you worried about her in Austin? Because I could have Isla check up on her, and you and I could even go back on the weekends—"

"No, it's not that." I turn and start putting away some of the laundry I left folded on top of the dresser, happy to have an activity that puts my back to him.

"Okay, then what is it?"

"It's silly. I shouldn't be jealous of my own sister. I want the best for McKenna."

"*You* want to go to Austin?"

I squeeze my eyes closed, annoyed that he can't read my mind. "No! That's stupid, I—"

"Want to go to college?"

I freeze, carefully assessing his words. Does he seem shocked? Incredulous at the idea? No, just curious.

I sigh, keeping my attention down on my hands as they toy with a button on one of his folded shirts. "Yes, actually. It's something I didn't get the chance to do, and I wish sometimes I were in McKenna's shoes. Things were different when I was in high school."

"Because of your mom and Lonny?"

I nod, glad I opened up to him the other day while we were in the bath. It feels better now that he knows more of my history.

"With only a high school diploma, I don't have many options. You've seen that firsthand. I worry about what jobs I can possibly hope to get in the future when I go back to Oak Dale. I refuse to go back to working at that motel."

"Well, there are a million colleges in Austin, so just apply to one of them."

I frown, unnerved by how easy he makes it sound. "Why in the world would I do that?"

"Because that's where we'll be living after this project wraps up."

I laugh then, shoving away from the dresser. "Oh my god, listen to yourself. You're such a control freak!"

"Oh, sorry. Here, let me try again: I think you and I should live in Austin, together. Was that better?"

"Not at all."

He catches me as I try to walk around him and squashes me against him. I have no hope of escaping. "Okay, so we'll talk about Austin later. Like next week."

"Next month."

"Tomorrow."

I groan, glad he swoops his mouth down to mine and effectively ends the discussion. I don't like talking about these things. I don't like pinning hope where none belongs.

I should be grateful for right now, for this job and my time with Ethan, especially because life has taught me time and time again how fleeting happiness can be.

CHAPTER TWENTY-NINE
TAYLOR

I know Ethan's partners are coming today because he woke up early then was ready and out of the cabin before I even managed to crawl out of bed. The client—the resort company behind this development—will be here too. I'm excited for them to see the progress of the build. So much has happened in the last few weeks. With the framing in progress, the hotel is starting to take shape, and they're moving on to other buildings as well.

The weather is working on our side. The trees and wildflowers are in full bloom along the path to the camp, and the cool morning breeze offsets the blazing sun.

Max is in the mess hall, finishing up his breakfast when I walk in. I smile and wave, and he shoots to his feet to join me in line.

"Hey, I was waiting for you."

I blanche, feeling bad for not waking up earlier. "Oh, sorry, I hope you didn't have to sit too long."

He shakes his head, and that's when I notice his usual happy disposition is noticeably dulled today. "What's going on?" I ask, nudging him with my shoulder. "You okay?"

"It's nothing. I just…" He laughs and drags a hand through his hair. "Listen, I've been trying to work up the nerve to ask you out again, and well, it seems like the courage will never come, so I'm just going to do it. Right now. This is…in fact, me asking you."

My eyes go wide.

What?!

His declaration is so out of left field that I don't know what to say first. Then, finally, I rush out my words. "Oh, Max, I'm really sorry. I just…I'm not—"

"Available?"

I swallow past the lump in my throat and glance away. A few of the guys in the mess hall are watching us, probably aware of what's happening. I wish Max had done this in private. I hate everyone knowing my business.

"You're not, right?" he continues. "Everyone's been saying you and Ethan are dating. That's why you two spend all your time in that cabin. You used to hang out with us after dinner, but now you scarf down your food like someone's about to steal it and then you're gone the rest of the night."

I'm blushing now, wishing I'd been more careful. I thought no one would realize what was happening if we kept our hands to ourselves on the site, but apparently, love isn't that easy to hide.

"It's not…" I sigh, feeling like I'm suddenly on trial. This wasn't supposed to happen this way. I wanted to keep my personal life separate from work, but in this setting, that's next to impossible. Still, I don't like the feeling of being backed into a corner, so instead of confirming Max's suspicions, I reroute. "I just don't think you and I would be a good fit."

It's true, regardless of whether or not I'm dating Ethan.

He doesn't buy it. He's hung up on the fact that I didn't outright deny my relationship.

"Do you really think that's a good idea?" He sneers. "Sleeping with the boss?"

I know he's saying these things because I rejected him and he's upset. I know he doesn't mean to sound so disgusted with me.

I open my mouth to apologize for not reciprocating his feelings. I know how badly that hurts, but he turns away before I get the chance, and the whole exchange makes me sick to my stomach.

I'm not hungry for breakfast after all, and as soon as Max goes to reclaim his seat by his friends, I head to find Ethan.

I'm in such a hurry, not paying attention as I rush out the door of the mess hall, and I collide against a hard chest, nearly falling back on my butt before two hands reach out to steady me.

"My bad," an amused voice says. "Jeez, you came out of nowhere."

I glance up and realize with dread that I've just run right into one of Ethan's partners. I recognize him from that night at the bar. He was another one of the suits sitting at the table.

He's slicker than Ethan. Even now, he's wearing a crisp white dress shirt with his jeans and boots, not a hair out of place. He's closer to my age and he'd be handsome if he weren't looking down at me with a sinister gleam in his gaze.

"Wait," he says, narrowing his eyes. "I know you."

I shake my head and try to step back, stomach twisting with dread, but his grip tightens as if he needs just another second of me standing in front of him to place me in his mind.

I look away, but it doesn't matter. His resulting chuckle makes me go perfectly still.

"You're the *thief*."

My heart leaps in my chest, misses a beat, and then thumps madly against my ribs.

"From the motel bar," he continues, letting his lazy gaze drag down my body.

I finally jerk my arms away from him and glance around, grateful that at least no one else heard him. Ethan is over near the trailer chatting with a few well-dressed people. His back is to us, and maybe that's for the best. What would he do if he saw his partner grabbing me like that?

"Does Ethan realize?" he continues.

"I have no idea what you're talking about," I say, speaking up for the first time and willing my voice to stay steady. I'm shaking in my boots and all I want to do is flee, but I won't give him the pleasure.

He smirks and shakes his head. "There's no point in trying to deny it. I'd remember your face anywhere. You know I wanted you that night just the same as Ethan did. I guess I lucked out in the end, though—and you did too. You'd have been disappointed if you lured me into that bathroom. I don't keep much cash on me."

An angry flush overtakes my cheeks.

"I'm Grant, by the way."

He holds out his hand, like I'd actually want to shake it after the snide remarks he just slung at me.

Instead, I let it hang there in the air before he laughs and lets it drop.

"Looks like Ethan has his hands full with you. I suppose it's no coincidence that you're here, though I would have appreciated if he'd told me. Maybe I would have come out here to check on the site sooner."

His double meaning is clear by the way he's leering down at me.

I'm dangerously close to losing it. Tears or fists are about to fly, but the first would make it so I could barely meet my own gaze in the mirror and the second would leave me without a job. I take a deep breath and force myself to stay calm as I glance up into his cold, haughty eyes.

"Whatever you think happened at that bar *didn't*. You should talk to Ethan."

"I'd rather talk to you."

"Taylor, Grant," Hudson shouts from a few yards away. "The meeting is about to start."

Of course, the meeting Grant will help run. I'm supposed to be present to take notes and provide any assistance if need be as we all crowd into the trailer together. Introductions are done quickly and I'm immediately intimidated by the group. There are two women and two men here as representatives of the luxury resort company, all more polished and put together than I could ever hope to be. I grab a notepad and pen, but Grant speaks up before I settle back into a chair in the corner.

"Taylor, I'd like some coffee. I left mine in the car."

The request might seem innocuous to everyone else, but not to me.

I don't say a word—knowing there's nothing *to* say—before I rise to fulfill his request. By the time I return, the meeting is in full swing. I walk quietly around the perimeter of chairs to hand it off to him, and he takes one look at it then wrinkles his nose. "Could you add some cream?"

There's no way to protest, no reason to. I'd look crazy if I did.

So I take that cup and rush back to the mess hall so I can add a splash of cream and not even an ounce of spit—which is really something I'm proud of—before I hurry back to the trailer.

He's still not happy. His mouth opens to object, but Ethan beats him to the punch.

"If you're that particular about your coffee, Grant, get up and get it yourself. You're disrupting the meeting."

Silence ensues as everyone turns to look at us.

Grant unfurls a smirk and holds up the cup in a silent cheers. “It’s fine. Continue.”

I hurry to my chair and try to make myself disappear, but it’s no use. Grant does everything possible to keep me involved. When everyone stands to tour the site, he insists I come along and stay by his side.

“I need you to take notes. You know how to do that right? Or does Ethan have you performing *other* duties?”

I hate that no one else hears him. I hate that I’m so close to making a scene.

Ethan is ahead of us, at the helm, talking with the clients. He’s running the show and though I want nothing more than to have a private word with him, it’s just not possible right now. He has a job to do, and so do I. I stay by Grant and keep my spine straight and my chin up. I fulfill my duties to the best of my ability and try hard to ignore the few tasteless comments he aims my way, insinuations about what I am to Ethan and what my role actually is here on site. He cloaks his accusations in euphemisms, but there’s no mistaking his malicious intent.

After lunch, I’m not sure I have the energy to continue. The clients are gone, but Ethan’s partners are still here. Apparently, they have more work to do before they head back to Austin. My stomach fills with dread. I have every intention of steering clear of the trailer, even if that means hiding out in the cabin.

I turn down the path and stop short when I spot Grant, Steven, and Brad walking toward me. Steven and Brad are wearing hard, angry expressions, but it’s Grant who captures my full attention as he leans over and spits blood into the grass.

Oh shit.

His mouth is puffed up like he's just eaten something he's allergic to. The lower half of his jaw is red and starting to bruise.

When he sees me, I expect the same treatment from this morning, but instead, his eyes widen in fear.

What the heck happened while I was at lunch!?

I stand stock-still, but they continue walking until we're only separated by a few feet. Then Steven nudges Grant forward with a shove.

He shoots the older man a searing glare over his shoulder and then straightens his shirt before coming to stand in front of me. For a few tense seconds, our eyes lock and I can feel his disdain for me pluming off him. Then he speaks and his tone is sharply clipped. "I'd like to apologize for what I insinuated this morning. I realize I was wrong about you."

My jaw drops.

His gaze flicks over my shoulder, out onto the path behind me, as he continues. It's clear he'd rather be eating dirt than apologizing to me right now. "I thought I was being funny, but my partners have pointed out that I was wrong."

"Say the rest," Brad adds with an unyielding tone.

"From this day forward, I won't talk to you—"

"*Or*," Steven goads.

"Or so much as look at you if it's not directly related to Lockwood Construction business."

It's obvious he's repeating words that were drilled into him, and I know without a shadow of a doubt that Ethan was behind his swollen lip.

My stomach knots with tension. "It's fine."

"It's really not," Steven insists, eyeing me gently. "He could have gotten this company into a hell of a lot of trouble if you'd decided to press harassment charges."

My gaze flicks back to Grant and I realize we're even now. He won't press charges against Ethan for a busted lip and I won't report him to HR—or worse, the media.

Grant glances down at me and frowns. "For what it's worth, this morning was more about getting under Ethan's skin than yours. He and I have always had a tenuous relationship. I realize now I took it too far."

I nod as Steven and Brad come up behind him, clapping him on the shoulder and pushing him forward brusquely. I step out of their way and watch as they disappear down the path.

When I make it to the cabin, I find Ethan sitting on the top stair, waiting for me.

He's fuming.

CHAPTER THIRTY
ETHAN

Boots crunching along the gravel path tug me out of my angry reverie. I look up just in time to watch Taylor make her way to the bottom of the stairs and stop on a dime. She's chewing her bottom lip. Her brown eyes are filled with guilt and she's got one arm wrapped around her stomach, her hand clutching her other elbow.

She looks like she's the one at fault for the events that transpired this morning, and I won't allow it.

"I suppose I should apologize for Grant. He's always been an ass, but this morning he went too far."

"You punched him?"

I flex my hand, surprised my knuckles don't ache. "Just once. I'll have you know, I've been wanting to do that for quite a while."

She doesn't let my smirk soothe her worries. "I really hate that guy."

"Truth be told, we all do. I doubt he'll be with Lockwood much longer."

Her eyes widen. "Hopefully not because of today?"

Of course she feels bad for him, a man who doesn't deserve an ounce of her pity. She doesn't know what he said to me after lunch, while we were surveying the cabin sites for phase two of construction. If she knew what Grant had called her…if she knew he asked me to pass her along to him when I was finished…

"Believe me, he doesn't deserve your pity."

She rocks back on her heels and looks away. “God, this has been a horrible morning.”

“Because of Grant?”

“Yes, and…” She shakes her head and sighs, long and heavy. “I found out the crew knows about us.”

I arch a brow. *Is that such a terrible thing?*

“Max sort of guessed it this morning, and I didn’t want to lie.”

“Good. I’d rather they know.”

Her gaze flies back to me. “Of course, because you never cared if they knew. It’s me who has to walk around this jobsite with everyone wondering why I’m here. I already seemed out of place before. Now it’s obvious I’m only here to amuse you, just like Grant said. It’s like I’m a groupie or a whor—”

“Don’t say it!”

My booming voice catches her off guard and she steps back.

I’m still angry that Grant used that word to describe her, and I don’t want to hear it again, much less from her own lips.

Unfortunately, it seems like we’re both stewing about more than just Grant. She’s upset the crew knows about us. I’m stressed about making all the right decisions where she’s concerned. This relationship has been on par with walking a tight rope from the very beginning.

She wants our relationship to be a secret, so I’ve done it.

She wants me to mind my own business and let her sort out her life herself, so I have.

She expects me to listen to her talk to her family and not help even though I’d barely have to lift a finger to solve her problems. It’s tearing me up inside. They’re working so hard to get that damn car out of the shop and I know it's a hulking piece of shit.

I want to provide for her and protect her and cherish her, and she wants none of it.

I stand up and stomp down the stairs, knowing we won't get anywhere right now. I still need to cool off.

"Take the afternoon off."

"No. There's work to do."

I shoot a glare at her. "Taylor, don't test me right now. I beg you, for once, listen to what I tell you."

She scowls. "I'll work here, cleaning the cabin. I'll stay out of your hair."

"Fine."

Taylor listens. *Barely*. She doesn't come into the trailer again, but she doesn't stay in the cabin either. When I walk back to camp after sending off Brad and Steven, I see her talking to Robert and the guys, rushing off to do their bidding. At various points in the day, I see her with a tape measure in hand, two coffees, a stack of blueprints, a level, and Hudson's laptop. She's running around being everything to everyone. She's more eager than ever to be useful, which I suppose is her way of ensuring everyone knows she's here for the right reasons.

I wish she'd trust that I have her best interests at heart. She thinks so little of this crew—expects them to act just like Grant—when in fact, none of them give two shits what she and I are doing in our personal life. Who cares if Max knows? If Hudson knows? They'll get over it.

But I've said my piece and I won't push her on it.

At dinner time, I walk into the mess hall and she's sitting with her friends, but her food goes untouched on her plate.

She spots me right away because her gaze was already pinned to the door. I know she was waiting for me, and I wonder if that seat beside her is empty because she wants me to sit in it. In the end, it doesn't matter because Hudson steals it before I can make a move.

Taylor's expression deflates, but I'm not sure why. Isn't this for the best? She wants us to fly under the radar, so that's what we'll do.

After we finish eating, I stay outside and chat with Robert and a few of the other guys. I'm having a pretty good time, right up until I watch Taylor walk out with Max.

Her gaze is aimed on the ground as he leans in to talk to her. What the fuck is so important he has to whisper it to her? He looks desperate for her to hear him out. His hands clasp together and I swear I see him say, "I'm sorry."

It's one thing for her to eat with her friends, but I'm not going to sit around watching her have an intimate conversation with Max. I push to stand. Taylor looks over, finds me, and I glance pointedly toward the path that leads to our cabin. The invitation is obvious and I don't wait around to see if she accepts, tossing a farewell to the guys and setting off down the path. Taylor arrives fifteen minutes later, after I've showered, just as the first round of thunder sounds in the distance.

We've been lucky with rain so far on this project, and I hope it stays that way. I don't want any delays.

I'm in the bathroom, brushing my teeth when she strolls in. I watch her in the reflection of the fogged mirror, aware of the tension she brought in with her. Maybe it's just the storm brewing outside, or maybe we're not done fighting. I spit and rinse my mouth then walk out to lean my shoulder against the post of the bunk bed. She's opening and slamming drawers, grabbing an oversized t-shirt.

I've calmed down a lot since this afternoon, but apparently, Taylor's even more worked up.

"Seems like you've got something on your mind," I say, unable to keep the amusement out of my voice.

I should have. It pisses her off.

She slams another drawer. "Yup."

"Want to talk about it?"

Her eyes narrow on me. "Not really."

Then she turns and locks herself in the bathroom while she showers.

I know I need to wipe the arrogant smirk off my face by the time she's done. She's upset, and I should be too, but I can't seem to fake the feeling. Taylor riles me up. This feisty side of her is just as compelling as the sweet, soft version she's shown me in recent weeks.

When that bathroom door opens again, I'm reading on the bottom bunk. I let the book fall on my chest and take her in: dark hair framing her alluring features as she walks over to the desk and grabs a bottle of lotion. Camille or Isla must have left it here, but she's using it now, moisturizing one leg and then the other. I watch her, mesmerized—imagining those long legs wrapped around my waist.

Last night, at this time, I was kissing my way down her body. Now, she won't even look at me. It's fine. I enjoy a challenge.

"Would you mind turning the lamp off when you're done? I'm going to bed early."

She shoots daggers at me over her shoulder.

Then, as quickly as she can, she yanks that lantern toward her and turns it off. We're plunged into darkness.

It was slightly premature on her part considering she hasn't finished getting ready for bed. That only makes her angrier—the fact that she has to tote that lantern with her into the bathroom so she can brush her teeth. When she walks back out, she slams it onto the desk, turns it off, and then walks toward the bunk, stubbing her toe in the process.

She curses under her breath and I ask if she's all right.

"*Fine*," she bites out.

She's about to pass me by to climb up the ladder, but I reach for her wrist and tug her closer.

"Sure you don't want to talk about today?"

"Positive."

"All right. Then, good night," I say, sitting up so my face is almost level with hers in the shallow darkness.

I want a goodnight kiss and she knows it, but even that small gesture is a concession on her part. She leans down quickly and kisses my cheek. I grin and keep my hand on her wrist as she tries to pull it away.

"Taylor."

"You're pushing your luck," she warns.

Ah, I'm learning so much about her. When she angry, she's even more stubborn than usual. She didn't have a good day and maybe she feels like I had something to do with that, or maybe she just wants to use me as a punching bag. Either way, I'm happy to push my luck.

I reach up to curve my other hand behind her neck, up under her hair. She shivers as I tug her down toward me and press a kiss to her lips. It's a kiss that says, *You can be mad at me all you want, but we're still in this together.*

She sighs and I release her so she can scale the ladder quickly and burrow under her covers.

Neither one of us goes to sleep easily.

The thunder picks up, and eventually, the rain starts.

I don't know how long I've been asleep when I hear rustling in the cabin. I blink my eyes open and there's Taylor, making a pallet for herself on the ground.

"What are you doing?" I ask, sleep evident in my voice.

"There's a leak in the roof and water was dripping on my head. My pillow's soaked."

"I can't fix it tonight," I say, still half-asleep and not thinking straight.

"I didn't ask you to fix it. I put a bucket up there for now. It's a slow enough leak that it should be fine until morning."

Right.

She growls as she tries to get her blanket to lie flat.

I dig at my eyes with the heels of my hands, trying to wake myself up. Then I wrestle the sheet off me.

"I'm not letting you sleep on the ground. Take my bunk. I'll go sleep somewhere else—"

A tree branch crashes against the windowpane. I'd be an idiot to leave this cabin right now.

"Or maybe I'll just take the floor."

"It's fine," she says, dropping down onto her thin palette and tugging her sheet up to her neck. It's adorable, the idea that she thinks I'll let her get away with sleeping there.

I lean down and haul her up off the ground, sheet and all.

"Ethan!" she protests, flinging her arms around my neck like she's scared I'll drop her.

I set her on the bottom bunk, push her toward the wall, and slide right in after her.

The bed feels tiny when I'm alone. With her, it's microscopic. The only way we'll both fit is if I gather her against me and envelop her in my arms, so I do. I feel better than I have all day.

Her head is nestled under my chin and her cheek is pressed against my chest. I can feel her eyelashes flutter against my skin. She's not closing her eyes and going to sleep like I want her to.

"Taylor?" I ask, one final time. "Tell me what's wrong."

My heart's breaking. Earlier today on the porch, I was worried I couldn't continue with the way things are between us, especially having to keep our relationship a secret. Now, having her in my arms, I realize I'm willing to do just about anything to keep her. Even if that means shutting up and acting like she doesn't exist during the day. Even if that means pretending she doesn't mean the fucking world to me when other people are around.

She shakes her head and stays quiet. It's obvious she has a lot on her mind, things she's not quite prepared to say out loud.

I whisper against her ear. "Tell me in the morning?"

The wind howls outside and the thunder rumbles.

She kisses my chest but never responds.

CHAPTER THIRTY-ONE
TAYLOR

I wake up the next morning to the sound of hammering.

Groggily, I push myself up out of bed and stumble onto the porch, peering up to find Ethan hard at work on the roof, repairing the leak. His t-shirt is already drenched in sweat. A toolbelt hangs around his waist and he's leaning over, slamming his hammer down onto a nail.

His brown hair needs a trim, but I secretly love the extra length. With it so disheveled, he looks like a farmhand about to drag me into a barn and have his wicked way with me.

Oh right, I'm supposed to be angry.

Why is that again?

Yesterday was a blur, one of those days where nothing goes right and everyone seems to be to blame. Max started the ball rolling then Grant made it ten times worse. Then I was annoyed with Ethan for ordering me to stay at the cabin and for not being more concerned about everyone knowing our business. It didn't help when he all but ignored me at dinner. Yeah, yeah, I realize I didn't give him much of a choice there, but what am I supposed to do? What happens when everyone knows about us and they all react just like Grant did?

I had every intention of picking up my anger right where I left it last night, but sleep did what sleep does, and now yesterday's fight just doesn't seem all that important in the light of day, not to mention I did a lot of thinking before I finally nodded off, and I managed to come to a few realizations.

Ethan finally notices I'm out here watching him, and he pauses, sitting back on his heels.

"You're a sight for sore eyes," he says, sounding like he means it.

I realize with my hand up, shielding my eyes from the sun, my t-shirt's hiked up on my thighs, all but revealing the bottom of my panties. I went to bed with my hair damp, so now it's a wild, curly mess. I'm sure I have bags under my eyes from lack of sleep and a pillow mark on my cheek, but his appreciative gaze makes me blush.

"Still angry with me?" he asks, tilting his head.

He looks like a devilish angel up there with the sun outlining him from behind and his dimpled smirk softening his handsome features. The oxymoron never fit a soul better.

"Maybe," I say, unable to keep the smile off my face.

He chuckles and shakes his head. "Suits me either way. Maybe when I'm finished with this roof, I'll come down there and coax you out of that bad mood."

It's a promise that has my spine tingling, and I decide maybe I won't throw in the towel just yet. If he's so intent on coaxing me, there's no point in telling him I'm not quite so mad anymore. In fact, I'm not mad at all.

I considered things quite a bit while I was lying awake in Ethan's arms, listening to the rain, not just about my relationship with him and how we'll navigate this tricky situation, but also about what could have happened if things had played out differently with Grant. If Ethan hadn't handled the situation, I would have been stuck dealing with him myself. How long would I have had to suffer? Grant wasn't the first man to mistreat me like that. I've dealt with men like him in all of my previous jobs, and it seems to be so easy for them to back me into a corner. They can say and do whatever they want because they know how badly I need the work. Without much education, I'm in a desperate position, and they take advantage.

I want things to be different, but they never will be. The root of the issue is that I have no options. My jobs have always been lifelines. As long as I'm living paycheck to paycheck, as long as I remain unqualified for any work with more stability and advancement opportunities, I'll find myself back in this position.

Helpless. Angry. Easily preyed upon.

My high school counselor handed me that pamphlet for online classes months ago and I disregarded it because, at the time, it seemed impossible.

Now, well…maybe it's not.

Suddenly, I'm rushing back into the cabin to throw on clothes.

"Hey, where are you going?" Ethan protests.

"I'll tell you later!" I shout, letting the door slam closed behind me. I feel panicky and excited and hopeful, like my chest might burst open. I haven't felt this way in a long time and I'm not going to stop to let doubt and insecurity wind their way through me. I throw on my jeans and boots and a t-shirt then I'm running back down the trail, my hair whipping in the wind behind me.

The ground is a muddy mess from all the rain and the crew is already getting started cleaning up what little damage the storm caused. The sunny skies will help dry things quickly, but even still, there are branches scattered around the jobsite and some debris that needs to be removed before they can continue working.

Hudson is overseeing everything and I run straight for him, heart thumping wildly in my chest.

"Hey Hudson! Would it be okay if I borrowed your laptop?"

He shrugs. "I'm barely on it. Use it for as long as you need."

"Thanks!" I say, already turning to run in the opposite direction.

"Hey, wait! Why are you in such a rush?"

I'm rushing because it feels imperative that I keep the ball rolling. No second-guessing myself, no debating whether or not this is actually possible.

In the trailer, I sit down at Hudson's desk, boot up his computer, and immediately pull up a website I haven't gone to in years. There, at the top of the page, I hover the cursor over *Course Calendar* and click.

That day, one major life decision rolls into another. I'm on fire, feeling like I haven't felt in years, possibly *ever*. After I finish on Hudson's computer, I borrow Ethan's phone to call my mom, confirm she got my most recent paycheck, and then inform her that I'll need her to leave a little bit of it in the bank for a bill I have coming in the next few weeks. With the rest, she'll still be able to get the car out of the shop, *finally*, and it couldn't have come at a better time. (Well, that's a lie…it would have been nice to have it these last few months, but I won't let anything spoil my positive mood.)

With only two weeks left in her program, she tells me she's already started shifting the furniture around in the trailer and carved out a little niche for a small salon. Right now, it's not much, just a mirror hanging on the wall over a small vanity she got for free from one of our neighbors. She mentions her school was selling off some of their used salon chairs and she hasn't purchased one yet, but I insist that she should, even if it means holding off on the car.

Her dream is to own a big salon one day, but right now, operating out of the trailer makes more sense. She'll be able to keep costs down for her clients since she won't have to spend money renting out a space.

She's always had a good eye when it comes to hair, and it won't be long until everyone in town is lining up to get an appointment with her.

After we hang up, I rush back into the trailer to hand off Ethan's phone. He's meeting with Hudson about the framing inspection they have coming up tomorrow, so I don't want to interrupt.

I set his cell on his desk and turn to hurry back out and see what Robert needed when he asked me to come find him earlier. Some windows were delivered yesterday and I think he wants them to be inventoried so we can confirm they're the exact style number the interiors team ordered.

"Taylor?" Ethan asks, catching my attention.

I glance over my shoulder, brows perked with eagerness. "Yes? Do you need anything?"

I sweep my gaze across his desk, seeing that he's still got some coffee and there's nothing in his outgoing tray for me to scan or file.

"You're running around like a chicken with your head cut off. What's gotten into you?"

What's gotten into me is largely thanks to stupid Grant and his stupid insinuations about my presence here on the jobsite. What he did to me yesterday was the last straw, the great big shove I needed to finally take control of my future.

I should actually send the man a thank you note, but I'd rather send him a steaming bag of dog poop.

I smile and nod toward the door. "I have to run and help Robert, but I'll find you at lunch, okay? How's that?"

I don't wait for him to reply, already running out of the trailer.

I feel bad for taking time this morning to handle some personal things, so I work my butt off until lunch, finish up everything Robert requests of me then trailing after Hudson with a tape measure while he double-checks the few changes the clients requested before the framing inspection gets underway tomorrow.

I don't have a second to catch my breath, but even when I stop to go get food, I still can't quite breathe easy. There's one more thing I know I need to do today, one more thing that should be accompanied by a tremendously kickass song and a group of spirit guides spurring me on.

I have nothing but my screaming nerves and my erratic heart telling me this might be a slightly impulsive idea. Then I stomp down on that train of thought. For weeks, I've worked side by side with a rowdy group of construction workers and I've tried my hardest to stand my ground with them and prove I'm not intimidated. I don't know why I've gotten it into my head that they can't know about my relationship with Ethan. They won't do what Grant did. He is a disgusting pig. These guys are my friends.

Also, so what if they make snide remarks or poke fun?

HELLO, I am having sex with a veritable god—who CARES what they think?

This morning my mouth *watered* when I saw him up on that roof. There is no going back. This is the only way.

When I tug open the door to the mess hall, I find Ethan standing in line. Around him are one thousand people. Okay, maybe less, but still…my hands start to shake as I make my way toward him. I was hoping for a small crowd, maybe one or two guys who could just pass the message on, but unfortunately, most of the crew is in here, scattered around the tables, talking and eating. It's a lively group and there's no way I can chicken out now.

Not after everything else I've done today.

I'll never forgive myself.

Ethan spots me and that dimple makes a wonderfully unexpected appearance when he sees how determined I am to get to him as I wind my way through a group of guys.

"Outta my way!" I shout teasingly.

A few of them put their hands up as they step back, like they're actually scared of me.

They probably should be at this point. I'd mow straight through them if I needed to. I've got a destination and that destination is a ruggedly handsome man I am hopelessly in love with.

Max shouts my name, showing me he's saved me a seat, and I wave and hold up a finger. *Yup, be there in a second, right after I make a huge public declaration and embarrass myself big time.*

Ethan is only a few yards away, then a few feet, and then I'm *there*, cutting the line to get to him.

There're moans of protest behind me. Hungry men want their lunch and I'm standing in the way of that, but I'm not here for a plate of spaghetti, though that garlic bread does smell damn good, so perhaps I will reward myself with some afterward. At the moment, I'm here for something else.

Without another thought, I press up onto my toes, grab Ethan by the front of his shirt, and lay one on him like I'm a soldier returning from war. Our lips collide and stars erupt. Somewhere in the distance, fireworks explode, I'm sure. Whoops and shouts go up around us and I should probably break it off now that I've made my point, but I'm not quite done. I press myself against him until our chests meet and then I kick one foot into the air, having accomplished exactly what I intended to do.

When I pull back, Ethan's grinning down at me, and sure, my cheeks are the color of ripe tomatoes, but my voice doesn't waver as I turn to the man standing behind us in line and find his eyes wide with shock.

"Did you hear? I'm dating the boss. Spread the word."

Ethan laughs then, wrapping a hand around my waist and tugging me against him.

"You know there was probably a more tactful way of informing everyone about our relationship."

"How? By sending out a company-wide memo? You have to admit, this had much more panache."

He shakes his head, amused. "I thought you wanted to keep things between us."

I pat his chest with a mocking smirk. "Ethan, Ethan, Ethan, that was *so* yesterday. Can't you keep up?"

That night, in the cabin, the events of the day finally catch up with me. I feel like all of my energy has been zapped away, like I'm a runner breaking through the finish line of a marathon then collapsing straight down onto the hard concrete. I'm happy though, happier and feeling lighter than I have in years. There's hope where there was none before, a plan that is feasible and scary all at the same time.

"Today was interesting, to say the least," Ethan says, drawing my attention over to his side of the porch. We're sitting with our backs to the posts on the top stair. The sun's still setting, but we've been here a while, enjoying the cool breeze before summer steals it away for good.

"You should have seen the way the guys treated me after lunch. I thought they would be disrespectful, but if anything, they're terrified of me now! Like if they so much as look at me the wrong way, you'll fire them. A few of them starting calling me *ma'am*!"

He grins. "Things will mellow out in a few days. Robert only made it worse when he stood up in the mess hall and told everyone to 'mind their own damn business'."

I chuckle, remembering the scene. We'd just walked over to join the others and everyone was staring at us, in shock after what I'd just done.

"It was kind of silly of me to do that, I know. I just didn't want you thinking I was ashamed of you or anything." I scrunch my brows. "It seemed really romantic in my head."

"You don't hear me complaining," Ethan says with a teasing smile. "Though we probably shouldn't make a habit of making out in the lunch line."

My cheeks grow warm under his gaze.

"Want to fill me in on the rest of your day? Maybe what had you running around all over the place this morning?"

Oh right.

I haven't told him yet.

I glance down at my water, feeling small all of a sudden. "Oh, um…it's nothing major."

"Tell me."

My finger traces the lid of my water bottle. "I signed up for two online classes through Austin Community College. They start in two weeks."

When I glance back, I find his brows arched.

Clearly, that wasn't what he was expecting.

"What did you sign up for?"

"English Comp and American history. I have to start with the basics." Then I realize he might be wondering how I'll manage it all. "Maybe I should have checked with you first, but it shouldn't affect my work or anything here. I'll be able to handle the reading assignments and homework in the evenings and on weekends."

He nods. "Of course. Let me know if Hudson's computer isn't fast enough and we'll see about getting you a new one."

I scowl, about to remind him that I don't want any favors, and he laughs.

"Oh, c'mon. It'll be Lockwood Construction property. I'll bolt it to the desk, how's that?"

I nod, careful to keep my face neutral. "I guess that would be okay."

"Do you have enough saved to cover tuition?" he asks lightly. "Or are you going to try for financial aid?"

I answer him carefully. "It actually isn't as ridiculously expensive as I thought it would be since it's just community college, and they have a payment program, so tuition isn't due all at once."

"But you'll tell me if you need anything?"

I shoot him a glare. "Ethan, I'll be fine."

He holds up his hands in innocence. "All right, but I'm your boyfriend, Taylor. It's not a crime for me to care about you or want to provide for you. I respect what you're doing and I'll honor your boundaries, but if you ever feel like you're in a place like you were that night at the bar, I want you to come to me. Don't let that stubborn streak of yours stand in your way. Why are you smiling like that? You should still be scowling."

"You said you're my boyfriend."

"I also said a lot of stuff after that—important stuff."

"I wasn't listening."

He growls, reaches over, and hauls me toward him so I collide with his chest. I expect my weight to topple him over, but he stays right where he is, with the post at his back and the golden hour casting him in a warm glow. He's beautiful.

"You'll have to repeat it," I continue, my attention on his lips.

"I can't, not now that you're on my lap," he says, moving his hand to cradle my chin and tilt it up. His thumb brushes across my bottom lip and I shiver.

"Sorry," I tease. "No time for seduction these days. I'm a college student now. I have books to read, papers to write, tests to ace."

He smirks. "If you had been in my classes in college, I would have failed every test."

"Really?" I shake my head, sure I have a more accurate representation of what the two of us would have been like in college together. "I think we would have developed a healthy competition. Who could get the better grades…that sort of thing. I'll have you know, I'm actually smarter than I look."

His grin widens. "Believe me, *I know*."

With that he scoops me up and stands, carrying me across the threshold of the cabin like we're husband and wife. It still feels like we have so much to discuss. We have crazy weeks ahead of us. I want to head back to Oak Dale for my mom's graduation, and when McKenna is ready to go to camp in Austin, I think it'd be fun if we drove her there. That way, she and Ethan can get to know each other a little better.

I don't start classes for a few weeks, but I'm eager to order my textbooks and start prepping. I want new pencils and a fresh planner and the course syllabus and my reading schedule, and mostly I just want a chance to be the kind of student I could have been if my life had been different in high school.

Ethan pushes the door closed, and that's when I notice something's different about the cabin.

Very different.

"When did you do this?!"

He's grinning. "After I finished the roof."

"How?"

"It was easy. The bunks each had a twin bed frame supported by posts. I unscrewed the post supports, separated them from the frames, and viola…"

Now, there's just one big bed shoved against the wall of the cabin, across from the desk. It's totally impractical. The cabin is small and now there's hardly any room to walk. We'll have to shimmy around the bed to get to the bathroom and the dresser, but somehow, I love it, and I wouldn't change a thing about any of it. That's the desk where I'll study, and that's the bed where Ethan will distract me, and this is where I'll start taking the steps to change my life.

Forever.

"Ethan?"

"Yeah?"

"Did I ever tell you how crazy it is that we ended up together? Me and *you*, the most coldhearted boss I've ever had. You, the man who drives me crazy. You, the person I think I'm starting to fall for."

"Starting to?"

"I don't want to scare you."

"Scare me," he commands.

"I think I've developed deep feelings for you," I say, chickening out.

"This from the woman who marched across the mess hall and mauled me today," he drawls with all the arrogance of a lion.

"I didn't maul you!"

"Just say it and put me out of my misery. I know how much you hated me, now tell me how much you love me."

"Okay. I really, really lo…ok forward to continuing to work on your crew. It's been a great experience."

"Try again."

"I really lo…se myself in your eyes. They're really pretty. Like chocolate, or poop."

He laughs and tosses me down onto the bed then crawls up over me.

He gives my hip a little love bite and I squeal.

"I've never heard such overtures of love before. I'm going to swoon."

He's working my t-shirt up and over my bra. Soon, it's yanked over my head.

"I really—*ah*!" I yelp when he unbuttons my jeans and tugs them roughly down my thighs. "Well I don't love you when you're doing that!" I tease, glaring down at him.

Then he tosses my jeans off the bed and settles his chest between my thighs so his mouth drops easily to my stomach, kissing the sensitive skin just below my navel, swirling soft circles just above the hem of my panties with his finger.

I'm sorry, what were we talking about…?

"It's fine," he says confidently. "You're not ready to say it…but I can be persuasive."

"Oh, really?"

He lowers his lips to my skin. "I made you a bed today," he says, as if that was part of his persuasion strategy.

I squint an eye skeptically. "Technically, you *dismantled* a bed today."

"I let you have half my cookie at lunch."

"You traded me your cookie for half my sandwich, and like I said, that trade is always available in the future, especially when the caterers do those white chocolate ones and when they're straight out of the oven and the chocolate's still kind of melted..."

He laughs against my skin then reins me back in to the topic at hand, tacking on one more reason for me to love him. "All right, how about this? I didn't take that kiss in the mess hall any further even though I was tempted to."

My eyes widen. "I would have killed you."

His brow arches and his fingers grip my panties just below my hips. He starts to tug them down and goose bumps bloom across my skin. "Would you have?"

I watch his every movement as he draws the silk down my thighs. His gaze falls heavy between my legs and my first instinct is to hide myself before I realize it's Ethan looking at me like that. *Ethan.*

None of it makes sense and yet...it all does.

Fate has such a funny way of conducting business sometimes. I would have appreciated a simple meet cute. Maybe he could have just offered to buy me a beer at that bar and we would have got to talking. Through polite conversation, he would have come to find out about my predicament and offered me a job here on his crew.

Instead, I stole his wallet.

And well...as much as it pains me to think something as cliché as this, the fact is, Ethan was the real thief in the end.

"Ethan?" I say, drawing his attention back up to my face.

I reach down and drag my hands through his hair, knowing there's definitely a better time to say this. We're half-naked and he's about to go down on me. It's not exactly roses and champagne in front of the Eiffel Tower, but I don't want to wait another second before telling him the last piece of truth I've been keeping locked away.

"I love you. I think I started falling for you the first night in that bar, which is why I got so carried away in the weeks that followed. We really let each other have it."

He smiles then, and the way it lights up his face makes my insides flip upside down.

"It does feel like we've been through a war."

No kidding.

"Truce?"

I hold up my hand for him to shake, and instead, he grabs my palm, turns it face up, and plants a kiss directly in the center.

"Truce."

EPILOGUE
TAYLOR

SIX YEARS LATER

"Taylor Larson Stone."

The announcer's voice rings out over the loudspeaker in the arena and I stand frozen for a millisecond before my brain screams, *That's you! GO!*

With shaking limbs, I start to cross the stage, knowing I have a little fan club somewhere watching. I kept thinking I'd be able to listen for them when it was my turn to get my diploma, but it all happens too fast. I walk to the center, shake the dean's hand, pose for a photo, and then they're on to the next person. I shouldn't be crying as I descend the steps. No one else is crying. In fact, the guy in front of me immediately starts texting again, bored out of his mind.

Maybe to some people, a college degree is a given.

For me, it wasn't.

I never thought I'd be here, a graduate of the University of Texas School of Engineering. For the last six years, I've been anything but the typical student. For my first couple of semesters, I took all my courses online while Ethan and I finished up work on Pine Wood Resort and then moved back to Austin together. There, I continued working for Lockwood Construction in a part-time position, all the while continuing to take courses at the community college.

Ethan was the one to convince me to apply to UT. It still felt like a pipe dream, especially considering McKenna was only a year away from applying herself. She was at the top of her class back in Oak Dale, president of everything. She had college in her future no matter how many ways you slice it.

Still, I applied, if nothing else so I could say, *Well, at least I tried!*

I didn't think I would get in. In fact, I was so sure of it that I didn't factor it into our plans. Ethan and I were both eager to take the next steps in our relationship. We wanted marriage and kids. We wanted a family of our own.

We had a tiny wedding ceremony back at Pine Wood, right on the edge of the lake where we used to spend our weekends swimming and reading. I stood across from him, pregnant, though I didn't know it at the time. We said our vows while the breeze from the lake rustled the flowers pinned in my hair. Mckenna and my mom cried the whole time, which in turn made me cry the whole time, but you better believe our hair looked *amazing*.

Ethan and I didn't have a honeymoon. There was no time. Lockwood Construction had a big project starting up—one I was going to help assist on—and then, well…everything happened all at once: I took a pregnancy test and found out I was pregnant the very same day my acceptance packet came from UT.

When Ethan got home that night, I was on the floor in our bathroom, crying and clutching the manila envelope in one hand and the test stick in the other. Apparently I looked like I was on the verge of a nervous breakdown because he hauled me onto his lap and started kissing my cheeks, my hair, anywhere within reach.

"Taylor," he said, desperately trying to get me to look at him. "It's okay. This will be okay. I know it's overwhelming, but don't be sad—"

That's when I finally spoke up, and to this day he still quotes me on this. With a smile and a broken sob, I said, "Are you kidding?! This is the best day of my life!"

Being a mom in college was as hilariously difficult as anyone would expect it to be. Late-night study sessions while breastfeeding an infant often had me seeing double the next day in class.

I had semesters where I only took one class and I had semesters where I crammed three courses into a shortened summer session and thought I was going to die from stress. Thankfully, Isla stepped up in a big way. I never had to think about hiring a nanny because she was there. I mean, really, at all hours of the day and night. I thought I'd never be able to repay her, but she's due to pop any day now, and I've already stocked her freezer full of meals and helped her set up the nursery. Tanner's a nervous wreck, so the plan is for me to be with her in the delivery room too, just in case he faints and has to be wheeled out.

I smile down at the fake diploma in my hand and then glance around me. Most of the students here had the standard college experience: four years of studying hard, taking risks, changing majors, finding themselves. Most of them are twenty-two, just babies. I know at twenty-eight, I'm not all that much older, and yet somehow I feel like I should be sitting here stroking a long gray beard.

The remainder of graduation passes by quickly now that the hard part is over with. Just before we stand up to toss our caps, my seatmate to the left leans over, smiling wide. "Got plans tonight? Me and my friends are throwing a party to celebrate graduating. We've got a house over in West Campus."

I'm tempted to flash him my diamond ring and tack on the fact that I'm not only a mom of one little boy, I'm expecting another. Beneath my graduation gown, there's an itty bitty bump, but honestly, I'm flattered by his invitation. It's good for the ego. So, instead, I smile and save him from having to awkwardly withdraw his offer. "Thanks, I appreciate it, but I have other plans."

Those other plans are waiting for me outside the arena with what looks like the entire contents of a party supply store. There are balloons and posters and bouquets of flowers. There are more people here than I was expecting, but I'm hung up on Ethan and Andrew looking like carbon copies of one another, standing at the front of the group. Andrew's wearing a clip-on bowtie and khakis, and his dark brown hair is styled back from his face, very fancy, just like his dad's. He's holding up a big poster that reads, *My mom is #1!*

It's so silly, with wobbly letters and cut-out stars half falling off of it, but here I am, tearing up again because Andrew made it just for me. Truthfully, he could glue a toothpick to a piece of paper and I'd think it was better than anything Picasso managed in his entire career.

"Mommy!" he shouts as he sees me, darting through the crowd and body-slamming into my legs.

I'd have completely lost my footing if the crowd wasn't so thick. Thankfully, a nice family catches my stumble and after quick apologies, Andrew is pulling me toward his dad as quickly as he can. I tell him there's no rush, but then, that's a lie, because I want to get back to Ethan as badly as he does.

He's standing just a few yards away in the center of the madness, holding a bouquet of wildflowers—a tradition we've kept up since our days in Rose Cabin. He looks devastatingly handsome in his suit, but then I suppose he always has. It's why we're all here in the first place.

His warm smile sends goose bumps down my arms, and though we're in a sea of people, the world falls out of focus behind him. When Andrew finishes tugging me over, I stand perfectly still for what feels like forever, just looking up at Ethan, reveling in this moment we've been working toward together as a family for so long. My burdens have been his burdens. My hardships have been equally shared. He's been my rock and I wish I could tell him so without breaking out in a full sob.

"Congratulations," he says, leaning in to kiss me. He covertly wipes away my tears while his face is pressed against mine, and I'm grateful for the sweet gesture. When he tries to step back, I don't let him. I squeeze him tight and hang on for just a little longer, needing his calming presence. His hand hits my stomach, right over our baby, and my eyes squeeze shut. Just like that, I feel like I can tackle the world again. I peel back and smile up at him.

"Thank you."

And though he stays by my side, that's the last chance we have for a private word because everyone else is rushing in now: Isla and Tanner, McKenna and my mom, even Jeremy and Khloe drove in from San Antonio with their daughter Mia, who Andrew happens to think is the coolest person he's ever met.

I get tugged aside for what I think is a photo with my mom, but McKenna's actually recording us instead.

"Okay! Here we are at Taylor's college graduation. Taylor, tell us what you majored in!" She sounds like one of those cheesy dads recording his family opening gifts on Christmas morning. *Timmy, tell the camera what Santa brought you!*

I roll my eyes but still play along. "Construction engineering and project management."

She laughs. "Wow, that's a mouthful! And what do you plan on doing now that you've officially graduated?"

"I'll be working as a project manager at Lockwood Construction."

Everyone already knows this. It's been the plan all along, ever since Robert took me under his wing and started showing me the ropes all those years ago.

"And tell us, are you nervous about taking on your new role? Knowing you might have to deal with stubborn men who don't like the idea of a woman running the show on a jobsite?"

My eyes find Ethan and he's visibly amused, knowing where my thoughts are headed before I even have to open my mouth.

"You know what? I like to think I've had some pretty good practice dealing with stubborn men."

Later that night, after the chaos of the day, Ethan and I are in the kitchen, tidying up. Well, *he's* tidying up and I'm sitting on a barstool, eating another piece of the cake McKenna and Isla made for my graduation party. There are layers of fresh fruit and homemade buttercream frosting and I've made it my life's mission to ensure that not a single crumb goes to waste. No crumbs left behind is my new motto.

"How are you doing over there, Mrs. Stone?" Ethan asks, smirking at me over his shoulder.

I give him a wide smile as I bring another forkful of cake to my mouth. "Just making sure the baby is well fed, that's all."

He arches a brow and shakes his head before turning back to rinse off the last dish.

He's absolutely delectable—maybe even more so than the cake.

His suit jacket and tie are long gone. His shirtsleeves are pushed up to his elbows, and his suit pants fit him to a T. I'm looking at his butt, filling my head with wicked ideas when my mom walks out of the hallway and interrupts my stream of thought.

"Okay, Andrew's officially asleep," she says, grabbing her purse off the kitchen counter and slinging it over her shoulder.

"Took you a while," I tease.

"Well, how am I supposed to say no when he asks for 'just one more book'? Before I realized it, we'd read a dozen, just like always. It's that charm of his—he has too much of it."

I smirk. "Blame his father."

"It's all Taylor," Ethan refutes.

My mom shakes her head and walks toward me, dropping a kiss on my forehead. "I'm proud of you, kiddo."

My throat squeezes tight with emotion as I offer up a little smile.

"Still need me to watch Andrew next Saturday?" she asks, heading for the door.

"If you can. We've got that fundraiser for his school."

"All right. I'll have Simone close the salon for me that day. I should be able to get here around dinner time."

For the one-thousandth time, I think of how grateful I am that my mom moved to Austin once McKenna started at UT. I love that we're all in the same city now.

"Thanks, that'd be great."

"Thanks again, Anne. Here, I'll walk you out," Ethan says, drying his hands on a towel so he can see her to her car.

When he walks back into the kitchen and meets my gaze, my dirty thoughts from a few moments ago come roaring back hotter than ever. It makes no sense. We've been married for years. We sleep in the same bed every night. The man has seen me give birth and breastfeed and cry and bleed, and yet he looks at me with the same level of need he did all those years ago, like I'm still the most seductive woman he's ever laid eyes on.

"All finished?" he taunts, swooping in to steal my plate and finish off the last bite.

"Hey!" I protest, reaching up to try to take it back.

He holds it over my head and then leans down, kissing me.

He steps closer, forcing me to lean back in my barstool so the countertop hits my lower back. He reigns over me, slanting his mouth and deepening the kiss. I fist his shirt, wrinkling it in my palm, and then his hands find the spaghetti straps on my dress so he can slide his fingers underneath them and push the silky material down my shoulders.

A shiver racks through me.

Our kiss is sinful, yet sweet thanks to the buttercream frosting.

If I wasn't already pregnant, we'd be fixing that tonight.

"Mommy?" a tired little voice says from down the hall. "Dad? Can I have some water?"

We break apart, half groaning, half laughing. It's part of the territory. There's very rarely a lazy session of lovemaking for us these days. More often than not, we're throwing on a TV show and running to the bedroom for an afternoon quickie, or we're locking the bathroom door and laughing as we collide against the tiled wall in the shower, hungry and rushed to have each other before parent duty calls again.

Ethan leans down and whispers a promise against the shell of my ear: "Later."

And then he's stepping back, walking over to the cabinet to get one of Andrew's cups for water.

I walk over to find our little boy standing in the door of his room, looking guilty for being out of bed. His brown hair is in disarray and he has his scruffy teddy bear tucked under one arm. I scoop him up, secretly happy to have another moment to squeeze him close today.

"Is Dad coming too?"

"I'm right here, bud," Ethan says, passing him the water cup over my shoulder.

"Will you guys tell me a story?"

"Didn't Nana read to you already?" I ask, smiling.

He nuzzles his head against my neck. "Just a little," he says, shattering my heart into a million pieces.

There's no way we're walking out of this room without telling him a story first. The boy has us wrapped around his finger.

"Okay, come lie down."

Once we're all settled on his bed with him tucked under the covers between us, Ethan starts us off.

"One time, there was a beautiful princess—"

Andrew cuts him off. "You're supposed to say '*Once upon a* time'!"

"Ah." Ethan nods reverently. "Of course. *Once upon a time*, there was a beautiful princess named Taylor."

"That's Mommy's name!" Andrew says, eyes wide with wonder.

I smile and shake my head, resting my head beside Andrew's on his pillow and closing my eyes as I listen to Ethan's deep voice when he continues.

"She was smart and clever, but her kingdom had fallen on hard times and she was the only one who could save it."

"What did she do?"

"She got a job so she could make money to help save the kingdom and all its people."

Andrew cracks up. "Princesses can't work, Dad!"

"Of course they can," he insists.

"What was her job?"

"She helped build castles—at least she wanted to help, but there was an evil coldhearted dragon standing in her way."

I chuckle, aware of where he's going with this.

"Oh no," Andrew gasps, fully invested.

"The evil dragon was mean to her and tried to stop her from saving her kingdom, but the princess didn't let that deter her—"

"*Deter*?" Andrew asks.

"She didn't let that *stop* her. She kept working hard, even when the dragon snarled and stomped and growled. And you know what happened?"

"What?!"

"Her bravery saved her kingdom after all, and on top of that, she managed to soften the heart of the dragon so much he fell in love with her."

"But he's a dragon!" Andrew protests. "Dragons can't love princesses!"

Ethan's hand gently strokes my hair as he replies, "This one did."

Find other R.S. Grey Books on Amazon!

Make Me Bad
Hotshot Doc
Not So Nice Guy
Arrogant Devil
The Beau & the Belle
The Fortunate Ones
The Foxe & the Hound
Anything You Can Do
A Place in the Sun
The Summer Games: Out of Bounds
The Summer Games: Settling the Score
The Allure of Dean Harper
The Allure of Julian Lefray
The Design
The Duet
Scoring Wilder
Chasing Spring
With This Heart
Behind His Lens

Made in the USA
San Bernardino, CA
23 January 2020